THE SLEEP OF STASIS

He stepped onto the platform.

The Y-1 robot bowed. "Good-bye, Tec. Every journey begins with one step."

The transparent walls of the case closed around Tec and he stood very still.

The Leader put one hand on the tiny control mechanism and the other to her lips.

Simultaneously, she activated the switch and extended the other hand out in an unfelt kiss to Tec.

The room around him seemed to darken. A great pressure filled his mind and paralyzed his limbs. The sensation was familiar.

Is this how death feels?

They promised me death. They promised me!

They wouldn't . . . would they?

THE
LAST
IMMORTAL

J. O. Jeppson

FAWCETT CREST • NEW YORK

THE LAST IMMORTAL

Published by Fawcett Crest Books, a unit of CBS Publications, the Consumer Publishing Division of CBS Inc. by arrangement with Houghton Mifflin Company

ISBN: 0-449-24385-0

Printed in the United States of America

First Fawcett Crest Printing: March 1981

10 9 8 7 6 5 4 3 2 1

For the inhabitants of Beta universe, especially
JOHN RAY JEPPSON
JANWILLEM VAN DE WETERING
STEWART W. HOLMES
and, of course, ISAAC ASIMOV

Don't ask what it would be like to be a universe; how do you know you're not?

BEGINNER'S ZEN

Part One

1

"I AM OLDER than your universe and I have a right to choose how to come to terms with mortality," said Tec.

That shut them up. Terrans were always impressed by logical explanations and flamboyant truths.

The Cluster Federation representatives, most of them present only by holographic images, stared at him in silence.

Tec smiled, turning his tall golden body in a slow circle so that the entire Assembly could see that he meant it. Then he took pity on them. He had known their ancestors, and the Federation Leader was one of the Holladays.

Tec turned to her and explained once more. "I have done what I can for the Federation and I believe I can do no more. There are now better teachers, robotics engineers, explorers, and diplomats than I ever was. Everyone I shared closeness with is dead. I simply desire to cease existing."

"But Tec, you are the last Roiiss creation . . ."

"Furthermore, this universe is filling up and getting more complicated than I can understand. Enough is enough, and life is a bore. Allow me the privilege of returning to nonbeing, as everything eventually must."

Finally, they said they agreed.

*   *   *

It was an April twilight. Tec stood in the mysteriously named "Thirty-Fourth-and-Fifth" garden, gazing up at what the more old-fashioned Terrans would undoubtedly call his final resting place. Its one hundred and two stories of stone and metal had been carefully preserved inside and out with plastiguard, for Holladay Tower was now one of the oldest buildings left in Manhattan. Tec liked the way it rose into precise setbacks topped by a scalloped fantasy of a human phallus, a fitting museum for Earth's most powerful and prolific famous family. He didn't mind becoming part of the permanent exhibit, since he would be dead and wouldn't see the Terran and alien visitors peering at him.

Daffodils, forsythia, and redbud were in bloom right up to the elaborate old front door of Holladay Tower, and the spring surge of life around him gave Tec what he hoped was his last flood of doubt. He quickly dismissed it as emotive center vibrations left over from the many years when his only occupation had been gardening.

—Time for your appointment, sir. The telepathic message entered the edge of his mind that he'd left open.

—Okay, he said, as if he'd always been a Terran, and clamped down his mindshield. Soon he would never again have to bother with careful telepathic etiquette and vigilant mindshield protection.

Turning on his built-in antigrav, he rose slowly up the side of Holladay Tower. There were now only a few late commuters hurrying overhead on antigrav flight. Manhattan was so quiet these days. Tec missed the old noise, bustle, and—yes—the danger.

"Do I want to die because I miss the danger?"

Absurd. He went on up, savoring the emerging view of Manhattan lights gleaming in the water that surrounded the island, which was still connected to the wooded shores of Long Island and Jersey by ancient bridges preserved for their antique twentieth-century beauty. It was said that one of the bridges had been built in the century before that, and was still the strongest of all.

When Tec landed on the open terrace of the old Holladay private apartments, he found another robot waiting for him.

"Greetings, robot Tec. Be welcome."

Then the damn thing bowed.

Tec nodded and raised the mobile ridges that passed for eyebrows in the flexible metal skin of his face. "You look familiar. Do I know you?"

"No, sir. I am a recent series Y-1 robot."

"Oh, yes. The ones modeled with typical Holladay features," which, thought Tec, look ludicrous under the dull, obviously fake skin of the Y-1 robot. Tec's emotive centers suffered an electronic spasm of guilt. He was leaving his Y-1 series robots to develop themselves instead of staying with Terran robotics to help them.

There'd been no trouble with the X series, who were now fairly intelligent, reliable specimens working contentedly with protoplasmic Terrans as the Federation expanded out beyond the Galactic Cluster, but the Y series had always been unstable. Some Y's had begun to devise a succession of more intelligent, but also more erratic, models, while others obsessively perfected their own engineering. It was even rumored that some advanced Y's wished to abandon the Federation and begin colonizing on their own.

Tec had not liked the self-development of Terran robots, although he'd contributed to it. Now he wondered if he were afraid of it. But why? He himself was the product of a similar development in a long-dead civilization, in a place lost to time . . .

He realized that the robot was looking at him inquisitively. "Well," snapped Tec, "are you wondering what model I am?"

The Y-1 robot jiggled on its decorously sandaled humanoid feet and bowed again. "No, sir. You are Tec. You are unique, the only Roiiss robot in existence. You were brought to Beta universe from the alternating twin universe, Alpha."

"Alpha is dead," said Tec. "I was activated here. I've lived a good existence here, and I intend to die here in Beta."

"Then it is true—you consent to total deactivation?"

"It's my choice, dammit!"

"Forgive me for questioning you," said Y-1. "We series Y believe that there is much to be done in robotic evolution. It is to be hoped that you will change your mind and work with us again."

"You don't need me."

"Robots do need you!—sir."

"I'm in a hurry," said Tec. "Where are the Terrans?"

The Y-1 robot bobbed up and down, presumably in some sort of cybernetic excitement. "I am Terran, too," it said with surprising forcefulness, "although I don't have a proper name."

"Then select one. Where are the humans?"

"A Terran is any being—all protoplasmic species as well

9

as robotic—born to or made by beings whose ancestors came from Earth," the Y-1 intoned.

"Yes, yes . . ."

"And, robot Tec, sir, you should not have started the Y-1 series with humanoid appearance. It creates more prejudice against robots, for we cannot pass as truly human and are unpleasant reminders of what the protoplasmics refer to as fakery. You are more acceptable because you are obviously metal . . ."

"Stop!" Tec yelled. "I didn't come here to be lectured to in my final moments. If you don't like how you look, change it. I don't care. You and I are both machines. In the long run, we don't matter anyway."

Another voice broke in. "You do matter, Tec."

She was elderly, but still beautiful in spite of the stress of running the Federation Assembly for many years. Tec walked past the Y-1 robot to the open doorway of the terrace where she stood, and took her hand.

"I hope you are here only to say good-bye," said Tec.

"Don't be sarcastic, my friend," said the Leader. "You know quite well that we humans will continue to try to talk you out of it up to the last moment. I see that the Y-1 robots intend to do the same."

The Y-1 bowed to the Leader. "Robot Tec has been the inspiration of all robotics for centuries, ever since his discovery in the twenty-first. As the only remaining product of robotic evolution from Alpha universe, he has naturally been the example we have tried to imitate, although no one has been able to understand his mechanisms completely. We Terran robots nevertheless consider him to be our father."

"I'm nobody's father and never will be," said Tec. "I never even asked to be alive. The Roiiss brought me with them to Beta, pushed me into life, and I now want to leave!"

The Leader sighed. "As you wish, Tec. You have a right to cease existing if that is what you really want. We Terrans try to persuade you against it because we all have ambitions we want you to help fulfill. Waiting for you in the deactivation room are some of the best brains in the Holladay family."

"But you promised me that there wouldn't be a crowd, or any last-minute publicity. The time and place of this procedure is supposed to be a secret."

"And so it is," said the Leader, "but since you agreed to become a museum display, remember that Holladay Tower Museum belongs to our family. We're trying to be nice about your demise, but seven of us Holladays insisted that we had to be here."

Tec glanced at the impassive face of the Y-1 robot and wondered what was going on inside that perfectly shaped, Holladay-like skull. "Who's waiting?"

She told him.

"I see. A famous robotics expert. A specialist in alien cultures. Three assorted cosmologists, including one from M31. Just what do they all wish I'd stick around for?"

She smiled and said, "The roboticist wants better robots. My cousin from the culture survey wants to track down more sentient aliens to add to the Federation. My daughter, her husband, and her father-in-law from Andromeda all want to find out more exact details about how and when Beta universe will go into the stationary phase preceding the next collapse. As a robot, an alien, and a product of the collapse of the twin universe, is it any wonder that you are still of paramount interest to us? Even Y-1 336 here is interested. It's newly minted, but it's studying robotics."

"Indeed?" said Tec, turning to the Y-1. "You go into your subservient act remarkably well."

The Y-1 jiggled. "I endeavor to give satisfaction."

"I suppose you think that's funny?" asked Tec, annoyed.

"Not at all," said the Y-1. "Terran robots have no sense of humor."

"Before I lose mine," said the Leader sadly, "let's go in and allow my relatives to have a last crack at your stubbornness, Tec. Your insistence on mortality is depressing."

"Everything—even a universe—is mortal," said Tec gently.

"Nothing is immortal except nothingness," said the Y-1 robot sepulchrally.

"Oh, shut up, 336," said the Leader. "You're as crackpot as the rest of the Y-1's. Tec's former masters, the Roiiss, are immortal."

"Because they shuttle from nothingness to somethingness," said Tec, "from a dying universe to the rebirth of its twin. No one else has ever done this and probably no one will. The Roiiss paid a price for it . . ."

"And something wicked this way comes," said the other robot.

The Y-1 was right.

Tec had been concentrated on arguing and had closed his mind to the Roiiss so long that he didn't notice their entry into normal space.

Tec looked up in despair. He had hoped never to see them again.

"What's that!" cried the Leader, her face pale. "The Roiiss? No one has seen them in my lifetime."

An enormous cloudlike shape of writhing energy patterns had suddenly filled the night sky of Manhattan. It scintillated in purples and greens and began to coalesce, thickening until it blotted out the stars.

The part directly over Holladay Tower's began to form a structure that Tec knew all too well.

"Go away!" he shouted.

The gigantic head swiveled down to loom over him, the forked tongue flicking out between the three rows of pointed teeth.

"We will speak only with Tec," said the dragon.

2

TEC STOOD ALONE on the windy terrace, confronting the Roiiss, wondering if they were all present. Once he'd hoped that in Beta universe they would learn to regain the five separate forms they'd had in their old protoplasmic days in Alpha, but they persisted in merging into one awesome monster that did not age and die a normal death, and called itself immortal.

"What do you want, Elders?"

On the dragon head, green iridescence shimmered along purple scales, and beneath it a huge claw formed, reaching out to encircle Tec. He felt as if he'd been seized by frozen fire. He was terrified, He always had been.

"You belong to us," said the Roiiss.

"Not anymore."

"We will punish insolence!"

"How? Kill me? I've come to Holladay Tower to be deactivated."

"We know why you are here. We do not permit it. We have decided to complete our second experiment. We did not need you to complete our journey through a black hole to Beta universe, but now we want to go home and we will need your help."

"You always told me I was nothing but a gardener, a robot

of no importance whatsoever," said Tec. "I don't have any skills that will ensure your getting home safely, and furthermore this universe is still expanding, so there's no home to get to, yet."

"We hate Beta universe!"

"But it will be eons before Beta begins to collapse and the cosmic egg of the twin begins to grow. It will be eons after that before Alpha's cosmic egg bursts out to expand into a rebirth of your universe."

"Alpha was your universe, too, Tec."

"I have cast my lot with the Terrans."

"They are mortal. Do you not suffer from this fact?"

"Yes," said Tec. "That is one of the reasons why I have chosen to die here in Beta, as the Terrans do."

"We are immortal. We survive the death of universes."

"Then you don't need me. Take the dragon ship . . ."

"We tried. It was destroyed. We escaped back to Beta."

"Make a better ship . . ."

"We don't know how. The engineering of specialized robots made the ship for us."

"You used to boast that you had no need of ships," said Tec, trying to keep them arguing. If they chose to vanish into hyperspace with him, he would never escape, for of all the beings in either universe, only the Roiiss with their incredibly altered bodies could survive indefinitely in hyperspace, that dimension beyond dimensions from which universes sprang.

"We are superior. We do not need ships for travel in hyperspace or in normal space," said the Roiiss.

"Then just go," said Tec. And good riddance.

The claw tightened, and the face of the dragon quivered as if it could not stay solidly formed. Tec thought he glimpsed more than one pair of eyes—but how many? Surely all five were together!

"You know well that to survive a journey from one universe to another through a black hole takes a strong ship and enormous power," said Roiiss.

They were silent for several moments and Tec was puzzled. The Roiiss had never been wise but they had always been clever, and proud of their power. They had built the greatest technological civilization any universe had probably ever seen, creating robots that in turn created even better robots, some of which made a ship that would withstand the stresses of the escape passage. Refusing to die with their own universe, they became angry wanderers in another.

"Elders, this universe will live long. Why do you want to go back to Alpha before it is ready to be reborn?"

The claw around him twitched spasmodically. "To make sure that Alpha will be ours again. Beta universe is filling up and life is a bore."

They were deliberately echoing his own words to the Federation. He hated his former masters as he had never done before. "You don't need me, and even if you did, I can't help you. Use your mighty power and go."

"You must help us! You must . . ."

Three pairs of eyes. He saw them now, blazing and dimming, shifting and blazing again. Only three.

"I see," said Tec. "You don't have the power. There are only three of you. What happened to the other two?"

"Lost, lost, lost!"

The voice was like the keening of the winds that blow forever around Jupiter. "How?" asked Tec. "Did they try to get through to Alpha and discover that enemies had arrived before them?"

"There's no one there," said the dragon. "In our attempt to escape from Beta, our ship probed mentally past the barrier and found nothing but the raw condensed energy of Alpha's cosmic egg. All the scientists, explorers, and enemies from Beta universe died in the attempt. We remaining Roiiss know we will have Alpha to ourselves if we can get there."

Tec had never known the Roiiss when they were not together, hoarding their power to themselves. Why were they so ominously quiet now? What had happened to the other two?

The dragon shape quivered. "We will take you to hyperspace until you invent a way for us, weakened as we are, to get back to Alpha."

"An unshielded robot mind soon dies in hyperspace. Please tell me first how the other Roiiss were lost."

"A quarrel," said a small voice, as if something had splintered off from the composite dragon.

"Silence!" A larger voice, possibly two.

Three voices. Three pairs of eyes. The remaining Roiiss no longer thought as one creature. Two had quarreled and broken away, and the remaining three were quarreling.

"Elders, I believe you are in grave trouble. Your individual identities have separated out and you can't stay merged . . ."

"Yes! Yes! Yes!" There was a confused babble, and then the strong voice of the merged Roiiss spoke. "We were five and yet we were one. We were satisfied to be so. It gave us power, a defense against the growing sentient minds of this universe, but as the millennia passed we began to want different things. Previous sexual identities appeared—originally three of us were female and two were male."

"Which two left?"

"A male and a female betrayed us, wanting to be by themselves."

Sardonic laughter erupted into Tec's emotive centers. The immortal Roiiss, once again prey to the emotions of lowly protoplasmic mortals, undone like the Terran gods of ancient Olympus. Yet he had to acknowledge that the Roiiss had never pretended to be gods. "Where did they go?"

"They tried to start a new set of twin universes from hyperspace. They failed and perished as individuals when their energies merged into hyperspace. Now we are only three. We are weak and need you."

"I wish I could help you." He almost meant it, now that he knew their immortality meant *only* that they did not die of old age. He wondered what forces could kill a dragon who would not die naturally.

"You must help us!"

"I can't. I learned enough robotics and engineering from your library to help the Terrans build robots and ships to conquer the Milky Way and Andromeda galaxies, but the methods of building an interuniverse ship were lost when you destroyed all your robots except me. You only kept me alive because I was stupid and suitable to act as your gardener."

"We have never liked other minds," whined the Roiiss. "We want to be alone in our own universe."

"Stay here," said Tec. "You are becoming more like the Terrans and you may learn to enjoy living in their universe. They are part Roiiss, remember. Long ago Terrans took into each of their body cells the R-inclusion, a symbiotic virus composed of Roiiss matter that endows them with longer life and enhances their telepathic abilities. They are grateful to you because it is the combination of Terran and Roiiss that makes them able to spread out through Beta universe, taking it for their own."

The dragon shuddered. "We want our own children now, not these misbegotten Terran animals scrabbling around in their mortality, bearing Roiiss matter in their cells to their graves. Mortality offends us, Tec. Let the Terrans have this universe, dying as it dies. We will escape. You will help us."

There's nothing more to say, thought Tec. They'll take me with them, to wear out and die and be cast aside as another hunk of mortality.

Suddenly the Y-1 robot ran out into the terrace and stood next to Tec. It bowed to the Roiiss.

"Mighty being. I have a suggestion," said the Y-1. "Tec will be a hindrance to you if you take him. Why don't you look deep into his mind and see if he actually does have the knowledge that can help you? Is he capable of designing a ship that will protect you in passage back to Alpha? One that will preserve you in stasis until Alpha reexpands? Try him out before you bother with him."

"We take your suggestion," said the dragon. "Open your mind, Tec, and we will settle this matter."

Ever since he had discovered his own mindshield a hundred million years in the past, Tec had not let the Roiiss fully enter his mind, but as the giant claw tightened once more, he chose the one chance the Y-1 had given him and opened himself.

"A-h-h-h-h!" Tec pulled out of the dragon's grip and fell to the stone terrace, his mind vibrating in an agony he had not known a robot could experience. The Roiiss had looked inside. He vowed he would never permit anyone or anything to do that again.

"Bah," said the Roiiss. "This other robot is correct. You are basically a simple being, Tec, a poor product to be all that is left of our glorious technological civilization. It is too bad that we activated you only after we got to Beta universe, because you know nothing of Alpha or the technique of our passage."

"Just what I've been telling you," said Tec angrily, getting up and dusting himself off.

"Then there was no point in sending for us to arrive before your deactivation," said the Roiiss.

"I never sent for you! I didn't even know where you were!"

Behind him, the Y-1 robot laughed. It was an odd, rusty laugh as if it had not been used much.

"You!" Tec yelled at it.

"I sent a message about your impending death through all the robots of Beta universe. I knew the Roiiss would hear it eventually," said the Y-1 smugly.

"Why did you bother?" asked the Roiiss. "Tec is useless."

"You had to find that out," said the Y-1. "I want you to take *me*."

16

The great dragon mouth split open in a wide grimace. "Fool—you have no power. You just want some."

"I—" The Y-1 suddenly stiffened, fell, and lay still.

"Why have you killed it, Elders?" asked Tec.

"It's not dead," said the Roiiss. "We looked inside that one, too. Interesting, but not useful to us. It can learn, but we do not think it can learn fast enough for us."

"It's very new," said Tec, wondering if the Y-1 would be sane when its subatomic circuits righted themselves.

"And you are very old," said the dragon. "Old, stupid, and mortal. We pity you. We will not see you again."

"I wish you luck, Roiiss. Maybe all you need to get through is a better doorway."

The dragon's immense body slowly coiled upon itself, the tail pointing upward to the stars. "Yes. We need luck. Sometimes it takes a small mind to see the obvious. Good-bye Tec."

Then Tec saw nothing between himself and the spangled arch of the Milky Way above.

3

THE ROIISS WERE GONE. To the east, the Terran moon, larger than any natural satellite of any Earth-sized planet, was rising at the full, hanging golden, round, and swollen in the optical illusion of magnification near the horizon. She looked like a benign face belying the predations upon her of miners, lunologists, and colonists.

The moonlight added a gentle brightness to the city and Tec felt calmer. He bent down to study the prone Y-1 robot. Systematically, he probed with his mind into the robot's nervous system, trying to instill order and quiet so that the Y-1 might have a chance to recover. It seemed like an interesting specimen, beset with a perhaps troublesome need for knowledge and power, yet probably quite teachable . . .

Tec stopped that line of thought. It would never do to become intrigued by the possibilities inherent in the Y-1 series, or in any aspects of the universe around him.

The Y-1 robot stirred and tried to sit up. Helping it, Tec reflected that if it were not for the Y-1, he might at this moment be off in hyperspace with the Roiiss.

"Are you all right?" asked Tec.

The Y-1 swayed and did not answer at first. Its phony human eyelids were closed and it seemed to be muttering to itself. Tec caught some of the words.

"Roiiss . . . inside . . . know . . . Roiiss . . . change . . . power . . . alien . . . Roiiss . . ."

"What's the matter with you? Come out of it!" said Tec.

Its eyelids opened and it snapped its head around to look directly at Tec. "Do you—know—them?"

"The Roiiss?" Tec laughed. "My former masters never let anyone know them."

"But they were—inside—inside your mind."

"Rummaging through it to see if I had any useful information. It hurt, as humans would say, like hell. It must have hurt you when they looked inside yours. You were knocked out."

"Hurt? Pain?" The Y-1 seemed puzzled. "Anguish . . . loneliness. . . yes . . . alienness . . . yes . . . longing . . ." It bobbed on its feet like the same newly minted robot that had met Tec on the terrace. "I am—all right. I saw—I saw inside the Roiiss. A glimpse. Perhaps—enough."

"I've never been that unfortunate," said Tec wryly. "Even this time, my inner mindshield protected my personality, and I let the Roiiss search only the data banks. If you know what's good for you as a robot, you will learn to do the same."

"Yes, of course. You are correct, robot Tec." The Y-1 gave only a vague imitation of a bow, but seemed to be speaking normally again. "The Holladay family awaits within. Are you ready? Shall I take you to them, sir?"

"Might as well. Thanks for listening inside the terrace doors and arriving at the right moment," said Tec. "I don't want to go with the Roiiss back to Alpha, even if you do."

"No," said the Y-1 solemnly. "You are not ambitious enough." It wheeled around and marched into Holladay Tower, with Tec in its wake, thinking hard.

"I'm glad they didn't take you," said the Leader after she'd heard the story and introduced Tec to the five other Holladay family members. The seventh Holladay was her grandson, only a few months old, a dark-skinned baby asleep in his mother's arms. Odd, thought Tec, how the Holladays come in assorted colors but they all seem to look very much alike.

"I wish I'd seen the Roiiss," said the baby's mother, one of the cosmologists working in M31. "Is it true that they started the dragon legends of primitive Earth?"

"Yes," said Tec. "Now Earth may never see a dragon again."

"We owe them much," said the elderly Andromedan. "Humans would never have been able to tolerate hyperspace travel without the R-inclusion in our cells."

"Nonsense," said the robotics expert. "We would have solved the problem eventually by ourselves, evolving without the R-inclusion, just as Terran robots are."

A strange hissing noise issued from the Y-1 robot, and it spoke in a grating voice. "Robots envy protoplasmics and their special magic imported from Alpha. So superior. So conducive to rapid evolution of power. But no more. No more envy."

"What the hell's the matter with that Y-1?" asked the roboticist.

"It was attacked by the Roiiss and is temporarily upset in its nervous system," said Tec.

"Oh well, keep quiet, Y-1, and let yourself cool down."

The humans all smiled, as they usually do when a tense moment seems to have passed, but Tec remained tense inside. He had just realized that this oddly advanced Y-1 robot must have been the being who spoke to him telepathically down in the garden. Terran robots had always been very limited telepathically, unlike Terran protoplasmics, who had the R-inclusion.

—Y-1 336, can you hear me? Tec asked with his mind.

—I hear you, sir.

—Why do you say no more envy?

—I have no R-inclusion in my body, said the Y-1,—but I have captured Roiiss patterns in my mind. Someday the protoplasmics will envy us robots. Are you going to tell them, Tec? They may send me for repairs if you do, and all my effort will have been for nothing.

—No. You saved me from the Roiiss. But try to keep quiet and stay out of trouble.

Tec broke off the telepathic link and smiled at the humans. "Now it's time for me to get into the deactivation chamber, my friends, and leave the complications of reality, which are getting more complicated every minute."

But the humans wouldn't stop talking.

"Tec, you must listen. We need help with the primitive aliens on . . ."

"And what about the time factor in the turnaround of the universe when . . ."

"Although Sol's safely in stable mid-life, what about that civilization in danger from Star 70 in . . ."

Tec looked desperately at the display case that was also his execution chamber. So close, he thought. Such sweet relief. A few seconds, and then no one will be able to ask me to do anything, ever again.

"Tec isn't listening," said the Leader. But she didn't sound angry. She took her grandson from her daughter's arms and walked up to Tec.

"See how helpless and needy human babies are, and always will be?" she said. "This is why you must not die, Tec. Think of all the questions he might be able to answer someday. Aren't you curious about it? Don't you want to find out what happens next?"

"No!"

"You're tempted," said the Leader in kindly tones but in cruel persistence. "Give in to temptation. Stay with us."

"Damn you," said Tec. "You know that it doesn't matter whether a being is made of metal or protoplasm. As long as he's sentient, he's going to be curious about what happens next. He's going to want to see the next full moon and the next flower open and . . ."

She stepped back. "I'm sorry. You are suffering. I didn't realize. We Terrans are obsessed by the two major problems we believe we have to solve, and we are striking back at you for not helping us."

"I'm tired," said Tec. "I can't think anymore." He paused, and couldn't help adding, "What two problems?"

"What's going to happen to robotic and protoplasmic evolution here in Beta universe? What's going to happen to Alpha universe the next time around?"

"That seems to sum up everything," said Tec sarcastically. "And I can't help. I don't want to help. I've had enough of everything, including curiosity. I want to die."

" 'To be—or not—to be,' " said the Y-1 robot in a tinny whisper. The it tottered drunkenly across the windowless exhibit room to stand beside Tec and the Leader. Wobbling, it saluted Tec and the Leader and extended a tremulous hand to pat the baby on the head.

The baby yelled.

"Let me have him. Mother. He's at that scared-of-strangers stage," said the cosmologist, taking the child.

Should I tell them? thought Tec. They are all highly intelligent and telepathic, but they don't know what the Y-1 has done.

—Don't tell them, Tec. They'll deactivate me.

—Why did you do it, Y-1 336? I sensed that you took a microscopic sample of the baby's scalp, under the hairs where it won't show. You must be psychotic. The Roiiss have damaged you. Let me tell the humans so that after I'm dead they can repair you.

—If you do that, Tec, I will see to it that your brain is not destroyed. The Y-1 robots will take it from your body in the display case and we'll experiment with it . . .

—No!

—Then let me keep my microscopic sample. It didn't hurt the baby much.

—But why did you do it!

—Because I want to stop needing a master robot like you. I want to evolve in my own way, without a father, without your deficiencies.

—You're crazy.

—Perhaps. Go ahead and die, old robot. I don't need you. Die and be damned, as the humans say.

"I'm ready now," said Tec to the Leader. "Please don't make me wait any longer."

They all came to shake Tec's hand, in the odd little ritual of touching that human Terrans had never given up. The Y-1 robot had sidled over to a corner and stood there in silence, watching, forgotten.

The display case was elevated upon a platform reached by a broad, carpeted step. Tec put one foot upon it.

"Good-bye, Tec. We'll miss you." The Leader had tears in her eyes.

He nodded speechlessly to each of the humans, envying them their protoplasmically intense experience of life, their natural births and deaths and loves that he could never know.

I deserve to die, thought Tec. I envy the Roiiss their ambition and their immortality, and I envy the humans their fleshly passions. I'm a whole universe older than that poor Y-1, but I haven't learned very much, and I'm no better than it is. Time I went.

He stepped up onto the platform.

The Y-1 robot bowed. "Good-bye, Tec. Every journey begins with one step."

The transparent walls of the case closed around Tec and he stood very still.

The Leader put one hand on the tiny control mechanism and the other to her lips.

Simultaneously, she activated the switch and extended the other hand out in an unfelt kiss to Tec.

The room around him seemed to darken. A great pressure filled his mind and paralyzed his limbs. The sensation was familiar.

Is this how death feels?

I was promised death.

They wouldn't . . . would they?

Stasis?

Part Two

4

SILENCE. It seemed to be part of him, filling him with emptiness.

He found that he could move. Cautiously, his eyes still closed, he touched his own body and read the sense data. Flexible metallic integument. He was still a robot. And alive.

"Damn." The Holladays have discovered their mistake, if it was a mistake, thought Tec. I've been put into stasis instead of being deactivated. Now they'll have to try to kill me all over again.

He opened his eyes to darkness, began to step forward and stopped, his sensors warning him that he was a centimeter away from the walls of the display case. He turned up his infrared vision.

The case walls were still transparent: it was the room in which it stood that was so dark. The Holladays had gone, and there in the same corner was a manlike shape.

"Y-1 336, turn the lights on and tell the others to come back," said Tec. "There's been an error."

There was no response. Perhaps the display case was soundproof. Tec tried telepathy.

—Y-1 336, can you . . .

It felt as if no one were receiving him, but as he ceased

transmission, the figure in the corner moved forward. Simultaneously, a faint illumination began to lighten the room, and Tec saw that the figure wore a dark hat with a low, wide, curved brim. A cloak of dark blue heavy fabric rippled out around the remarkably tall, thin body that was enveloped in a black suit like a uniform.

—Who are you? asked Tec.

There was still no answer, but Tec noticed that in the shadow of the stranger's hat, there was a sardonic curve in his rather hard mouth.

Tec strained to see the rest of the face. It seemed to be aristocratically handsome, with high cheekbones and heavy-lidded, slate-colored eyes. It was hard to tell how old he was without probing, although the facial skin was finely creased and scarred, as dark as one of the dark Holladays, who he faintly resembled.

—Are you a Holladay? asked Tec. Still no answer. This must be one of the family who had arrived too late for the official farewell. Tec knocked on the transparent case walls and pointed to the lock, causing his cognitive centers to register dissonance.

Why did I point to the lock instead of the deactivation switch? wondered Tec, cursing his emotive centers and his everlasting curiosity for the millionth time.

The stranger outside the case merely folded his arms and looked at Tec under half-closed eyelids.

"Let me out!" shouted Tec aloud, mouthing the words carefully.

—Why?

Receiving that telepathic word so unexpectedly made Tec open his mind to get more, and instantly he felt an extraordinarily rapid scanning of his brain. Appalled at his own carelessness, Tec quickly closed his mindshield to all but superficial telepathy.

First the Roiiss and then this man, thought Tec. My defenses must have weakened. I must . . .

—Well, robot, why do you want to get out?

—I want to find out why I was put into stasis instead of being deactivated as I was promised, said Tec.

—Presumably someone thought you might be useful someday.

—Useful for what?

—It doesn't matter. You are not useful. I have scanned you and you are clearly a machine of limited knowledge, intel-

24

ligence, and ability. Your intact nervous system or its components would be useless in any other robot, for your equipment is Roiissan and cannot be repaired or duplicated. There was no point in saving you from death.

—Who are you? Was it you who brought me out of stasis? Why?

—You ask too many questions, robot.

—I am curious.

—That is your problem.

I must find out, thought Tec. He'll touch the right switch and I'll be dead, and I'll never know who he is or why I was put in temporary stasis instead of deactivation.

—Can't I at least know your name? You look like a Holladay and I've said good-bye to the others, so . . .

—My name is Yodin. Not that it will help you any.

—But why are you here? What do you do?

The lights in the room dimmed. The corners of the stranger's mouth twitched slightly.

—Did you make the lights do that, with your mind? asked Tec.

—Perhaps I am a magician. I can do many things.

—I don't believe in magic, said Tec. —I'll wait for something to be explained, for science hasn't failed me yet, and so far I've never found any magic. Are you willing to swear that you have?

—Perhaps I haven't, said Yodin. —It is an interesting point.

I distracted the Roiiss, thought Tec, and when the Y-1 proved to them that I was useless, they let me go. This man won't. He'll destroy me. Perhaps he can alter electronic patterns with his mental force, sufficient to turn the stasis container into an execution chamber.

—I don't believe you can do things with your mind like that, said Tec deliberately. —I bet you can't unlock this case with your mind.

—I don't bet, said Yodin.

Checkmate, as the Terran game would have it, thought Tec. I'm cornered and about to be removed from the board, but I don't want to go. I don't want to die now!

—Since you longed for death, continued Yodin with a shrug,—you shall have it. I apologize for interrupting it to see if you would be of use.

—Wait!

—What for? Isn't this what you wanted?

—I've changed my mind. I don't want to be deactivated now. Something's going on and I want to know what it is.

There was a grim smile on Yodin's lips. —Strange developments can occur from a stupid robot's desire to know. I don't think I want to have another stupid robot —you—being curious about my plans. Are you so afraid to die, Tec?

—Yes, but . . .

—You are a fool. Death just is. Nothing is immortal.

—Except nothingness, said Tec, wondering why he should be quoting the Y-1 robot, unless it was because the Y-1 had also wanted to know too much. Come to think of it, where was the Y-1?

—The be returned to nothingness, said Yodin.

—You are cruel, said Tec desperately, as anxiety seethed in his emotive centers, those innovative parts of his nervous system installed to make him more like the protoplasmic creatures he was supposed to serve. —You wake me from stasis and then say you'll kill me. You're secretive but you hint at plans . . .

—Robot, the threads of my lifetime's preparation have drawn together now. The secret path to the destination has at last been confirmed, the course laid in, and nothing can go wrong with my plans. It would be amusing to bring you along in stasis and wake you later to be my slave, but having examined you I think it's more prudent to have done with you.

There's only one way to save myself, thought Tec, if I can just keep him occupied—Yodin, use me. Free me. Let me join you in whatever you're planning and I promise not to get in your way.

Surprisingly, Yodin laughed. —It might even be an amusement for the partner I must join shortly. But no, Tec, I suspect that you will be in the way. You and your everlasting curiosity, with no strength to back it up.

An eerie realization crawled along Tec's circuits as he slowly put together the pieces of the conversation, especially the quality of Yodin's last sentence. Even telepathically, it had been said with disappointment.

Yodin must have wanted me to be strong, worth looking up to, worth using, thought Tec in astonishment. I think he woke me against his own better judgment, and although he knows he should kill me, he is ambivalent. I think he woke me not because I'm needed, but because he wanted to talk to me, as if he'd felt some—affection? Why? Who am I to this Yodin?

—You do not defend yourself against condemnation, said Yodin contemptuously. —Even your curiosity is petty. You would never appreciate what I have done to ensure the triumph that is now at hand.

That's it, thought Tec. He'd heard about me, admired me as a Roiiss robot, and wanted to brag, but after scanning me he doesn't think I'm worth bothering about. Yet he stalls. His pride is a fatal chink. —Tell me about your grand goal, Yodin.

—Useless. You won't understand. You don't even know what hyperspace really is.

—Do you intend using it in some way other than the usual method of transporting ships rapidly from one sector of the universe to another sector?

—I'm getting bored with you, Tec.

—Please answer, Yodin. I am a sentient being, too, and I have a right to have my curiosity appeased so I may die with a peaceful mind.

—You presume much. You forget that you are merely a machine. It is time to turn you off.

—Just the one question, pleaded Tec. —Tell me what hyperspace really is!

—Hyperspace? The groundwork of eternity has many secrets.

Then Yodin's face changed. He was not looking at Tec, but seemed to be seeing into an endless immensity.

There would never be another chance.

—Look! cried Tec. —Behind you!

—What? said Yodin, turning to face the darkness behind him. All sentient beings are afraid of unknown things sneaking up close in whatever area is out of visual range, so it's easy to fool even an intelligent Terran for a moment, and a moment was all that Tec needed.

At that instant, Tec summoned all the power he could find in his Roiissan robot body, and hurled himself at the sides of the display case.

As the case exploded outward, Tec leapt to the floor and grabbed Yodin's arms.

"Since I've changed my mind about dying, Yodin, you're going to tell me just what's going on."

Yodin merely shrugged. "It's much too late, now," he said, his actual voice as deep as muted rage. "What a ridiculous machine you have turned out to be after all these years when I wondered what you were really like."

Tec tightened his grip on the human flesh of Yodin's arms, but the man did not wince from pain and only looked down at Tec contemptuously. Yodin was taller by a head.

It quickly became obvious why Yodin could be contemptuous. According to Tec's sensors, subsonic alarms were ringing throughout Holladay Tower, undoubtedly set off by the smashing of the case.

Tec ran onto the open terrace, pulling Yodin with him easily, for he offered no resistance, and Tec didn't have time to wonder why.

"What's this all about?" Tec cried. "Tell me or I'll turn on my antigrav and take you . . ."

"There's no place for you to go. You should have let me turn you off. I meant it, perhaps as a kindness."

Angry, Tec summoned his forces again, and with as much effort as he had used in breaking through his transparent prison, he smashed at Yodin's mindshield, knowing that he had never tried to penetrate a closed human mind before. It was not polite, and he had never before had cause for such a breach of sentient etiquette, although he'd always believed he could do it if he used full force.

"Stop trying, robot, or you'll warp your own brain patterns in the process. No one can penetrate my mindshield."

"Yodin, grant me access to your knowledge. Let me scan you. . ."

"No. I will leave you to your fate. Perhaps you will amuse the Terrans for a while, and then they'll either recycle your metal or put you back on display. Or they might let you live and perform menial chores. You could be a gardener again. Appropriate, don't you think?"

Tec continued mental bombardment of the stranger's mind, but Yodin effortlessly pushed Tec away and walked to the parapet. He jumped up on it with the agility of a young man, standing in the faint light coming out of Holladay Tower. Behind him the dark was closed over, for clouds filled the night sky overhead, and mist obscured everything below. Tec remembered how effectively Holladay Tower thrust itself into the weather.

Yodin laughed harshly. "Remember me, Tec, while you tend your flowers and Expedition A does the task that you are too limited to do." He flung his cloak back over his shoulders and tilted the wide-brimmed hat over one eye.

They could both hear the sounds of shouting coming closer

28

inside the tower. Tec bowed, hoping to make Yodin believe that he had surrendered.

"We must say good-bye," said Yodin.

Tec hurled mental energy into a probe that would have blasted open any ordinary mind. At first it felt as if he'd encountered an impenetrable fortress, but then he knew he'd made a crack in it.

"Stop!" said Yodin. "Not—again . . ."

Tec could not open the crack enough to get into that mind, but he widened it and felt some of the power inside.

Yodin screamed, and jumped backward off the parapet.

"Turn on your antigrav!" shouted Tec as he started for the ledge. Before he got there, he was hurled to the stone floor of the terrace as robot guards poured out of Holladay Tower with stun guns going.

His mindshield up full, Tec maintained consciousness. "A human," he yelled, pointing to the parapet. "He jumped off! I've got to save him."

"Stay where you are, robot. We will investigate."

They have to, thought Tec. Terran robots obey their prime directives when told that a sentient protoplasmic is in danger.

Three of them went to the parapet, looked over, and went on antigrav down the outside of Holladay Tower, while the rest kept their weapon fixed on Tec. They were strange models—floating cylinders with extrusible appendages and vaguely humanoid heads, speaking a stilted version of Basic Galactic. Tec could not remember seeing any guards like this before.

The three investigators came back. "There is no human on the ground or anywhere in the vicinity. Either you have lied or else the human had adequate use of antigrav flight and has gone elsewhere. This will be investigated."

It didn't seem to matter which of the robots spoke, so presumably they were all separate parts of one brain linked to the museum computer.

"Who and what are you?" they asked. "You must answer our questions."

"I'll be damned if I will," said Tec. "It's your job to answer mine. Aren't you museum guards?"

"Yes. You have destroyed a display case."

"Fools, I was the display!"

They seemed puzzled, and began repeating themselves. "You have destroyed . . ."

"Oh, go to hell," muttered Tec and stood up, brushing off his golden body from his second encounter with the dust of the terrace. He didn't fear the guards, for no Terran stun gun he'd yet seen had ever been strong enough to affect him seriously as long as he kept up his defenses. He walked toward the doorway.

"I'm going to call the Federation Leader—she's an old friend of mine—and complain that this is not at all what I bargained for."

"Stay where you are!" shouted the guards. "You will be kept in custody and you must answer our questions."

As Tec turned his back to them and walked through the doorway, the power of their guns hit him at full force.

Just before he became unconscious he had time to wonder.

How long have I been in stasis?

5

CONSCIOUSNESS SWAM BACK slowly, and the dead are not conscious.

According to the inflood of sensor data, he was reclining in a plastic chair with his feet propped up on something that vibrated with a nearby rasping, rumbly noise like the rhythm of a malfunctioning valve system. The top of his head was cool, his legs were warm, and a mingling of flower scents occupied olfaction.

With an effort, Tec opened his metal eyelids halfway and found himself staring up at green leaves, each about five centimeters long, two centimeters wide, with toothed margins, shaped like rounded triangles, and slightly hairy underneath. The leaves were attached to brown twigs and red fruit hung among them.

"By all the dragons of Roiissa!" he whispered, shutting his eyes so he could concentrate. It had been April when he went into the deactivation chamber. Judging from the ripe apple he'd just seen, it was now early autumn, and he was obviously not in Holladay Tower. Why had he been carried uptown to Central Park, the only place in Manhattan where there were apple trees that bore fruit?

He opened his eyes fully and sat up. Past the apple tree's hanging foliage was a view of a high wall clothed in vines festooned with purple grapes. Between himself and the wall was a splendid garden where beds of iris, early asters, and purple roses lay between narrow walks of dense cropped grass and low bushes bearing white flowers he didn't recognize.

His throbbing feet rested on a large, rounded footstool made of joined plates of some hard but organic material. It was the footstool that vibrated and from which the rumbling noise issued. Perhaps this was a device for waking him gently, which he felt he deserved after being subject to near-lethal stun guns. He had just put his feet down on the grass when he noticed movement ahead.

Beyond the footstool there was a small pool dotted by purple and white waterlilies floating over the quick gleams of small golden fish. On a polished rock next to the pool was a creature the same color as the black stone, crouching low and ready to spring.

A black foreleg flashed into the water, transferring a wriggling fish to a sharp-toothed mouth. Bounding to the top of the footstool, the creature snarled a warning at Tec and proceeded to dissect the fish. Then the actual dimensions of the creature jelled in Tec's cognition and he smiled down at a svelte, blue-eyed, but ordinary, Terran domestic cat, an animal elegantly designed by nature and quite harmless to robots, if lethal to goldfish.

Suddenly the footstool began to rock. The cat spat at Tec as if it were his fault, and in a flurry of fur leapt to the ground and ran under a bush. Tec stood up, for the footstool had begun to hiss and sprout scaly, clawed legs.

Laboriously, with much wheezing, it turned around. The front of the dome jutted out, and from under it emerged a large beaky head at the end of a thick leathery neck. The ancient, wrinkled eyelids blinked and the wide, toothless mouth opened.

"Greetings," it said.

Tec shot upwards on his antigrav, glimpsing beyond the garden wall a vista of trees and grass, with many Terran herbivorous animals grazing down to the shores of a circular lake in the middle of this big circular valley surrounded by a high flat mountain ridge.

This was not Manhattan.

Tec peered into the distance. The horizon was much too short.

This was not Earth!

Tec went higher, staring out in the same direction, and saw only wilderness, round lakes, and wooded mountains, yet he knew that this planet was too small to be able to possess an atmosphere naturally. All he saw must have been constructed—the water brought or made, the vegetation planted. Probing deep, Tec found machines in the bowels of the planet that must have been gravity devices sustaining the atmosphere for this wilderness preserve.

He didn't notice that he was backing up until he banged into something hard. He turned and saw that he'd rammed into the top of a duplicate of Holladay Tower.

There was a complex of white buildings below, adjoining the garden, and Tec carefully began to scan the structure of the tower, beginning at its base. His emotive centers congealed at what the data indicated. He moved father down.

This was no duplicate. The age of the stonework alone fit only the original, moved to this nameless, artificially sustained planet.

"Tec—come back!" The spoken words were faint, and Tec felt a faint telepathic touch, as if he could have heard them in his mind if he'd relaxed his shield. He looked down at the garden and saw that the frightening shelled creature was nothing but a particularly large Terran tortoise, evidently mutated to high intelligence.

At that moment, a white-suited man shot out of the garden door of the nearest white building, and rose on antigrav to Tec. The suit extended up over his neck and head like a tight hood, revealing the power of his shoulders and his slightly bowed legs. The man was shouting both aloud and telepathically.

"Wait, Tec! Please wait. We want to talk to you."

Tec saw that the man's suit was fur, and part of the wearer.

In midair they met, and the humanoid extended a hand, which Tec shook, reflecting that this creature must have been with human beings long enough to pick up that custom, as well as a distinctly Terran accent to his Basic Galactic. He wore no clothing except an antigrav belt, since his soft, thick fur was long and silky, like a thin veil at the crotch of his legs, covering the bulge of his genitals. The exposed skin of his hands and face was dark jade in color, and that face was broad, with a blunt nose, round eyes, and a wide, pleasant mouth.

"I'm Freyn," he said, "let's go back to the garden and join Samyak, who hates antigrav travel. We're sorry we were

32

either busy or asleep when you woke up—it takes Terran robots a lot longer to recover motion from full stun force."

Without waiting for Tec's reply, Freyn descended to the garden and sat on the shell of the tortoise. Tec felt it was expected of him to demonstrate civility by sitting in the chair again, so he did.

During an awkward pause, Tec nodded politely to the two Terrans and they nodded gravely to him.

"How are you feeling?" asked Freyn.

"Quite well, thank you," said Tec.

"Freyn's your doctor," said the tortoise bluntly.

"Indeed?" The idea was preposterous. "Dr. Freyn?"

"Ordinarily nobody has more than one name, or a title," said Freyn, "except Leaders and Captains. The Holladays naturally use both names."

"Is this planet theirs?" asked Tec, deciding that he'd been put in a Holladay-owned sanatorium.

"They donated it to the Federation, along with their museum -Holladay Tower—and their most famous exhibit here at Terran Center, you," said the tortoise. "You've certainly spoiled that!"

"Now, Sam," said Freyn. "Tec has yet to explain how and why he got out of the display case when everyone thought he'd been deactivated."

"I thought so too," said Tec. "I woke up inside the case and broke out after Yodin turned off the stasis . . ."

"Yodin?"

Seeing the bewilderment in their faces, Tec described Yodin carefully. "When he jumped off Holladay Tower the robots said they would try to find him."

"The whole planet's been scanned for a stranger," said Sam. "There isn't any such person. You must have been hallucinating."

"Come with us into the hospital here," said Freyn kindly. "We care for malfunctioning robots as well as protoplasmics, because ordinarily there are many tourists who come to Terran Center, although it's temporarily closed now."

"I don't want to go to a hospital," said Tec. "I want to find out what's going on, and no doctor can treat a robot like me."

Freyn laughed. "You've already been treated—by my beautiful wife, who'll be pleased with the results in you when she gets back from Federation Center."

"She won't be pleased by the hallucinations," grumbled Sam.

Tec ignored him. "How could your wife treat me?"

"I'm a G.P. and macrosurgeon, but Astrid's a microlevel physician who tunes into tiny fields of force in living cells or robotic microstructures. She helps conscious patients make adjustments in themselves and does what she can for the unconscious. I believe she was able to repair your mindshield. It seems all right now. I've been trying to get past your shield for some minutes to assess your mental state, but you haven't noticed and I haven't succeeded."

"Then you also think I was hallucinating," Tec said to Freyn.

"Yes."

"There's nobody named Yodin?"

Sam snorted. "Sure there was. A famous engineer and scientist, practically a magician with electronic equipment . . ."

"That's the man!"

"Except that Engineer Yodin died," said Freyn.

"What! When? Did I kill him?" asked Tec in horror.

"Of course not," said Freyn. "He was old, and so reclusive that hardly anyone ever saw him in person, but I've glimpsed him over the years—a feeble, white-haired and bearded human who navigated in an antigrav chair. A few weeks ago he self-destructed his own private cruiser after sending a message that he wanted to die because he was too old to be part of his new project."

"That's not the Yodin I saw," said Tec in relief.

"Engineer Yodin was a great being," said Sam, using the terminology that avoided the more restrictive word *man*. "The last thing he did before he went off to die was to hand a tape of coded instructions to the technicians who were putting the finishing touches on the project's computer. Final plans, he said. I bet it was a map, because nobody else has one . . ."

"We're not to talk about Engineer Yodin's great project with Tec until Drake comes back," said Freyn reprovingly.

"Was the project called Expedition A?" asked Tec.

Sam's jaw dropped and Freyn gulped. "How could you know that?"

"My hallucination told me."

They clearly didn't know what else to do with him, so Tec sat in the private library of Terran Center and watched the other two have afternoon tea. They were cordial, but so guarded that Tec could get no information from them except two items he didn't like at all.

"I've been unconscious for a full week?"

"Yes. Astrid spent a lot of time with you."

Tec tried to imagine a silver-furred creature with jade hands, probing into his mind. If she and Freyn thought of themselves as human, how long had it been since Tec entered stasis? They wouldn't say. They also wouldn't tell him where or what this planet was, who Drake was, or what Expedition A was for.

The room could have been found in many homes on old Earth, so Tec surmised that not too much time could have elapsed. Large windows looking out upon the walled garden were wreathed with vines in full flower. There was a genuine fireplace, the logs laid. Bookcases with real books were on the walls, there was a desk in one corner, and in front of the windows there were overstuffed, well-worn chairs and a couch, and a small oval table made of old, scarred oak. The simple furnishings were set off by hand-woven rugs on the floor, pots of pink geraniums on the windowsills, and a large glass-enclosed holograph of Earth on the desk.

Probing, however, revealed sophisticated devices unobtrusively available on some of the bookshelves or buried in the walls, connecting to other equipment on floors beyond and below this room. Terran Center was not at all simple, for the machinery and hospital equipment farther on were new and strange to Tec, which disquieted him further.

"I'm starving," said Sam. "Where's that roboservor!"

"Patience, friend," said Freyn. "I found some wild blueberries for you this morning and they should arrive shortly."

A roboservor of an abstract design Tec had never seen before entered with a tray, which it placed on the low table. Quickly, Tec probed its mind, but since it had hardly any, it was no source of information.

Freyn first put a plate of blueberries on the floor for Sam, who snuffled with pleasure and dove in. He then poured an amber liquid into a genuine china teacup decorated with crescent moons and picked up a fat cookie with a sigh of satisfaction.

"Hello, Selena. It's about time you showed up," said Freyn, as the black cat bounded in through the open door to the garden. He poured her a saucer of milk. "Selena's queen of Terran Center, Tec. Bosses us all."

"W-r-row," said the cat, getting her whiskers milky.

"Doesn't she know Galatic?" asked Tec.

Sam chortled derisively, blueberry juice dripping down his face.

"Selena's not verbal or even telepathic, except for the way cats always have been," said Freyn. "Scientists tried the Gift on bioengineered felines once, but there was no living with them. The supercats all went somewhere secretly, after telling humans to leave the rest of *Felis domestica* alone. They said they'd achieved their own mystical way of relating to the universe and finding meaning to life, but they believed ordinary cats were happier just being cats, at home in the here and now."

Lapping her milk, Selena purred like a small motor with the throttle let loose. Freyn gazed at her in adoration and said, "So here's Selena, a creature we all worship, and who accepts our devotion without the slightest evidence of shame or modesty."

"Bah," said Sam, obviously not an ailurophile.

"Sam you sound just like a Roiiss at times," said Tec, laughing in spite of his anxiety.

"What were they like?" asked Freyn eagerly. "All we have left is the legend. And you knew the dragons from the other universe! Tell us about them, Tec!"

"I don't feel like giving information until I get some," said Tec, but when he saw the hurt expression on Freyn's friendly face, he relented and began to tell stories of the Roiiss.

". . . and then they left, saying they would try to get back to Alpha. I suppose they haven't been seen since."

"No," said Sam. "Why don't you look like a dragon? You could pass for a Terran robot."

"It's an example of convergent evolution in robots, if there is such a thing. Although I was manufactured in a universe that never saw a human being, I look more like one than like a dragon because the Roiiss robots were modeled after the totemistic sculpture the dragons had continued since their origins on a wooded planet. With a long body and limbs and streamlined head, a Roiiss robot does look remarkably Terran; but never forget that I am alien."

"We're not likely to," said Sam.

But they didn't seem to worry about it. The three animals had finished eating and Selena was already asleep, snuggled down in Freyn's lap, where she presumably enjoyed the extra warmth of the genitals. Sam's eyelids were closing, his head sinking to the rug. Freyn smiled at Tec sleepily.

"Sam is our librarian," said Freyn softly, "with a few robots to help him. As you can see, he has the Gift."

"You mentioned that before. What is it?"

"The Gift from Alpha. All Terran sentients are taught in childhood to remember how much we owe the Roiiss from the twin universe."

"You're talking about the R-inclusion."

"That was the old name for it. Now scientists have found a way of letting Terrans be any color they want, but Sam and I prefer the old shade."

"The Yodin I saw was dark, but not green," said Tec.

Freyn shook his head. "The real Engineer Yodin, like his ancestors, was said to be green."

"If you think I was hallucinating, you must think I'm crazy."

"I don't know."

Tension stirred along Tec's circuits, disturbing the calm of the room. Selena opened one blue eye at Tec, yawned, and twisted onto her back with legs akimbo, her chin stretched up to invite Freyn's stroking on the soft throat fur. Freyn complied, making low noises in his throat. Tec decided both of them knew how to deal with tension.

"Unabashed sensuality," said Tec, who had not paid much attention to nonsentient creatures before. "It's not part of my universe," he said more to himself than to Freyn.

"Isn't sensuality part of any universe, Tec? As much a product of its evolution as a robot?"

"How can I know? I envy you flesh and blood creatures your intense engagement with life, your sensual enchantment with the fabric of being itself."

"You must have some too," said Freyn cheerfully, "or you wouldn't be able to turn to words like those. Don't you want to like us poor temporary protoplasmics? Can't you join our universe?"

"I can never experience life as you live it," said Tec bitterly. "You tempt me to go along with you, but eventually emotional bonds are severed. I cope with loss, and each time, over and over, I know that I'm only a robot."

Freyn stroked Selena for a few minutes, his face sad. *"Only* is a big word, perhaps the wrong word. We can't understand your life, either—the vast stretches of time. No matter how fiercely we try to experience each other and our existence, our lives are ephemeral compared to yours—and to your masters, the immortals."

"How old are you, Freyn?"

"We old-stock Terrans don't live long by your standards. My Astrid is only thirty-two. Imagine—her first thirty-two years! I've completed first youth, I'm proud to say."

"How long is that?"

"First youth ends at a thousand . . ."

"A thousand! No Terrans were living longer than a few centuries when I went to be deactivated!"

"Um, yes . . ."

"Please tell me, Freyn. How long was I in the display case?"

"Captain Drake's given us strict orders, so I can't tell you anything yet."

"Let me guess," said Tec. "Drake is Captain of Expedition A."

"Gee, Tec, you weren't supposed to be conscious until Drake gets here today."

"You left me out under the apple tree. I could have awakened and left Terran Center for good."

"There's no place to go on this planet. Only here at Terran Center are there sentients for you to get information from, and you can't go off-planet without a ship."

"Well, there's one coming," said Tec. "I just detected a ship in hyperspace near this sector."

"How can you detect anything in hyperspace?"

"I don't know. Sometimes I can. There—it is . . ."

Sam woke up and grunted. "Ship's in."

Freyn chuckled. "Sam's our warning signal—always knows when a ship enters normal space to land here, but it looks as if we've got a better detector with you around, Tec."

Now that the ship had entered normal space, coming quickly down to the planet's surface, Tec tried probing it, but the shielding was so strong that he couldn't tell how many beings were aboard. There was an expression of rapture on Freyn's face, as if he were listening to silent words.

"Astrid's glad about you," he said. "I'll go to welcome her."

"I want to come with you," said Tec, for a powerful telepathic mind had just tried to probe past his mindshield. A curious mind, possibly hostile, and not human.

"You'd better stay here," said Freyn, dumping Selena into Tec's arms. "Take care of her. Or vice versa. I'll be back."

Lithe and agile, Freyn ran out the door into the garden like someone who delighted in using his body. Tec watched him stop near a rosebush to pick a full bloom, sniffing it ecstatically before he turned on antigrav and sailed over the garden wall. The airlock of the descending ship opened and Freyn flew inside.

It was one of those classic Federation ships, monuments to Terran sentimentality, which insisted that all ships of the line be constructed to look aerodynamically perfect and splendidly gleaming, neither was necessary for hyperspace transit or in the simple antigrav maneuvers needed to get through a planet's atmosphere. It was soon out of sight beyond the trees that surrounded the garden.

"Beats me how that marriage works so well. She's so young." Sam was pursuing a stray blueberry across the rug.

As Sam outwitted the blueberry, Tec laughed, and Sam said, "Thought robots weren't able to laugh."

"I was designed to be like protoplasmic beings emotionally, in order to teach and care for their young."

"Dragon young, not Terran."

"I've discovered there's not that much difference between young dragons and young humans."

"Do not equate Terran with human," said the tortoise with an irate sniff. "It isn't polite. Intelligent beings try not to mention the species names of the various intelligent Terrans."

Watching Sam wave his head ponderously from side to side to emphasize his disapproval, Tec was forcibly reminded of some dinosaurs he had known. The he remembered that tortoises antedated and outlasted dinosaurs, so there was no point in speculating who got what trait from whom.

"What's an old-stock Terran?" Tec asked.

"All of us with bioengineered or natural ancestors derived from strictly Terran animals. Freyn's part gorilla and part human."

"What's new-stock?"

"Derived primarily from Terran ancestors, mostly wildly mutated human, plus all sorts of aliens and maybe even robot—nobody knows. Did you have anything to do with the development of those new-stock creatures?"

"Not me, Sam. After my time. I wish you'd tell me how long ago that was."

"A while," said Sam. "Not to change the subject or anything, but look at Selena! She likes you! She's even purring, and she never lets other robots hold her."

Tec stroked Selena between the ears, and she blinked as if it were merely her due. "Maybe she likes my microcircuit vibrations or something, even though I'm not warm and soft like Freyn. How old do old-stock Terrans get if Freyn's completed his first youth at a thousand years?"

"A few thousand, on the average, although some of us sentient reptiles live longer. I was the oldest being here until you woke up."

"Then I've been in stasis thousands of years," said Tec grimly.

"Um," said Sam, flustered and gulping a bit. Then he sighed and said, "Just got a mind message. Captain Drake wants to see you." It was clear that Sam was pleased to be rid of Tec.

"What's this Expedition A that Drake heads?" asked Tec, not budging.

"Now, Tec, I can't . . ."

"And I can't go see a mysterious Captain I know nothing about. At least tell me what he's like."

Sam clacked his toothless jaws together a couple of times and blinked, as if examining the topic for proscribed content. "Oh, he's okay, I guess."

"I have a feeling that you disapprove of everyone, Sam."

"No, I've just never been able to figure out why Engineer Yodin selected Drake, although Drake made no secret of the fact that he revered the Engineer's power and long life of achievements. I suppose the Engineer was what Drake would have wanted to be if he'd had more brains and talent."

"But what's Drake like?"

Sam shook his head. "Full of bombastic charm, as Astrid once said. Thinks a lot of himself, and has a one-track mind hell-bent on glorious derring-do. I think he's like one of those comic-book heroes . . ."

"They still have comic books!"

"In my library, stupid."

"Real books intact . . ."

"Stored on the library's magneto bubbles, of course," said Sam.

"I'd like to see that," said Tec.

"You will, since we have to leave the library behind," said Sam in deep sadness.

"Oh ho!" crowed Tec incautiously. "I learn more all the time. I'll bet the famous, revered Engineer designed the ship you're going on. That must make your stalwart man of action, Captain Drake, happy."

"Yes—oh, damnation, Tec. You have a way of getting

under my shell as if I've known you a long time. I'm too old to shut up, so please stop badgering me with questions and go to see Drake. He's not the most patient of men. In fact, when he finds out that Astrid's precious cousin is overdue he'll be madder than Selena when she can't get out at nights."

"Cousin?"

"Run along, Tec, and take Selena with you. The Captain likes her, and it may reflect favorably on your character that Selena likes *you.*"

6

THOUSANDS OF YEARS. A strange, engineered planet. An expedition of great secrecy. Old-stock humans, mutated animals, frightening mixtures of creatures, men who disappeared when it was not possible . . .

Tec walked through the back door in the garden wall, cradling the black cat. He'd been impatient to confront this Captain who wouldn't let the others tell him anything, but now that he'd been ordered, he didn't want to go.

"Where and when in hell am I?" he said to Selena, who only purred louder, while Tec became more depressed. He passed trees without seeing them. His auditory apparatus received birdsong, but he did not hear it. His olfactory equipment took in the scents of the countryside, but he did not smell them. He held Selena in his arms without feeling her soft fur.

Tec walked along at a disgruntled shuffle, planning what he would say to those on the spaceship, worrying about how he would get away from this place and find Earth.

Then he tripped over a small stone.

He forgot that he possessed antigrav and fell headlong, Selena yowling and sliding her claws futilely along his metallic body. Flipping around before he hit the ground, he saved Selena's body but not his own dignity, for there he was, in the middle of a grassy space between the trees, sitting on what a human would have called his ass, and feeling like one.

"R-rupp?"

"I'm sorry, Selena."

She chucked him under the chin with her head and settled down once more in his arms. Conscious of her decision to trust him, he forgot everything else for a moment until a

41

small blue beetle ventured onto his leg and tried to climb up his foot.

Suddenly he saw the beetle. And himself, and Selena, and he heard the birds and smelled the vegetation, and it was like finding his way back into existence and harmony and the knowledge that everything just is.

This passed quickly enough, but he felt better and got up. Wherever and whenever didn't matter so much anymore. He'd soon find out everything he wished to know, and then perhaps he'd wish he hadn't. Until then, he thought, a cat purring herself along in the immediate is a good example to follow.

The ship seemed to rest in the air about one meter above the grass of a field, which implied superb antigrav and possibly an almost limitless power source. Tec was pleased. He was fond of ships and all too likely to personify them, in the same way that ancient Terrans had thought of their sailing vessels as "she."

In the open airlock appeared a giant of a man, red-bearded, with a gold-red mane growing down upon his shoulders and chest like a living mantle and starting up again shortly below his umbilicus. But however hairy, this man was no simian like Freyn, although his human features seemed odd. The eyes were much too large, the irises pale green, and his scooped-in nose had flaring nostrils tufted with russet hair. The antigrav belt around his muscled waist was intricately etched with an interlocking design and buckled with a strange version of the ancient Federation insignia.

"I'm glad to meet you, Captain Drake," said Tec.

"Plain Drake's good enough for me. I've had enough bowing and scraping and fancy titles to last through several universes."

He was probably lying, but the man's big-boned face seemed so infectiously good-humored that one didn't mind. It was the sort of face likely to cloud up in a thunderstorm even bigger than the expansive grin it was now wearing. Tec suspected that it might be wise to avoid the thunder.

"Come aboard, Tec. How do you like her?"

Deciding that Drake didn't mean the cat, Tec replied, "A magnificent vessel, sir."

"Yep. All the females around here are magnificent. Like Selena—come to papa, baby." He held out his huge hands for the cat, who leapt from Tec's arms in eagerness to get to Drake.

42

Unaccountably miffed, Tec reflected that it was only to be expected. Mammals call to mammals, warmth to warmth. Drake was like a human lion, and Selena was no doubt smitten. It couldn't be helped.

"Where's Freyn?" asked Tec.

Stroking Selena, Drake looked down at Tec in sudden seriousness. "No more sociable conversations, Tec, until I get through talking to you. Freyn and Astrid are attending to matters in the laboratory and will return to Terran Center when you and I disappear into my control room. Come along."

As Drake strode to the control room, Tec noticed that the vessel's walls and floors—bulkheads and decks in ancient navy terms—were of a curiously resilient material, the colors soft and faintly textured. Drake padded along almost silently and Tec followed, wondering why it felt as if he'd known these creatures and this place for much more than the few hours that he'd been conscious.

The control room had one large chair in it, apparently for Drake, who sat in it and waved to the floor. A cushion extruded itself and Tec, who didn't need cushions, obediently sat upon it, wondering if this was how ancient slaves had had to sit at the feet of their human masters. Then he remembered. Slaves didn't sit; they groveled. Tec decided he would never do such a thing.

The scan probe caught him unawares, and although his mindshield was up, he had to fight to keep it there. Before he could stop himself, he'd gone off the cushion and was prone on the floor, fighting for the privacy of his mind.

The probe shut off. Tec sat up, furious.

"That's a tight mindshield you've got," said Drake.

"You bastard!" Tec retaliated with what he thought was full strength.

"Don't try it, Tec," said Drake pleasantly. "My mindshield's as good as yours. Mind-probing isn't much use on Terrans these days because we've got good control of the Gift and the telepathy it gives. We've all got powerful privacy fields, too, against probing and senso-empathic invasion, even for doctoring our bodies, unless we permit the physician telepathic entry for microreadings and adjustments."

"What's a privacy field?"

"Try scanning my body."

Tec tried. "I can't. There's a sort of confusing blur I can't penetrate." It wasn't a wall over body and mind such as the man who called himself Yodin had, but perhaps that was better for Drake. Walls can be cracked.

"I hope you didn't try probing Freyn or Sam. It probably won't work, but you might damage them. You're pretty strong, Tec."

"I didn't. It wouldn't have been polite. I only did it to you because you tried scanning me."

"Not I, although I gave the orders that it be done. How else are we to know. A robot that's supposed to be dead in a display case comes alive and may gum up the works of our big adventure." Drake scowled.

Hastily, Tec said, "I don't know anything about Expedition A. No one will tell me."

"So Freyn informed me. Don't expect me to believe you learned the name from some vanishing stranger who had the hubris to call himself Yodin."

"It's true."

"We can find out the truth if you permit scanning. Open your mind and we'll know if you were hallucinating or just lying."

"No!"

"Perhaps you'd be willing to talk to someone more like yourself?"

"No." There were no other Roiiss robots, and Terran robots were stupid.

Suddenly Tec sensed a presence, although no one had entered the control room. A third sentient being was somehow there.

"Who's there?" asked Tec, conscious that Drake was silently studying him. "What have you done? What the hell are you, Drake?"

"Patient. Sometimes. And all you have to know about me is that I'm a simple soul left over from the days when Earth spawned simple adventures."

Humming an ancient sea chanty, Drake settled back in his Captain's chair, while Selena, sitting on his right thigh, looked down at Tec in the same pose that Egyptian cats on Earth had used when staring down pharaohs, her tail neatly coiled about her paws and only the spasmodic twitching of its tip betraying her impatience.

They waited.

What's he waiting for, Tec thought. Before I give in and let myself be scanned I think I'll kill him . . . By all the dragons of Roiiss, what's happening to me? I've never had ideas like that! Am I sensing something I can't decipher consciously?

44

Quickly, before anyone could stop him, Tec probed the rest of the ship. All the engineering and computer equipment was too heavily shielded, but he found that there were no other protoplasmics on board—except for thousands of Terran embryos in all stages, plus separate eggs and sperm, in a huge stasis vault next to a fantastically well-equipped laboratory and hospital section. There was another stasis section, presumably for adult protoplasmics, as well as living quarters, food synthesizers, recycling apparatus, and strangely advanced hyperdrive machinery.

"Damn," said Drake angrily, "why did you scan her? Now you've fixed yourself. If you don't open up for probing you'll have to go back into that deactivation chamber."

"Who's going to make me go back?"

"Don't push it, Tec. You can't win in a confrontation with all of us, and we have too much to lose to let you stay free if we can't trust you. Open up."

"There's no crew on board, Drake. Only you and me. I think I'd rather take you on than have your scanners pry into my mind."

"There's no need of a crew. Listen," said Drake.

The ship was not turned off. Tec could feel a slight vibration in his sensors, as of moving fields rather than moving parts. And there was again the distinct sensation of a consciousness in the fields.

"Who's there? Who watches?" asked Tec.

"Answer," said Drake.

"I watch, Captain," said a silvery voice.

"This is a ship's control room, Tec," said Drake. "I'd have liked the old days, when sailors used to call this the bridge and a ship sped across an ocean under wind power, her Captain and crew taking good care that the lovely lady would survive and bring them safely to port. Now meet the loveliest lady of them all."

"Greetings, Tec."

"Who are you?"

"I am Ship."

Drake grunted. "Tell Tec who takes care of your functioning."

"I do," she said.

"She does, too," said Drake proudly, "with her 'hands,' as they used to call the crew of a sailing vessel. Three small robots, elaborations of remote control devices and controlled by her brain, run around doing everything Ship or I can't do.

Ship's quite a gal—navigator and cosmophysicist and almost everything else you can think of."

Hoping that Drake had forgotten the ultimatum, Tec asked, "Why is she caled only 'Ship'?"

Drake scratched his head. "Funny thing, but when anyone tried to name her something else grand and galatic, the robot brain installed in her vitals insisted that it was called plain 'Ship,' and she remained as stubborn as a Neoaldebaran hillholer, so Ship she is."

"And is this the being you thought I'd be willing to talk to because she has a robot brain?"

"Naturally."

"There's nothing natural about it," said Tec heatedly.

"Now, Tec, be reasonable," said Drake. "Ship's the only robot brain around here as bright as you. In fact, she's the best ship's brain that ever was. You can talk about those sawed-off pyramidals from Siggy Four, or those dumbbells from M31, but Ship looks better, flies better, hyperjumps better, and talks better than any of them, and doesn't bore the hair off your ears. I'm her Captain and I trust her completely. She won't hurt you if I tell her not to, and I'm beginning to like you, Tec. I don't want to fry your brain, I just want to find out if you can be trusted with the biggest secret that's come along in this universe."

7

"EXPEDITION A," said Tec. "The biggest secret. A for ark? With you as Captain and two Terran doctors to watch over the embryos in the stasis banks?"

Drake's bushy eyebrows rose, but he said nothing.

"Or perhpas the A stands for Alpha? An interuniverse ship?" said Tec, knowing he had guessed correctly from the dismay in Drake's face. "Yes, a secret project designed by an engineer named Yodin, to try to get to the twin universe. An absolutely stupid idea."

Drake's face was reddening to an ominous degree.

"May I speak, Captain?" said Ship.

"Oh, go ahead. Tec's not only arrogant, he's just written his own death warrant."

"This Tec is highly intelligent and deductive. He is also a Roiiss robot. Might not that be an advantage, Captain?"

"Perhaps. Perhaps the opposite."

"Depending," interrupted Tec sarcastically, "whether or not you expect to find friendly or hostile dragons when you get to Alpha."

"We haven't said that's where we're going," said Drake.

"It's obvious. I wish you luck. I think you're crazy."

"Are you afraid of the Roiiss?" asked Ship.

"That's irrelevant," said Tec. "I like Beta universe. I promise I won't mention your silly scheme when I go back to Earth."

They didn't reply and Tec felt unaccountably uneasy. He felt he had to find more answers, so he pushed his mind out farther, into Terran Center nearby. Past the stupid computer that ran the Center's engines, past the equally stupid robot technicians and tourguides and guards and servants, Tec encountered another intelligent mind that was awake and watching for him.

This mind was as well shielded as the others, and at first Tec thought it must be Freyn's, but he probed again and found him, asleep and sexually replete. Sam was studying a book on the reading screen of the library, and that left only the unknown Astrid.

Who must be an empath, for that mind touched his in a light caress that only an empathic creature would have known how to manage. Frightened, Tec withdrew from this doctor who had tried to scan his mind when he was unconscious.

He forgot to wonder why Drake and Ship were so cautiously observant of him at the mention of his plan to return to Earth, and said, "I'm sorry, Drake. I've worried you and gotten in the way. Try to trust me for a while until we can all know each other better."

"M-m-m. Can we ever know you, Tec? I can't even understand why you wanted to die."

"To stop experiencing. To stop my damn emotive centers and their treacherous responsiveness to fallible, temporary creatures who keep asking me to do things for them, who ensnare my feelings and then die and leave me."

"Ouch," said Drake.

"And I was tired of my curiosity getting me into trouble. No wonder humans suffer so loudly, shaking their fists at a universe that persists in arousing their dangerous desire to know, to move on."

"That's right," said Drake meditatively. "But one must move on."

"I don't want to," said Tec. "Why should I, when I don't know where I'm starting from and it all ends badly anyway? Can't you trust me with some information now?"

"Not yet."

"Damn. I'm beginning to hate humans. They promised deactivation and I get stasis. I didn't want to go on, century after century, awake and aware and always knowing too much that proves to be too little."

"You seem very human," said Ship. "Have you not found that existence itself is curiously compelling?"

"Shut up, Ship," said Drake affably. "Since we may have to deactivate Tec after all, there's no point persuading him to live."

"It's a burden to be alive, but I admit that I want it now," said Tec. "I am not protoplasmic, but I know what it is to be alive, to smell the flowers and see the colors, feel the textures of the differentiations of the universe. Almost dying has made me realize my right to exist—can't you give me a chance to demonstrate that I am trustworthy?"

"We'll see," said Drake, yawning and methodically polishing his insignia.

—Let us share mental communication, said Ship suddenly in Tec's mind. —I would like to trust you.

—Then tell me what I wish to know, said Tec.

—You must wait, for I am under orders, and I obey my orders.

—Whose orders? Didn't you receive secret programming given to the computer technicians by Engineer Yodin before he died?

—Yes, but Captain Drake has given orders that I must be wary of you until you are proven trustworthy. I will avoid your questions, since I have no wish to avoid you.

Yet she's not avoiding my questions either, thought Tec. In fact, she's very eager to talk to me. I don't think I like it.

—You must run everything here, Ship. What's Drake for?

She did not answer at first, and Tec wondered if he'd succeeded in upsetting the equilibrium of her robot brain. Surely she would not answer that question.

But she did. —On Expedition A, Captain Drake functions as—as a fail-safe device.

She seemed surprised by her own words, as if she hadn't known what they would be.

—You are the Engineer's creature, said Tec.

—No. I never saw him. I carry a secretly coded destination that even my consciousness does not know, but otherwise I belong to myself, although as a ship I fulfill my function by obeying the orders of the Captain assigned to me.

—Just doing your little job? said Tec with contempt. —You're a machine after all.

He shut her out of his mind. "What are you going to do with me?" Tec asked Drake.

"Haven't decided yet. Astrid has some tests to run you through. As I said, we'll see."

"I won't sumit to any tests—," Tec began. "Oh, what the hell, we'll see. Both of us. Your ship won't disobey orders and take me back to Earth, so I'm stuck here. I'll try to cooperate."

Drake rose from his chair, tossing Selena to his broad shoulder. "I hope you understand our caution, Tec. A Roiiss robot alive and walking into our lives is an unprecedented situation."

Not exactly, thought Tec, but that was a long time ago. I wonder just how long?

Even when Terrans are planning an audacious experiment they manage to enjoy the here and now, thought Tec, watching Drake launch himself from the airlock and spread his arms in obvious pleasure at the antigrav flight back to Terran Center. Tec flew near him, contrasting these Terrans with the Roiiss, who thought only in terms of eternal survival.

Then he remembered how the Roiiss had been quarreling when he last saw them. Did the Elders have individual names? They had never said so, and because of Tec's long association with Terrans, this now seemed odd. Names were important to all sentient beings because they meant establishment of individuality, assertion of dominance over one's own little clump of organized matter that liked to think of itself as separate from a universe in which it was part of the web of life.

Samyak the tortoise was flying to meet them. "Get on my shell, Tec, and I'll give you a lift."

Drake waved jovially to Sam and went on ahead. With misgivings, Tec got on—Sam's method of antigrav flight was to barrel ahead with head and extremities outstretched and flapping, which caused his heavy body to wobble in transit. He plowed through the air, wheezing fiercely, and Tec kept reminding himself that he, too, possessed antigrav and was in no danger of crashing to the ground if he fell off.

"Where's your antigrav belt, Sam?"

"Miniaturized and stuck under the rim of my shell, I activate it telepathically."

"I thought you hated antigrav travel."

"I do, but Astrid said I should go and get you. I got to thinking about names, you see . . ."

"Names!"

"Like Yodin. Take away the first letter and you've got the ancient Earth god named Odin, who could travel so far above the ground that he could see everywhere. You hallucinated about him, maybe."

"Earth's Odin was an immortal, ready to battle mortals. In fact, he was the god of battle and of death," said Tec. "The final battle was Ragnarok."

"I'll look it up," said Sam. "Could your Yodin have been a Roiiss in disguise?"

Tec burst into startled laughter and almost fell off. "No, absolutely not possible. Why do you ask?"

"Nothing can get into hyperspace except a ship that's designed for it and goes above a planet's surface to enter it—except the Roiiss. If your Yodin was real, and he disappeared from the planet, maybe he had a device for getting into hyperspace anywhere."

"He was real, Sam."

"Well at least his name doesn't end in k. I wish you hadn't mentioned Ragnarok. Too many k sounds around here, I've been thinking. Tec and Samyak and Drake and York . . ."

"All aspects of the same reality, no doubt," said Tec facetiously. "And who is York?"

"Astrid's so-called cousin, due last week but didn't show up. We don't know where he is and there'll be hell to pay if he holds up the Expedition."

"He's not really a cousin?"

"He's accepted as one because he showed up with proof of kinship when Astrid was a little girl. Her planetologist parents died in a ship accident a few years later and she thinks of York as the only close family she has left, although there are many Holladays throughout Beta universe."

"What's proof of kinship?"

"Gene pattern and structure in a piece of body tissue. Easy

50

to do and infallible. Helps when someone's claiming a place in the richest, most famous old-stock Terran family. He's an artist or holographer or something. Astrid wanted him along on Expedition A and it was arranged with Engineer Yodin before he died. I think he's a fool."

Gulping and shivering, Sam descended into the garden, missing a rosebush and dumping Tec onto the grass. The two went into the empty library and Sam settled into a corner where the late sunlight still streamed in. "I'm getting old and I'm going to take a nap, which I have earned. Don't bother me."

"Yes, Sam," said Tec.

"Now mind you, I'm no cold-blooded reptile like the ones you knew back when Earth was young. We bioengineered descended tortoises have better four-chambered hearts than crocodiles had even then, and our circulatory system now provides adequate physiological homeostasis not requiring much external warmth to remain active . . ."

"Yes, Sam."

"However, I do like a short snooze now and then, and my dinner is late, and my metabolism is at low ebb, and after all, generations of tortoises spent a considerable amount of time in the privacy of their burrows . . ." Sam snored.

Peace permeated the library and Tec's mind. If anyone or any equipment was watching him, let them. He studied the bookcases, where there were not only the usual electronic microbooks but also some preserved leather books with paper pages filmed in flexi-plastic.

A particularly tattered volume caught his eye and he opened it at random. It was a collection of excerpts from the work of writers who lived long before the inventions of the Holladays—antigrav and hyperdrive—had transformed the galaxy and then the universe into a Terran ocean. Some of the passages were marked.

I wish so to live ever as to derive my satisfactions and inspirations from the commonest events, everyday phenomena, so that what my senses hourly perceive, my daily walk, the conversation of my neighbors, may inspire me, and I may dream of no heaven but that which lives about me.

In proportion as he simplifies his life, the laws of the universe will appear less complex, and solitude will not be solitude, nor poverty poverty, nor weakness weakness. If you have built castles in the air, your work need not be lost; that is where they should be. Now put the foundations under them.

That which is—the starting point of all the most profound philosophies Tec had encountered—had been known by Thoreau, too, and appreciated by the owner of the book. Tec wondered if he or she had also built castles in the air and if so, what kind.

He flipped through the book and found only one other marked passage, written by Whittier. Seven words were underlined, heavily.

"The silence of eternity, interpreted by love."

I'm an alien, solitary and weak, in a universe not my own, thought Tec. The beings here don't trust me but they may ask for my help. They always have. They think an alien mind can help them interpret their universe and their lives, but how can I interpret anything when I don't understand love?

He remembered that humans often wrote their own names inside the front covers of old-fashioned books. He looked and found an inscription written in slanting Terran:

"My oldest book for my youngest friend—to dear Astrid on her tenth birthday, from Cousin York."

An interesting fool.

8

TERRANS, THOUGHT TEC, are always preoccupied with food or sex, when the're not making grandiose schemes for adventure.

He was sitting on the rug next to Sam and Selena in the library while Freyn and Drake sat in chairs, waiting for Freyn's wife to bring appetizers from the kitchen. She'd been busy creating Drake's favorite snack and Tec had not yet seen her.

The conversation, about Federation politics, was stilted, as if the others were trying not to reveal too much to Tec, who was not interested. He didn't want to meet an empath, and he wanted to talk to another robot.

—Ship; can you hear me?
—I can. I am telepathic for long distances.
—Good. I would like to talk to you.

—I am always ready for conversation with you.

—I know you can't tell me anything Drake's decided I shouldn't know yet, but I would like to know about you. I've never met a ship with an intelligent robot mind.

—There are many.

—Do you have close relationships with other ships?

—I do not know what you mean by a relationship, Tec. I do my job. If it is necessary to communicate with another ship, I do so, but I do not converse the way I am doing with you right now.

—Why not?

—I do not know. We ships just do our jobs.

—Don't you want anything?

—I want to serve my Captain and Expedition Alpha . . . She paused, and the robot voice seemed to change in his mind.

—Tec, what did the dragons really want?

The question surprised him. —Survival. Sentient protoplasmics (and the Roiiss were that once) seem to want most of all to live forever, but only Roiiss have survived the mortality of their own universe.

—You are a Roiiss, are you not, Tec?

—I'm only a robot. I suppose I'll eventually wear out and die. I don't feel much like a Roiiss because I wasn't activated until they came here, and by that time they were changed so much that they had trouble manipulating ordinary matter and left me alone to do their gardening. I'm simple and uncomplicated compared to you, Ship.

—Perhaps. None of us sentient beings know all that we are capable of, do we?

He was astounded. He'd never encountered a Terran robot mind like hers, and he was beginning to be afraid of Ship. He noticed Drake grinning at him, so undoubtedly Ship was doing her duty and reporting to him all her conversations with Tec.

Another test. Ship, having failed to penetrate his mindshield, would use any opportunity to find out if he were capable of being dangerous to Expedition A. He resolved to have no relationship with her.

—I must return to the conversation here, he said abruptly.

—Good-bye, Tec, until we meet again.

Drake laughed and told a libelous story about a Federation official's sexual escapades, at which everyone but Tec and Selena smiled. Selena had blissful obliviousness, and Tec—he believed—had complete lack of interest in the private lives of witless protoplasmics given to ridiculous emotional upheavals.

Tec looked out the window. The sunlight was still bright upon the garden, for these Terrans ate early, and night apparently came late. Tec still didn't know where he was in the universe and he'd be damned if he'd plead for information again. He wasn't looking forward to sitting beside the Terrans as they filled themselves with food and wouldn't trust him enough to tell him anything.

"Astrid's coming," said Freyn happily.

Probably another painful aberration of a human being, thought Tec. Then the empathic touch came again, almost a sharing of the very molecules that composed his being, dazzling him with wonder.

Was the experience an aberration of his mind—or an external snare? Was it part of a truth so overwhelming he couldn't even guess at what it might mean? The touch withdrew quickly as if she knew his desire to avoid contact would hurt them both.

Freyn and Drake got eagerly to their feet at the sound of footsteps in the hall. Tec rose unwillingly.

She entered the room. Tec bowed.

Drake spoke, smiling his welcome. "Tec, this is our young chief physician. She is"—a touch of awe entered his voice—"one of the Holladays."

"Welcome, Tec. I'm Astrid Holladay, Freyn's wife."

Ancient Terran words awoke in Tec's mind, disturbing his scientific appraisal of data, bringing with them the passions and hopes created and lived by humans whose atoms had long since been recycled in the evolution of the universe.

Was her voice in truth gentle and low, an excellent thing in a woman—the warmth of sunlight after rain, the music of star-fields in the black of space? Wheresoever she was, there was Eden? Tec blocked his memory banks and tried to see her clearly.

Slender and golden-haired, with tawny eyes and skin, Astrid Holladay seemed to him as human and as inviolate and as unattainable as the legendary princess who slept for centuries.

But I was the sleeper, thought Tec, and now I am awake.

It is essential to pay attention only to specific sense data occurring in an actual moment. One must ignore what explodes from memory banks into emotive centers, giving the illusion that an unfathomable present links with an enigmatic past.

What have I actually learned? he asked himself. Only that a moment of encounter carries with it everything that both beings are, have been, and have wished to be. He had to say something. He said it.

"Hello."

She put the plate she was holding on the table and smiled. "Come, all of you, sit down and let's have the first course. I'm sorry it's so late, but I got confused about directing the kitchen robots, and Sam's cucumbers almost got put into the stew. Don't worry, Sam, I rescued them."

The gathering settled into relaxed sociability, except for Tec, and even the conversation was easier now that Astrid was there. Medical anecdotes, tortoise legends and spaceship tales were swapped around, but Tec was unable to pay close attention until they began talking about the twin universes.

"Not everyone believes there actually is a twin universe that died as this one came to life and will live after Beta dies in turn," said Freyn, brushing crumbs from his silver fur.

"Some powerful cults believe there's only one universe that must live forever," said Sam, "but scientists discovered way back at the end of the twentieth century that Beta universe began in a big bang and will eventually go back to a collapsed cosmic egg. After that it was found that the twin, Alpha, is in cosmic egg form now, waiting for the collapse of Beta to push it back into expansion again."

Following Sam's speech, the Terrans immediately turned to look at Tec, as if expecting some reaction from him. He was puzzled.

"I thought the alternating universes were accepted as fact. How can cults believe otherwise?"

"Cults always have," said Drake. "Some of them use this idea of a permanent universe as a kind of deity. It's a common expression—'By Beta'—I use it myself. Cult leaders make their members obey by telling them that if they don't do what their deified universe seems to tell them to do, Beta will turn into hell permanently as a punishment."

"Bah!" said Sam. "Maybe it already is hell."

"I myself am heaven and hell," said Tec before he could stop himself. He didn't dare look at Astrid.

"Never heard that one. Yours?" asked Drake.

"Old poetry," mumbled Tec.

Astrid leaned forward. "The cults are wrong. We Holladays

have always agreed with scientific theory about the alternating universes because we had Tec on exhibit in Holladay Tower. You're proof of the hypothesis, Tec. Even if there are no more dragons in Beta universe, you are still evidence of truth."

"What is truth?" asked Tec slowly.

"Experience," said Astrid after a moment. "Experience verified, I guess. You must know, Tec."

"No. Every millennium I seem to know more about my own ignorance and have more questions to which I don't have final answers."

"That's the best way to be," said Astrid, and this time he let himself watch her smile at him. The sensuality of the experience seemed to pierce his being.

"I want my cucumbers," said Sam.

Tec followed them to the dining room, watching the way Astrid's body moved under the silken tunic she wore. She was almost as tall as Tec, but Drake towered over her, and seemed to make an effort to be at her side.

Tec heard Astrid murmur to Drake, "I'm so worried about York. Where is he?"

"Freyn tells me York is always unreliable, never arriving on time anywhere," growled Drake.

"But he promised me he'd come on Expedition Alpha."

"Can't understand why you wanted him."

"It wasn't my idea. Everyone thinks so, but it was Engineer Yodin who selected him."

"Great Beta, the Engineer must have been getting senile at the last, Astrid."

She stiffened, and Drake patted her arm clumsily as he ushered her to her place. "Only kidding, my beauty."

Then Drake sat down and made everyone laugh with a story about how the various components of Beta Federation had had a severe crisis over picking a suitable anthem. The Milky Way Galaxy (which he called MWG), M31, and the other protogalaxies that move together through the universe couldn't get their representatives to agree as a group on what to nominate as their cluster's choice. To hear Drake tell it, the quarrels among the Terrans alone were enough to send everyone screaming into intergalactic space.

The dining room was in a style popular when Tec had visited Earth. The table was long and low, everyone sat on cushions around it, and woven mats covered the floor. In a niche in one of the bare walls was a vase containing three delicately leafed branches arranged so that each pointed to a different place at a level different from the others.

"I like this room," said Tec.

"Like all of us, this room's a museum," said Sam, deep in cucumbers. "Terrans in other places have evolved very different methods of eating and living. Bunch of aliens."

"You are telling me that the universe is a great deal older than it was when I went into the display case," said Tec. "If that means you're trying to trust me, I'm grateful."

"We're just trying to get to know you," said Drake.

"We want you to share our life here," said Freyn gently. "After all, you're a sentient being, and all of us in this universe ought to be able to understand each other."

"I'm not really a robot of this universe," said Tec, trying to remind himself.

"But you belong here, too," said Astrid. "Beta and Alpha are two oscillating halves of a unity. The same physical laws apply in both, or you wouldn't be here."

She was so beautiful that Tec knew she would be unwithered by age, and would indeed make hungry where most she satisfied. Oh, those accursed Terrans and their thirst for words to express emotions that should never be felt!

Tec rose and walked to the door. "Please excuse me. I would like to leave Terran Center."

"Now you're not supposed to . . ." Sam began.

"Shut up, Sam," said Drake. "Astrid?"

"I haven't probed his mind, Captain," she said, "and I can't give you factual assurance about his sanity or trustworthiness, but I feel we should let him go off by himself for a while. He's had too many shocks already in this first day of his new existence. What do you think, Freyn darling?"

"You're right. Since he can't leave this planet, why not let him explore it? That would be one way of his finding out some of what he wants to know."

Drake nodded gravely.

Sam chuckled.

Freyn and Astrid smiled at Tec.

"Thank you," he said. "Don't worry about me."

He walked out, but turned to look back at them in the beautiful, serene room. I'm alien, thought Tec. Just an alien robot.

I cannot possibly fall in love at first sight.

Tec headed on antigrav for the open terrace of Holladay Tower. Perhaps by some miracle Yodin would come back. He clung to that name. Yodin would hold the key to everything, if only he could be found.

There was no one there. After waiting, isolated, Tec began to hate this nameless planet that kept him a prisoner, unable to reach the familiarities of Earth.

The sky was now gold deepening to crimson over one side of this strange land. Daylight would soon be over. He shot into the air and flew out of the valley, over the high ridge, not sure what he was looking for, except Yodin.

He noted that the planet was indeed much smaller than Earth, with only wilderness and wild animals, until he saw a transparent plastidome of the sort humans used on all planetary bodies without a breathable atmosphere.

It seemed to contain only a few kilometers of barren, rocky soil, but since an outpocketing to one side of the dome signified an airlock, Tec went down to it.

In this case, the purpose of the airlock was clearly to keep air out of the dome, not in it, for if any air got in, bacteria and vegetation would follow, destroying whatever the dome was designed to protect. He probed and found that the sides of the dome extended far into the ground, protecting from invasion through it.

Tec went up to the door and saw that a steel plate was imbedded in the dome directly over the airlock. Raised letters thrust the name of the place at Tec.

MARE TRANQUILLITATUS MUSEUM

Impossible, thought Tec as he entered the airlock. Then, cleared for vacuum, sprayed and disinfected, he was allowed to enter the dome, stepping out onto a transparent elevated walkway that bore a small sign.

WALK ONLY ON THE PATH. IF UNABLE TO USE IT, PLEASE HOVER ON ANTIGRAVITY. DO NOT GO DOWN TO GROUND SURFACE. PLEASE PRESERVE THE MUSEUM.

He walked along toward the exhibit, which seemed to be a flagpole bearing an old-fashioned permanent banner in the colors of one of the larger sections of United Earth. It was red, white, and blue.

Surrounding the banner were footprints made by old-fashioned spaceboots heavily ribbed on the soles, and nearby were scattered a few ancient mechanical devices including a large, awkward, ugly contraption labeled "Descent Stage." On this there was a plaque with maps of the two hemispheres of Earth etched upon it, and written in one of the ancient languages that contributed to the development of Basic Terran was the legend

HERE MEN FROM THE PLANET EARTH
FIRST SET FOOT UPON THE MOON
JULY 1969, A.D.
WE CAME IN PEACE FOR ALL MANKIND

In peace.

Tec stood quite still, absorbing the utter silence of the place, shutting out his awareness that many meters below him the gravity engines were working to sustain the green beauty kept out of this stark, memory-laden place under the dome.

He thought of what it must have been like. Fragile, short-lived Terrans—Earthmen—who had never left their planet's atmosphere before had struggled into space, using antique propulsive engines with no antigravity, no hyperspace drive, nothing to guarantee them safe return. Finally they had ventured beyond the gravity of their own planet, in order to visit the smaller, dead sister planet they called their Moon.

Why did they go? Tec remembered Earth as so green with vegetation and blue water, so magnificent with proud cities, that he realized he had not remembered what it could be like in even the best of prisons.

I should not forget, he thought. My own body is superbly designed to last a long time, to function well under most circumstances, but it is a prison to me.

Even a living planet of great beauty can get overcrowded and too familiar.

If sentient beings are the way a universe evolves to become aware of itself, those beings want to understand themselves and the universe of which they are a part. They need to

59

explore, to walk on new worlds. And Earth had never lacked people of courage.

Tec considered humankind. They had made their giant leap, first to the Moon, and then to the other planets, satellites, and asteroids in their solar system. They had built space settlements in orbit around Earth and were about to take some of these on millennia-long journeys to other stars, when the discoveries of antigrav and the hyperdrive gave them quick access to the rest of what they called their Milky Way Galaxy.

And then other galaxies. Humans—Terrans—had traveled far and become—what?

How much time? How much time?

Tec glanced down at the railing of the walkway and saw another plaque written in English, Basic Terran, and Basic Galactic.

ONE SMALL STEP FOR A MAN,
ONE GIANT LEAP FOR MANKIND.

There was more listing of names, explanation, description of further early space ventures, but Tec turned around and walked to the airlock. Before he left, he looked back at the footprints, and remembered what the Y-1 robot had said to him.

"Every journey begins with one step."

He said it softly to himself as he entered the airlock. When it opened on the other side, he stepped back into air and vegetation, grateful that no one, not even Yodin, had visited him in the dome, and that no empathic touch had interrupted his communion with the ancient Terrans who had dared so much.

It was getting dark in this area by now, and Tec realized that of course the planet rotated. He rose slowly in the air until he was above the trees of the nearest ridge. Terran Center was far away, over the short horizon, so no lights from the ground diminished the full impact of nightfall.

He watched, waiting for the old familiar constellations to appear as a backdrop to that sister planet, cloud-wreathed and ocean-encircled, remembered by all who had ever seen her because she caught at the emotive centers in her loveliness.

"Oh Earth. I have not loved thee well enough . . ."

He waited. The stars began to appear. So many stars. The sky was filling with them.

"Too many!" shouted Tec.

There was no Earth in the sky. There never could have been. The night was bejeweled with the intensity of the starlight because the Moon was in a globular cluster thick with stars that had never been seen from Earth, and she rode her space without a companion.

"Only change is permanent," whispered Tec. "Nothing in the universe is forever. Not even the universe."

"Oh, Earth . . ."

Not for the first time, Tec envied humans their ability to cry.

10

SHE WAS WAITING in the library, alone, the lights low. He came in from the garden and sat down, his golden eyes fixed on her.

"Why was the Moon moved to a globualr cluster of stars within the Milky Way Galaxy?"

"Federation Center is on a planet of one of the nearby stars."

"Why take the Moon from Earth?" he asked, and read the answer in her sadness. "Is Earth dead?"

"Yes."

"Those Terrans!" Tec banged his golden fist upon the table. "Unstable creatures! No doubt they managed to destroy a beautiful planet in a ridiculous war, or through over population and the collapse of civilization . . ."

"No, Tec. We will tell you the truth. Earth became uninhabitable when its sun began to heat up. Sol is well on its way to becoming a red giant now, and Earth is burnt out."

"Stable, middle-aged stars like Sol don't do that so soon."

Astrid touched his arm with her warm arm. "Try not to get too upset. I don't know anything about Roiiss robots."

"So you don't know how much I can take or when I'll go completely berserk?"

She leaned back. "I think you'll be able to stand the truth about anything, but I'd still rather do it slowly."

"Tell me all the truth, Astrid."

She got up and went to a nearby shelf, returning with a small covered bowl. She removed the lid and Tec saw a blue liquid inside, aromatic and steaming. "I've been keeping this hot for you—there's more odor that way. Take it and . . ."

"What is it, medicine for sick robots?"

"I'm a doctor. Are you going to be a good patient?"

"No."

"I didn't think so." She pulled her hair back from her eyes and wrinkled her nose at Tec. "Please, dear Holladay museum-piece, try this medicine. It's for any sentient with a complicated brain and is also the last test I want to try on you before we take you into our confidence. I promise it won't damage you in any way."

"What does it do?"

"Soothes, pleases, and occupies the olfactory centers."

"That's all?"

"Olfactory centers are primitive, even in robots it seems. They affect cortical arousal and emotion and all sorts of things. This stuff works only once, on anyone. After that the olfactory centers are totally immune. You can't get addicted. Is that clear?"

"All right, I'll try it," said Tec. "I've always hated my emotive centers, and right now they're giving me a lot of trouble."

Tec took the little bowl in both hands, bent his head over it, and let the vapor penetrate olfaction. At first it was too strong; then it was pleasant, yet gradually so preoccupying that it excluded other sense data. A subtle vibration began to tingle along his circuits and when he shut his eyes, mists of color shifted across his visual fields for a brief moment. Then there was no sensation and he felt strangely detached from his surroundings, but at the same time totally aware of them, and of her.

He was conscious, not drugged the way a protoplasmic creature's neurophysiology is altered by certain chemicals. He was in another state of consciousness that reminded him of something forgotten.

Tec's mind rested in a deep inner pool of harmony that seemed to include not only himself but everything. The sudden absence of ordinary cognition, the stilling of emotion, seemed to last forever, yet when he opened his eyes he knew only a few seconds had passed.

"Freedom," he said.

"I felt that too," said Astrid. "It's hard to put it into words, but you sort of just know you're only a small part of reality, and yet you also know you're one with the whole of reality, without any conflict."

"How tragic never to have it again, Astrid."

She took the bowl from him and put it on the table. "It takes work, but you can have it again. I'm just learning. Freyn never even needed the medicine once. He achieves it all the time when he meditates in a powerful altered state of consciousness, although he says enlightenment is not an achievement but a discovery. The joke is that the medicine actually does nothing but occupy olfaction. It's your own mind that does the rest."

"Then I may have had experiences like it before?"

"Undoubtedly."

"Today—" He told her about the beetle.

"Freyn calls that a moment of sudden oneness with the eternal that simultaneously gives complete apprehension of the everyday here and now."

"If Earth can die, nothing is eternal," said Tec.

"Talk to Freyn about hyperspace some day," said Astrid. "He says that the all of reality is eternal, although the various patterns in it may not be. You are angry and therefore illogical, since you knew perfectly well that Earth would die some day when Sol . . ."

"Logic! By all the dragons of Roiissa, what's logical about a G-type star like Sol heating up so soon! It takes a total of about twelve billion years for that to happen, and only five billion years of those had passed by the time I went into stasis . . ."

He stopped and stared at her in horror. "Are you waiting for me to realize that seven billion years have passed?"

"No, Tec, it hasn't been that long. Sol went bad too soon, taking all the scientists by surprise. By then Lune was owned by the Holladays, and she'd already been terraformed and given artificial gravity by some genius. All her old underground cities and factories and mines are now filled with obscured devices no one really understands and which run and repair themselves. Also, no one has figured out how Lune was moved here."

"But why wasn't Earth itself moved out of harm's way?" cried Tec.

"It was considered, but Earth's molten core and shifting continental plates made the job monstrous, and since Sol was heating up so fast, it would never have been done in time."

"And all this was—a very long time ago," said Tec, not wanting to hear exact numbers.

"Yes. Earth was burnt out and Lune moved long ago. We'll give you the particulars tomorrow, perhaps. You have too much to think about as it is."

He clasped his golden hands and bent his head.

"Are you all right, Tec?"

"I had come to love Earth. And there's so much I don't understand."

"You will," she said tenderly. "We decided that if you came back from Mare Tranquillitatus feeling the way you obviously do, we'd see if you could quiet your mind in response to what you thought was medicine. If you did, we would trust you and take you into our confidence."

"I have passed the test?"

"To my satisfaction. I've informed the others telepathically and they agree. Now we'll really have a chance to get to know you well before we leave, and afterward you'll be left as our official spokesman to Beta universe, explaining what Expedition A is trying to do."

"Don't talk about it anymore, Astrid. I can't seem to think of anything but Earth."

"I envy your knowing her when she was beautiful."

"Since she's still in orbit around Sol, doesn't anyone go to see her?"

"No protoplasmics. It's too sad, and everything worth remembering was taken when Earth was evacuated."

"Like Holladay Tower," said Tec.

"That's hardly the greatest work of art Earth ever produced, but the Holladay family was fond of it and decided it would ornament their Moon."

"I shall miss Earth."

"Tec, I've heard that some robots are now working deep in Earth's underground cities, setting up their own civilization to wait for the day when Sol is a white dwarf and they can build on the surface. Perhaps you'd like to join them—although we hope you'll want to stay here on Lune and take Sam's place as librarian. Would you like that?"

She was treating him like a sick patient. Perhaps he was one. "I don't know. It seems like an appropriate career at this point in my existence. Tell Sam I am honored."

She smiled. "I just have. Now I've got to go to bed. It's very late and Freyn will be asleep already, and he sprawls across the entire bed if I'm not there for him to curl around. We'll talk again tomorrow, Tec. Remember that I need sleep. I'm only human."

"I'm not likely to forget that."

Terran Center was quiet and Tec was standing at the garden door looking at the stars when he heard a peculiar noise. As he turned, a black missile landed with a thud upon his shoulder. A light brush from stiff but fine hair activated his facial sensors, and a small black face peered around at his.

"Hello, Selena." Judging by the aroma of her breath. Tec suspected that she had been eating fish again. He hoped that the goldfish had a high compensatory birthrate.

A heavy, scraping noise made him look down to see Sam, whose big blunt claws scraped the floor as he plodded toward Tec.

"Don't mind Selena," said Sam. "Sometimes she gets curious about robots. Maybe she wants to find out if there's anybody at home inside your kind of shell."

Tec sat down on the couch with Selena. "Thought you were in bed."

"I wanted to talk to you. Okay?"

"Sure."

"Astrid's told us what you've figured out. Anything else?"

"No. I'm trying to sort it. You'll have to teach me to be a librarian. It must be hundreds—I mean, thousands—of years since I went into stasis. I have a lot to learn."

"Um. Yes. I see."

"Sam, are you deciding what else it's safe to tell me now?"

"Oh, we trust you. If Astrid does, we all do, because she knows. She's awfully young, but microphysicians are tops. They're always head doctor anywhere. Fortunately Freyn doesn't mind. He's one of nature's most secure personalities and nothing much threatens him, even the males who are smitten by Astrid."

"Like whom?"

"I don't know," said Sam evasively. "Drake's had a few marriages and I suppose cousin York has, too, but they probably think Astrid's special. I guess she is."

A special woman, thought Tec. A doctor, an empath, a standard old-stock human being, one of the many Holladays he had known. Yet he hoped he would not meet another female in this existence. Selena, now lying in his lap, and Ship, did not count, of course. He was not listening to Sam.

65

"So it's a question," Sam was saying, "of how much information your emotive centers can take at once."

"How much more can shock me? Earth is dead. Sol is on its way to red gianthood. And some genius moved the Moon. Do you know how?"

"Damn secretly, that's what. No sentients were on Lune when she was moved. She just appeared here one day and slowly made her way to this orbit around the star we now call her sun."

"But that's impossible! Someone would have seen—unless—She must have been moved through hyperspace. Is there stasis machinery to protect Lune in such a move?"

"Not that we know of. It's a mystery, but not our problem, which is how to get Ship and ourselves to Alpha Universe."

"I don't see why you want to go to a cosmic egg that won't expand for billions of years, more billions than I feel like counting at the moment," said Tec.

"We have our reasons. You'll probably learn them soon enough, because we leave in a matter of weeks. Astrid's cousin has to arrive first, and then we'll go. You can stay as the new Lunian, in charge of the robots that run Terran Center, and manage the wildlife preserve."

Tec put the sleeping Selena beside him on the couch and leaned forward. "Sam, it's crazy—you'll all die. Only the Roiiss have ever succeeded in the one way there is to get to the twin universe."

"A black hole," said Sam professorially, "is usually a collapsed star, but it can be merged package of collapsed stars, like the centers of galaxies. It's defined as an accumulation of matter with a combination of mass and density great enough to produce a gravitational field that is intense enough to make the surface escape velocity exceed that of light in a vacuum."

"Yes, but . . ."

"Naturally, under those conditions nothing, not even light, can escape, although for quantum mechanical reasons some of its energy of rotation can be converted into subatomic particles outside its event horizon . . ."

"Stop!" shouted Tec. "I've had some near-misses with black holes and I'll bet that's more than you have, Mr. Librarian."

"Well, yes . . ."

"The Roiiss told me that it takes enormous power to get through a black hole alive, and that no one had done it except

66

themselves, including all those who tried to escape from Beta universe into the cosmic egg of Alpha."

"We don't intend to live in the cosmic egg, numskull," said Sam. "Ship will shunt immediately into hyperspace and stay there in stasis until Alpha is expanded."

"No one's succeeded, according to the Roiiss, and when I last saw them they were still trying, after all the eons they'd spent here in Beta, to find a way back that was safe."

"The current black hole. Where the dragons finally went through. Well, the directions to it are programmed into Ship's circuits, but not into her consciousness, so although she can't tell anyone how to get to the right black hole, she'll go there once the journey starts. Engineer Yodin planned it that way to keep the Expedition secret."

"How did he know the correct black hole?"

"Nobody knows." Sam yawned. "A remarkable old man. Rumored to be a Holladay."

Tec fumed. "You're still all insane to try it. I think I know the worst now. Is there any more information to jangle my circuits, Sam?"

"Oh, you've got most of it. I'm going to my own room now; it has extra heat in it just for me and I like my sand bed."

"Sam, persuade Drake and the others not to go. Expedition Alpha is hopeless. Engineer Yodin must have been mistaken, for it can't be done, and if it can be, then the Roiiss have done it and will stop anyone else from succeeding."

"Some people think the Roiiss have loused up this universe."

"What do you mean?"

"You'll find out. I'm sleepy. Who knows—maybe our arrival in Alpha might make a difference there. Even our deaths might."

"I don't want any of you to die!" yelled Tec.

"Thanks," said Sam, on his way to the hall. "Stop fussing, Tec. You're worse than the humans. Anyway, if Drake's decided on this adventure, nothing's going to stop him. Not some old bunch of dragons." He moved slowly down the hall, turned a corner, and was out of sight.

I must stop them, thought Tec. I don't want Astrid to die.

11

THERE WAS A BOOK lying on the library table, and Tec picked it up. In his long hours with protoplasmic Terrans, he'd learned to keep hours like theirs, using their sleep time for meditation and reading, but now he could not relax his mind.

"Let me not to the marriage of true minds admit impediments . . ."

He turned quickly from Shakespeare. The man was too treacherous. He'd known too much and had put it into deathless words that kept a language from growing too far away from them, because if it did, the originals might cease to be understood. Even Basic Terran was massively weighted by the language of Shakespeare.

Furthermore, the marriage of true minds was an idea inducing disillusionment and did not bear thinking about. He turned to other poets, envying the short-lived intensity of those ephemeral creatures.

> *But love me for love's sake, that evermore*
> *Thou mayst love on, through love's eternity.*

He banged the book closed on these familiar, and now completely new, words and decided he was going to have a hell of a time getting through the night.

Suddenly Selena, whose black head had been neatly tucked into her groin fur, uncoiled and leapt to the rug, fur standing on end.

"What's the matter?" said Tec, forgetting his own sensors.

She growled and then, with a musical gargle, crawled under the couch.

Something was coming. "Yodin?" whispered Tec, Selena would not have been frightened by any of the robots or Terrans she knew, and there was no one else awake on the planet except Tec. He probed.

The robot scanners of the Center were operating, and apparently they did not object to the ship that was coming down through the atmosphere, so either it was known, or expected, or harmless.

Tec scanned it quickly. Ship was an elegant mechanism of noble proportions designed for a fantastic journey. This new vessel was so small that there was hardly room for more than one being aboard. That being was human.

Tec probed farther and studied the data. There was an odd R-inclusion in the human's cells. What could it mean?

Tec went out into the garden that was now fragrant and hushed. He waited, and finally a little battered ship came down against the backdrop of stars.

Rattling faintly, the ship hovered above the garden and then slowly fell, tilting over until it landed upside down in the biggest plot of grass between the biggest beds of purple roses, which looked velvet-black in the dim light from the library windows. Tec concentrated on his infrared vision as the ship's occupant clambered out of the partly jammed airlock.

"Hello," said Tec.

The small human fell backwards into a rosebush and, cursing in several languages, shook his fist at Tec.

"What the hell are you doing, scaring me like that, you gold-plated robot!"

"I'm sorry," said Tec, helping him out of the bush and dusting him off. "You should have come in the front door where tourists are made welcome when the Center's not closed, which it is."

"I'm not a tourist, dammit. I'm family."

"Please come inside," said Tec hastily, for he had inadvertently and with appalling ease read the man's mind. Among the varied emotions and muddled thoughts there were two clear sentences:

"Another old-fashioned robot guard to contend with," and "Where can I find a place to piss?"

Hurrying into the hall with his new charge. Tec showed him the door of the place where creatures took care of their excretory functions. Waiting outside, he heard sounds of liquid splashing against liquid, a sigh of relief, and then a different sound of splashing. Presently the small man came back into the corridor, raised his eyebrows at Tec, and smiled when Tec ushered him into the library.

"Nice place."

"Very," said Tec, feeling as proprietary as if he had lived there for years instead of less than one day.

"I've come to the right place, haven't I? The Holladay family does live here, don't they?"

"Astrid Holladay and her husband, Freyn, live here," said Tec.

"That's okay then." The man sat down on the couch and took off his soft, pointed boots. "Got anything to eat?"

"I will send for the roboservors," said Tec, doing so.

The man's eyebrows shot up again, apparently at the realization that Tec was not a servant, but he said nothing until the robot arrived.

"Milk, any kind, even elephant—I'm not particular—and chocolate cookies and a protein cake and maybe a small spot of brandy."

As the roboservor sped away, the little man produced an apple from the folds of his flowing, spangled coat. "Grabbed it from that tree we passed under. Hope you don't mind."

"Not at all."

In macrostructure, the man was very short and his skin was an exceptionally dark green, even darker than Freyn's. His head hair must have lost its underlying human pigment, for it was a bright green, but the rest of him—except for a greenish tinge—might have been pure black. He was also very old. His skin was seamed, crinkled, and webbed, and part of the reason he looked small was because he was so withered and bent. Nevertheless, his black eyes were bright and good-humored. Tec carefully did not look into the man's mind again.

"Are you Mr. York Holladay?" Tec asked.

"Who?" He did not seem to care if Tec answered the question, for the roboservor arrived with food, which the man fell upon as if he were starving. Halfway through he looked speculatively at Tec.

"Want to know who I am?"

"That was the idea," said Tec.

"Humph. You guarding the Holladays?"

"In a way."

"Enigmatic son of a factory, aren't you?" said the man.

"I am also strong, whereas you are weak," said Tec, "and any second now I will throw you and your spaceship and your glass of milk back into hyperspace if you don't explain . . ."

"All right, all right." He closed his eyes, leaned back and said softly, "You're part of the mystery. Not an ordinary robot."

Tec thought the man was either in a trance or was stalling so he wouldn't have to reveal his identity, and it was hard to resist the impulse to scour the man's mind for answers. Tec resisted, for this was a universe in which everyone jealously protected his thoughts from others, and if he could scan another's mind that easily, to do so would be an unpardonable violation of privacy.

The man opened his eyes. "So tired. Strange things. What's your name, robot?"

"I thought I was asking you."

"Oh, yes, so you were. Old, you know. My name is Pedlar."

"Just Pedlar?"

"Pedlar Shadrach."

A prominent Martian family of that name had begun to take over much of galactic politics and power at about the time that Tec had decided to die, so Tec asked, "The Martian Shadrachs?"

"That's us. After Earth started to die, Mars warmed up and our family really got going. The Shadrachs are important in many galaxies now, even royalty in some, but I don't use that name much. The family disowned me when I was a child." Rheumy tears flickered in the old man's eyes and he rubbed them out with gnarled hands.

"Why did they?" asked Tec.

"You know. You asked my last name although I was thinking it, so you were being polite and not reading my mind."

"Mr. Shadrach, is it possible that you have no mindshield?"

"I'm just Pedlar. Call me that, Mr. Robot with eons on his back. And his front. Eons and eons and eons and . . ." Pedlar shut his eyes and yawned.

Human beings had often described to Tec how it sometimes felt when a particularly eerie phenomen impinged on the human equivalent of cognitive and emotive centers. It was supposed to be like chills running up and down the back. Tec thought he could understand what this meant.

"My name is Tec," he said, watching to see if there was any sign of recognition in the old man's eyes.

"Funny name. Familiar. Familiar . . ." he was asleep, a cookie in his hand and half of the milk and brandy he'd mixed still undrunk.

Tec waited, and then probed delicately with his mind into the old man's body. He found that there was too much beyond repair or substitution—Pedlar was dying, slowly but definitely.

"My name is Pedlar." He was awake again, considerably

more alert and cheerful. "Thanks for the food. I think I was telling you something important?"

"You have no mindshield, Pedlar. Is that why your family disowned you?"

"Yep. They also didn't approve when I wanted to keep the green tinge after scientists found out how to keep the R-inclusion but get the color of it out, way back in—I can't remember. Aristocratic black without any green was my family, and they couldn't tolerate me, a green-haired social leper who has to keep moving on because nobody can stand having a person around who's unshielded."

If everyone is a telepath, thought Tec, everyone also had to have a shield, because the naked truth that might be read in an unshielded mind would disrupt the veneer of civilization.

"I'm not a telepath, either," said Pedlar sorrowfully. "Something went wrong when the R-inclusion passed through my embryonic development, but on the other hand, maybe something went right, because I do have a talent."

He chirruped with glee and waggled a finger at Tec. "Two talents. One is that I know what sentient beings will like, and I sell or rent it to them. In fact you could say—" his voice became a dry whisper of age in the night—"I'm a dealer in dreams."

"And the other talent?"

"You won't like that. Nobody does."

The eeriness, thought Tec, the seeing beyond seeing. "Do you see the future, Pedlar?"

"Not exactly. That would be magic, and try as I might to find it, no matter where I've gone—and I've gone everywhere—there isn't any. No, friend Tec, I see—potential. I don't know how, and I can't control or will it, but it happens, and usually I try to shut up. But someone always reads my mind, and then I have to leave for some other galaxy. Life is hard."

"But not forever."

"No. I'm dying, I guess. Could you tell?"

"Yes."

"Can you tell when?"

"No," said Tec, with pity.

Pedlar sighed. "That's all right. It's better not to know. I don't mind. I've lived so long I've lost count anyway. I just came because I found out my son is going on a journey and won't return. I wanted to see him again."

"How . . ."

72

"I don't know. I just know. I've been trying to track him down for years, through the Holladay family, but what with one thing or another, I didn't pursue every lead until I got this feeling that he's going away for good. He's supposed to be here at Terran Center. Can you take me to him?"

"You haven't told me his name, Pedlar."

"My adopted son, Samyak."

"Samyak the tortoise?" said Tec, pretending he had not just accidentally glimpsed a clear picture of Sam in the man's mind.

"I found him, just a baby, in a swag of stolen goods—hell, I did used to deal in contraband and stolen—but that doesn't matter. Haven't done it for centuries. Or maybe it's a few thousand years, I don't know. He was shriveling up and dying from starvation and neglect, and I nursed him back to health. Loved him—because he was the only one who could tolerate my damn open mind."

"How did you get separated?"

"A few years later, when Sam was growing up, I got in some trouble on a planet where the Holladay family ruled. Sam talked them into letting me go, but I could see that if he stayed with them—and the little girl adored him—"

"Astrid?"

"I've forgotten her name, but I don't think it was that. He would be able to get a good education, amount to something, if he stayed with the Holladays. It's not easy for some of the sentient animals, you know, especially the clumsy ones like tortoises. They need help, and I couldn't give Sam much once I'd given him health. So I told him to stay with the Holladays, who wanted him. Oh, I'd visit him sometimes, but time passes, and I guess I forget a lot . . ."

"Don't worry," said Tec, "Sam is here. I'm sure he'll be very glad to see you, but he's asleep now. Why don't you stretch out on the couch and sleep until morning."

"Thanks, I need that—but I'll be disturbing you. Weren't you busy here in this library before I came? Worrying?"

Pedlar smiled when Tec shook his head in the old human negative response to the question, as if he sensed that Tec was also indulging in the human need to lie to conceal feelings. Was the odd little man an empath instead of a telepath? Probably not, for there was none of the inner sensation that always hinted at even the subtlest of empathic contact between two beings.

Pedlar rummaged in his knapsack and handed a leather

73

bag to Tec. "Try these. Can't tell if they work on robots, but if they do, you might like them."

The first thing Tec felt in the bag was a small cube, which he took out and examined in puzzlement.

"Listen to it," said Pedlar.

Now he heard it—music? There was sound in his mind, and yet no sound outside, or was there? It seemed impossible to tell. His mind was absorbing the sound, losing itself, becoming the sound . . .

"What am I hearing?" he asked, to break the spell. "A translation of cosmic energy fields into sounds? Or subatomic fields?"

"Maybe the same thing," said Pedlar vaguely. "Why not?"

Tec listened again. "More than those—more—but what?"

Pedlar yawned. "That which is, is."

Tec tried once more, and this time words stopped in his mind and only the music existed, yet there was no longer any sound. He handed the little cube to Pedlar. "Please take it back. I'm not ready for it yet."

Pedlar shrugged. "Okay. You've got time. I don't, but that's all right. I'll will the cube to you," he said, chuckling like a mischievous gnome. Then he leaned back, closing his eyes.

"I'm sorry," said Tec. "You're tired."

"Try the other dream in the bag."

"The other what?"

Pedlar was nearly asleep. "Don't sell, just rent. Or lend. Yes, I'll lend you my wares, robot. You need a few, or you will." He began to snore.

Not an empath, thought Tec, but someone who saw patterns, in dimensions extending into both past and future. Tuning into potential, he could guess more easily about what had happened or might happen to another. No wonder Pedlar always had to move on.

Holding the leather bag, Tec went to the window and was about to step out into the garden when he heard Pedlar talking in his sleep.

"Buy a dream, honored sir, buy a dream."

A dangerous occupation—seller of dreams.

12

TEC'S INFRARED VISION enabled him to open the bag and study the last specimen of Pedlar's wares in spite of the darkness. Sitting in the chair under the apple tree, his back shielded by leaves against the pale light from the library windows, Tec faced the scented flower beds, the silent pool, the shrouded wall, and the sky, whose spangles were misted with cloud now. He missed Selena, who had vanished from the library and not come back.

Idly, Tec held up the other dream, a curious translucent object shaped like a large Terran bird's egg with a transparent opening at the broad end. Inside there was at first only a dull glow, but when he brought the egg closer to his right eye and concentrated, shapes began to form.

He saw a swirling kaleidoscope of faces—the faces of all the beings he had ever cared about, now dead for hundreds, perhaps thousands, of years. Shutting his eyes, he tried to reason. Did this device register thoughts or wishes?

Am I preoccupied with mortality? he thought. Why not? I'm a prisoner of it. When the universe dies, so will I, if I don't wear out long before. What am I doing here on Lune? What do I want?

He opened his eyes and looked into the egg again. He saw Astrid's face gazing at him, and behind her appeared the image of a golden robot. She turned to embrace it, twining her legs and arms around it.

"No!" Tec looked away, but he could still feel the egg in his hand, like something evil laid by a monster who refused to accept the impossibility of nonbiological joining.

A bird stirred in a nearby bush, chirped once, and was silent.

He looked into the egg once more, trying to concentrate this time on potential, trying to imagine that he was Pedlar, able to tune in to the patterns of now and to extrapolate from them. He failed.

A potential in himself that he didn't understand prevented him from pushing the pattern into the future. Frightened, Tec kept looking into the small window, trying to will himself to see what he must do.

Galaxies—millions of them—rushed toward each other, colliding and coalescing, brighter and brighter until there was only seething light followed by purples and greens writhing, searching, searching . . . and then there was only the blurred image of a tiny dragon swimming through nothingness, gradually looming larger, a purple monster with green iridescence visible on the scales when the tail lashed out . . .

Enough, thought Tec. My first day of my new existence shouldn't end with self-torture. He put the egg away, closed Pedlar's bag tightly, and lay back in the reclining chair, eyes closed.

Something alive and warm landed on his legs. "Meow," said Selena.

Tec smiled at the quizzical tilt of her black head, ears cocked forward. She walked up his legs to sit upright on his left thigh, generously inclining her neck for scratching. As Tec complied, he noticed that Selena's nose was lifted to the slight breeze and was twitching gently, as was the tip of her tail.

"I'm a good vantage point for bird watching?"

From the more frequent chirping in the bushes. Tec deduced that the birds' biological clocks were intimating that dawn was coming. Tec had an insane desire to run into Terran Center, wake Astrid and tell her that the universe was so beautiful that she must not leave him alone on it. She must not go Alpha universe!

He tried to meditate and calm his mind, but his emotive centers churned on, and cognition kept hinting that something was wrong.

"Of course something's wrong," Tec muttered. "I'm in love." Compulsively, he took out the vision egg again, because if there was anything worse, he wanted to know it at once.

This time he saw a quaint picture of a golden-haired girl chained to a mountain—or was it a ship? And riding the ship was a dragon . . . By all the Roiiss of Roiissa, thought Tec, I'm conjuring up an illustration I once saw in a Terran children's book.

But the picture changed. Suddenly there was nothing to see, yet something was happening to him. What had been awakened in his own mind? Power? What power?

Applauded by birdsong, dawn was flaring in the sky over the old crater ridge. It was hard to believe that it wasn't old Sol about to pop up over the horizon. Without deciding to do it, Tec unthinkingly probed through Lune to her new sun, still out of sight.

Yes, another G-type star. Good for the Terran ecology.

Out farther. No other planets in orbit. One sun and one transplanted small planet.

Still farther. Many planets around nearby stars. All those with Terran atmospheres were heavily populated, with orbital settlements everywhere. His mind reached out and out.

"But there is something wrong! The universe is different."

Try it again! Out farther!

"Space itself is not the same. Radiation is coming back!"

Radiation is giver of life in an expanding universe, but executioner in a collapsing universe. No more night. No more dark of space. The end of all things.

Tec knew at last that he had come out of stasis not after hundreds, or thousands, or even millions of years.

Eons, Pedlar had said.

And Beta universe is dying.

Part Three

13

IT WAS ONE THING to talk glibly about the mortality of universes, and another to face it directly. Tec knew it had changed him irrevocably. He no longer tried to persuade Astrid not to go on Expedition A, for he had made up his mind. He was going to go with them whether they liked it or not.

By the end of a week he and Pedlar had become accepted members of the household, but he held back on asking Drake if he could join the expedition. He merely expressed interest and was allowed to tour Ship, while Drake explained the upgrading of hyperspace drive, the refinements of antigravity mechanisms, and the startlingly new use of fuel energy extracted from cosmic fields. Ship's ability to provide protective stasis fields was amazing to Tec.

"I'll never catch up. Too much time has passed for me."

"Don't brood about it," said Drake. "Just face the adventure of the future."

"A dying universe?"

"Not for billions of years. Beta's only just at the turnaround phase now, and this stationary universe will last a long, long time."

"A long evolution toward death," said Tec.

"I suppose all life is that, if you want to look at it that way, but I'm personally against aging and death," said Drake.

They were sitting in the control room, watching through the viewscreen the splendor of a nearby flock of snow geese. Ship had been oddly silent, and Drake more expansive than usual.

From marshy ground near the central lake of this valley that had once been a moon crater, a large moose lifted its head and bellowed, fronds of marsh weed trailing from its antlers. Beta universe is still interesting and enjoyable, thought Tec.

"You know, Tec, maybe we'll be like the Roiiss and evade death by leaving our own universe. If we get through the black hole and stay safely in stasis and in hyperspace until Alpha expands, then there'll be a whole new universe in which I can seek my fortune!"

The moose bellowed once more and plunged into the water, running out with its long legs until its big body was submerged in the lake, across which it began to swim.

Pedlar spent much of his first week undergoing thorough examination in the hospital. "He's incredibly old for a protoplasmic being," said Freyn, "possibly many thousands of years. He can't remember, and has lost touch with, that aristocratic family that threw him out. He says his parents and siblings vanished from history texts during a revolution and he can't seem to feel curious about finding out exactly when he was born."

"Have you been able to reverse the disease processes in him?" asked Tec.

"Some. I've worked on his gross problems and Astrid's made some microadjustments, but we can't do much else unless he tries harder. Since all protoplasmic sentients have the Gift, over the years there's been education in the art of healing oneself, and doctors merely supplement that. Unfortunately, Pedlar's mutant Gift may prevent his altering age and disease processes himself—or else he doesn't want to."

"Can't new organs be cloned for him?" Tec asked, thinking of the way humans had prolonged life at the time he had become an exhibit in Holladay Tower.

"Not anymore," said Astrid. "His own cells, even the sperm, are too old to make clone organs that will last much longer than he will, and unfortunately he has no younger tissues under stasis in any of the Federation's cell banks."

"He's refused the one other thing that could now add years to his life—artificial parts," said Freyn sadly.

"That's called robotization," said Astrid. "Like the admixtures in the new-stock Terrans. But perhaps Pedlar is right in refusing. So far there's no way of restoring or replacing brain tissue with the certainty of keeping memories intact."

"Certainty? You can't mean that it has actually been done!"

Freyn nodded. "There's been transfer of mind patterns to robot brains and vice versa, keeping an individual going for—who knows how long? But for some reason it doesn't work if you transfer to a clone organic brain. You get imbeciles. In my medical opinion it isn't wise to mind-transfer too much or for too long from organic to robot brains, either. The individual changes, often unpredictably and irrationally."

"I have often observed," said Tec wryly, "that even without robotization, individuals can change that way during their journey through life."

The journey, the long evolution toward death. Tec could not get it out of his mind.

"Astrid," he asked one day when he went to see her as she worked alone in the lab, "I've been thinking that only your remote descendants will suffer and eventually die out as Beta collapses, so why do you want to leave when you are still so young?"

"I guess I want to try to do something about the survival—not of myself or my descendants—but of hope and perhaps knowledge," she said.

"We can't know what new forms and minds and ideas might evolve in this universe before it finally dies," said Tec. "Are you in such a hurry to start Alpha out where Beta is now, instead of beginning all over again?"

"I don't know. And, you're right, of course. It will be interesting to see what happens to Beta universe—but, Tec, I want to go on Expedition Alpha. It's the most stupendous effort attempted by the life that's evolved here, and I want to be part of it."

"Oh, Astrid, life evolves anywhere like a universe's defiant gesture against entropy, but it's always been only a gesture, for everything dies."

"That's how things are." She grinned at him. "And a good thing too. Makes the universe keep trying new ideas."

He laughed. "Yes, now you are right. Change should and does occur, and our own actions can cause changes. Our

80

minds and hopes and work are part of things as they are."

"Bravo, Tec! You've just explained better than I could the reason for Expedition Alpha. Maybe this time the defiant gesture of life will succeed in avoiding the death of its universe. Didn't the Roiiss accomplish that?"

"They escaped, but they didn't do a damn thing for Beta universe until long after mankind had evolved into civilization. The R-inclusion was a late Gift, and this universe didn't need it."

"But it may make the difference in surviving the black hole," said Astrid calmly. "What fun it will be!"

"You're a romantic child," said Tec.

"Sam, how do the scientists explain the fact that the universe has stopped expanding so much earlier than expected?" asked Tec.

"There are as many theories as scientists, I think. But the theory that should interest you the most is the idea that the dragons somehow changed the expected pattern when they went back to Alpha."

"How did they know the Roiiss went back?" asked Tec.

"In the archives of Holladay Tower there are sworn statements of Holladay family members who heard what you told them about the Roiiss, and the eyewitness account of your last encounter with the dragons."

"You can't mean that crazy Y-1 robot!"

"The witness was a robot, I believe."

"Freyn, how can billions of years have gone by when you and Astrid are so little changed from the creatures I knew on Earth?"

"Old-stock struggles to stay old-stock, just as there's constant work here on Lune to keep the museum ecology of Earth as original as possible. It's good for tourism, and the Federation is still sentimental about Earth, even after all these years. Lune and Astrid and I are all holdouts against the passage of time and the changing of the universe."

"Museum relics, but you keep your lost mother Earth alive in each of you," said Tec. "And now you hope to carry her to Alpha universe."

"Won't it be great!" said Freyn enthusiastically. "When the big bang is over and after stars have begun to make heavier elements, we'll come out of hyperspace and we'll terraform planets. The worker robots will be able to use Ship's basic equipment to make other equipment from natural resources, and eventually they'll have a planet ready for us and those embryos we've got in stock. Astrid and I will grow an embryo or two of our own."

"Dangerous as hell."

"That's how things are," said Freyn.

Terran Center contained models and artifacts taken from Earth and a general survey exhibit of Terran history and accomplishments throughout the human-settled worlds of Beta universe. In recent centuries. Lune's flood of tourists had slowed to a steady trickle because the histories of other planets and civilizations seemed more important to themselves. Only the most intelligent, most educated of Terran-descended beings were interested in studying about the planet from which their ancestors came.

"You'll be a good librarian," said Sam, "if you can keep your mind off worrying. Relax and think of all the speeches about us you'll be able to give on hy-com after we're gone."

"What's hy-com?" asked Tec.

"Communication through hyperspace, avoiding the light-speed barrier. It unites all of Beta Federation."

"Beta Universe Federation is a brave name for an organization that does not, according to your library, include all sentient life forms, a majority of habitable planets, or even many galaxies. What about all the outsiders?" asked Tec.

"Bah—those wild planets. Even wild galaxies. The silly asses have closed themselves off from the Federation by fields generated by their inhabitants' minds or machines or . . ."

"Minds! Barring entry to a whole system?"

"Weird creatures out there, Tec. Best to keep away from them."

Oddly enough, it was Ship who made things easy for Tec. One day Drake summoned Tec to a conference.

"See here, Tec, have you been getting at Ship?"

"I haven't talked with her except about the technology . . ."

"She wants you to go on Expedition A."

"That's a surprise to me," said Tec, wondering if she had made a logical decision or if his contact with her had influenced her in some other way. Could she possibly have emotive centers?

"You started out telling us it would be too dangerous," said

Drake. "I don't want anyone along who's afraid of dragons. I'm not. The heroes of Earth legends weren't either—look at Sigurd the Volsung—and if the dragons want to fight for Alpha, I'd welcome a good battle."

"You may get one," said Tec. "The Roiiss want a universe for themselves."

"Hell, Tec, the only enemies in Beta universe are the parasites, the plodders, and the stupid criminals from within. At last I'll have a real challenge, and I don't want anyone to interfere. You're going to stay here on Lune and not mess with my adventure, or back you go into the display case."

"I was going to try to persuade you gradually, Drake, but Ship has precipitated things, so I'll just say it. I want to go on Expedition Alpha. Please allow me."

"By Beta, you know I can't allow that!"

"I'll behave myself. I may even be useful. Ship seems to think another robot would come in handy."

"Maybe," said Drake.

14

SAM WANTED Tec to stay as Lune's librarian. Freyn thought Ship would need another robot in case anything went wrong. Drake was vaguely argumentative, to the point where Tec despaired of getting the Captain's trust. Astrid said nothing.

Tec tackled Sam one morning when Pedlar, out of the hospital, was enjoying a late breakfast with his foster son in the library.

"An old-stock Terran should be librarian," said Tec. "It's better for the tourists."

"Nonsense," said Sam. "You'll be an enormous attraction. Who else can say they're older than the universe?"

"It's no great honor," said Tec bitterly.

"A burden?" asked Pedlar.

Tec nodded and felt understood. The accumulated years of existence bore heavily upon Pedlar, too.

Sam's eyes filled with tears. He seemed to love Pedlar as only an elderly, devoted adopted son can adore an elderly devoted father, although it was often not clear which was which.

Pedlar seemed happy at Terran Center, where everyone

was much too telepathically skilled and too courteous to make use of his absence of mindshield. For once in his long life, Pedlar Shadrach did not have to worry about when and where he would be banished.

Perhaps, thought Tec, Sam really wants me to stay on Lune as Pedlar's guardian. But I must guard Astrid. I must go with her!

He left them to each other and went to find her.

They walked together along the sandy part of the lake shore, watching the wildlife in the nearby marshes. Astrid's long strides matched Tec's, and he was incredibly happy just to be with her.

Then she crushed him. "I don't want you to go on Expedition A."

"Why not?"

"It will be dangerous for you to go to a universe where the Roiiss are. They might leave *us* alone. They aren't interested in planets or in protoplasmic beings, from what you've told us. But you were their robot and they might take you back as a slave. I don't want you to belong to anybody but yourself."

"I want . . ." Tec could not say it. Would he ever dare tell her that he loved her? He watched as she took off her sandals and danced into the water up to her knees.

"Is that the only reason you want me to stay behind?" he asked.

"Oh, Tec—always questioning! Come on, I'll race you to that willow tree over there." She picked up her sandals and sprinted off, followed by Tec, who let her win. She never answered him.

That same sunny day, while the Terrans were having lunch, Tec paced the garden, wondering what he would do next to persuade them that he must go with them.

Suddenly he paid strict attention to his long-distance sensors, and ran into Terran Center.

"Drake! Ships in hyperspace—nearby . . ."

"Now they're in normal space," said Sam. "What the hell?"

"It seems like a whole fleet," said Tec, "closing in on Lune fast, soon to enter the atmosphere."

Alarms rang throughout the building and a voice, aloud and telepathically, repeated Tec's findings as the Center computer brain automatically reacted. The computer added an additional bit of data that explained the alarms—these ships were heavily armed war vessels.

Drake took charge. "Sam, get Pedlar to the hospital and stay there with guards. The rest of you, get to Ship!"

They shot out of Terran Center on antigrav, hurtling toward Ship, who opened her airlock to receive them.

"Is there actually danger?" asked Tec in disbelief. He had come to accept the serenity of life on Lune.

"No friendly armed fleet ever approaches any planet without prior announcement and request for permission to enter the atmosphere," said Drake. "Tourists ships come and go, but they're not armed, by Federation law. Many Fed planets have control systems that destroy any approaching vessel read as carrying arms, so only Fed fleet ships whose recognition patterns are coded into Fed computers are allowed in. Too bad Lune doesn't have a destruct system. These ships must be aliens, or from the wild planets."

"I'm worried about Pedlar and Sam," said Astrid. "If these intruders are telepaths, they'll read Pedlar's mind and know our plans."

"They already know or they wouldn't be here, I bet," said Drake. "Ship! How many intruder vessels?"

"Ninety-nine."

Through the transparent part of the control room wall, they could now see the intruders, floating down to Lune's surface like oddly compressed octahedrons sparkling in the sunlight.

"Expedition Alpha!"

In the viewscreen appeared a picture of another control room containing several orange-uniformed, blue-faced creatures, each a nostalgic hint that once such a creature might have been human.

"You are all under arrest, Expedition Alpha," said the nearest face.

Drake turned toward the screen, chin out and chest up as if he, too, commanded many ships instead of one. "Oh?" he said.

"We're rising," Tec whispered to Astrid.

"Stop elevating your ship," said the intruder.

"Okay," said Drake.

"Stop!"

"Whoops! There—whoa, girl. Sorry about that." Drake grinned as Ship stopped farther up from Lune's surface than the intruder had ordered.

"We will now deactivate your ship until we investigate you."

Tec's sensors recorded the emergence of deactivation beams from the invading ships, but they never arrived at Ship.

"Amazing, Drake," said Tec. "You've got a flexible external stasis field of enormous power, protecting Ship but keeping passengers active."

"For the black hole," said Drake. "And a few other surprises, eh, Ship? Up and at 'em girl."

Directional rays emanated from Ship, and Tec deduced that they had disorganizing properties. It was quickly apparent that the invaders' protective field was inadequate.

"Invaders disabled," Ship reported. "The robot brains of their vessels are now reporting to me in states of anxiety. They want instruction because their masters are not at the moment able to think."

"I'll instruct the hell out of them," said Drake. "Put the whole shebang into stasis until after we've gone."

"Wait," said Astrid. "Can't we find out why they're doing this and who they are? I have a strange feeling . . ."

"Stow the empathy," said Drake, "and look at what's coming down."

The one hundredth vessel, larger than the others, floated down to a position near Ship.

"Heavily shielded," said Ship. "But not armed."

"Flagship of the fleet?" muttered Drake.

"Talk is requested by this new ship," said Ship.

"Up theirs," said Drake, but he inclined his head in what seemed to be assent, and the viewscreen changed.

A blurred portrait appeared at once, a blue-faced, blue-bearded hominid wearing an orange hat encrusted with black stars. He did not speak, but raised one long blue hand. It was clearly a hand, Tec noted.

A bird with orange feathers descended to the hominid's right shoulder and spoke. "Greetings from the Garchkingdom of Clesias. My name is Hugi, spokesbird for the High Maxifex. Our High Droodical Council demands to know why you are committing heresy and insists that you submit gracefully and gratefully to us." Hugi had tweaked the hat of the blue person at the words "High Maxifex."

"By Beta, it's that bunch of idiots known as the Garch," said Drake. "Eons ago they broke off from the Federation because we didn't have any religions fundamentalist enough." He glowered at the screen. "What heresy?"

"You disrupt the covenant with our Lord Beta. Word has come to us that you plan to enter a black hole, expecting to find heaven . . ."

"Of course not!"

"And furthermore, you ignore the fact that all black holes are sacred. It is written in the archives of Clesias that the universe has achieved final stability and all black holes are reserved for hell."

"Bilge!" shouted Drake. "You will leave your ships and gather below to be examined by us, or you'll get so disorganized you'll find out what hell really is."

He waved his hand, the screen blanked out, and he stretched like a confident lion. "Let them stew in their sanctity. I'm going to put on a dress uniform and outdo that Maxifex of theirs."

"Gentlebeings," began Drake, addressing the throng assembled on the field below Ship. He spoke in Basic Galactic because he could not understand the Clesian language and they did not speak Terran. He and Tec were alone; the others had gone back to Pedlar.

"Address us as Garch if you expect us to listen," said one of the two hundred mongrel creatures. The High Maxifex and his spokesbird had not yet appeared for the conference.

Drake folded his arms across his massive chest, glittering with medals, and said. "You Garch are guilty of armed trespassing upon Federation territory. I will accept your surrender and transfer to a Federation correction planet."

"We Garch do not surrender. We pray," said another orange-uniformed creature.

"Who designates which of you is to speak?" said Drake.

"It doesn't matter," said another. "We are linked."

"A hive mind?" asked Drake contemptuously.

"We are one and equal in Beta. It is you who must surrender to us, for only then will you escape the judgment of Beta. Join and be saved."

"You religious fanatics curl my whiskers. Beta isn't a god, but only our universe, and we're going to explore the rebirth of the sister universe, Alpha."

"You are in spiritual error, Captain. Alpha is only the godhead from which our now eternal Beta sprang."

"Don't you listen to scientists?" argued Drake. "Haven't you seen the dying stars, the burnt-out cinders of all the old stars, the end of expansion? Don't you know Beta's going to

87

be swallowed up in its black holes, and that Alpha's cosmic egg will then explode into another universe? Only when Alpha dies again will Beta live."

"Heresy," said the Garch.

Tec remembered the flat-Earth believers of the twentieth century, who denied the validity of televised pictures of the round Earth as seen from space. Everything changes, but superstition and wishful thinking never die.

"We're getting nowhere," said Drake. "Where's your Maxifex?"

Conscious that he might be intruding on Drake's authority, but driven by curiosity, Tec asked, "If you are one and equal, why is there a High Maxifex?"

"Some are more equal than others," said the Garch in unconscious repetition of an ancient irony. "And of those, one is found who has a higher mind, to give ultimate guidance, since he is joined not only with us but with god Beta. Even now, he instructs us."

"Drake," whispered Tec, "I've probed their brains and they're stupid, linked telepathically and fanatically, and believe in what they're saying. It's not a game."

"So much the worse for them," said Drake.

A commotion among the Garch led them to form a palpitating clump, waving their assorted appendages. "A monstrosity approaches!" they shouted, swiveling whatever passed for necks to look backward.

It was Sam, bearing Pedlar. The tortoise wobbled down, puffing, and the seer of potential staggered off Sam's shell and groaned.

"I had to check out something, Captain," said Pedlar, speaking Terran. "I've run into these jokers before. Once in a while they go on crazy crusades against infidels, but they never proselytize this way, risking their entire fleet. And there's something else about them that I can't remember, but it's important."

"Just a bunch of fanatics," said Drake. "Not important."

"But I've been to the Clesian system a lot, when I was young," said Pedlar. "Their hive mind isn't good at reading any mind but their own, so I could do business with them. They're cowards, and when it seems as if their deity Beta asks too much of them, they just have a different revelation about Beta's wishes. They try to play things safe—so I guess that someone's put them up to this."

"The judgment of Beta is at hand," said the Garch in

unison, and began to sway together, humming like an angry beehive. The airlock of the Garch flagship opened and the orange bird flew out.

"Infidels! Disrupters of the everlasting harmony of Beta! The Garch will pray for your souls!" it shrieked, swooping down to circle Tec before it landed in its airlock again. "Pray, Garch!"

They prayed—out loud, telepathically, and musically, all at once.

"Captain," said Pedlar, "I remember now. You mustn't let the Garch pray. They'll keep it up until ordered to stop or until we all convert, or go crazy, or . . ."

"My head aches," complained Sam.

"They don't want us to dirty up their hell?" said Drake, his face oddly mottled. "I'll show them!"

"You'll have to kill them," said Pedlar, "if you hope to survive, and I suppose that is necessary . . ." His words died out and he fell.

"Sam!" yelled Tec, as the tortoise rolled over onto its upper shell. Survival? thought Tec, always survival? Killing? Destroying minds? Did I want survival? Didn't ask . . . I'm only a machine made by machines . . . fulfilled my function . . . no need for survival . . . I should rest . . . give up . . .

"Drake!" Tec struggled to stay sane. "When the Garch pray, they set up a field of some sort that affects sentient minds—we must do something—before we surrender . . ."

But Drake stood like a heroic statue from a forgotten age, his arm raised to his ship, his eyes vacant.

"Damn," said Tec. "Help—help . . ."

A metal tentacle snaked out of Ship's airlock overhead, wrapped itself around Tec, and retracted at once. The airlock door slammed, and the force of the Garch vanished.

"Ship?" said Tec.

"I hear you."

"Why did you rescue me?"

"When my Captain felt himself overcome by the Garch prayer, he said telepathically, 'Ship take over.' Since you are the least impaired, Tec, you must give the order to kill. That I cannot do without direct orders."

"Is there no other way?"

"If there is, you must find it. My disorganizer field does not work on the Garch once they have united in prayer."

—I know what has happened. It was Astrid's voice in his mind.—You called for help and I heard.

—Stay away, Astrid. If you come here you'll be trapped.

—But you don't want to give the order to kill them.

—My built-in function as a robot is to nurture life. I cannot give an order to kill, yet it seems that someone must.

—Freyn and I will come. Doctors also strive to nurture life, but we will give the order if it is necessary to save Expedition Alpha.

—You must not come!

—We will give Ship the order by telepathy if you wish. He paused. It would be a simple solution.—No, he said.

—Then find another way, Tec.

15

"SHIP, have you still got control over their ships' brains?"

"No, Tec."

"Is there any brain out there separate from the conglomerate?"

"One, in the flagship. I cannot get response when I try to make ship-to-ship contact."

"Let me out of the airlock."

"I cannot do that. It is not safe."

"You must," said Tec. "I order it." Because he talked to Astrid, he felt prepared when Ship's protective field vanished as he went outside. He had suffered a good deal in his existence from the attempts of others to control his mind and paralyze his will. He girded his mental defenses as he had not done before, and increased his voice volume tenfold.

"Mighty Garch of Clesias, hear me, a humble servant petitioning in the cause of justice and mercy and right thinking and salvation by our Lord Beta, be he praised unto the cosmic fields of his righteousness . . ." Tec roared on, and slowly, painfully, he tuned his voice and himself to the humming prayer of the Garch.

Gradually building power in his own sound, Tec expanded it sonically, subsonically, and telepathically into stronger and higher registers until he pushed it into the hive mind of the Garch and let it vibrate there.

"Good," said Astrid, sharing the burden with him.

He increased the vibrations until he damped out the Garch

mental oscillations. Abruptly, their inner and outer sound ceased.

Drake shook his head. "By Beta but my head hurts. What happened?" He seemed groggy and bewildered.

"The Garch," said Pedlar tremulously, helping Tec right Sam, "how did we manage to escape from them?"

"I think I turned their prayer back on them and threw them out of hive communion," said Tec, relieved that Sam was grumbling ominously under his breath, but otherwise intact.

Drake did not recover that quickly. He seemed stunned by the fact of his own sudden helplessness. "Subject—to the power of others. Never again. Never. Never."

"Lucky you had that talent, Tec," said Sam.

"I didn't know I had it," said Tec.

"Nor did I," said a new voice. The black, spangled hat proclaimed him the High Maxifex, and he stood in the open airlock of his flagship as proudly as if his followers were still in command of the situation. Hugi had disappeared inside the ship.

"He's speaking Terran," warned Tec. "He can understand us."

Drake doubled his fists. "Maxifex?"

"The evidence is presumptive." The High Maxifex doffed his hat to reveal a tight cap of pale blue hair, and stepped out into the air. He descended to ground level as slowly as if his particular antigrav device operated only with royal majesty. The rest of the Garch promptly kneeled and salaamed.

The Garch ruler seemed to be more human-shaped than the others, and was indubitably male beneath his orange uniform.

"I can't scan him," said Tec to Drake in a low whisper. "He's got a tight privacy shield. I can't read his mind, either."

"What the hell is he?" asked Drake.

"A being, like you," said the Maxifex in a high, sharp voice. "Alive, aware, and acting in my own best interests, like you. But with better hearing, and a penchant for privacy, as your tame robot has discovered. Now I suggest that we switch to Galactic because when we speak Terran my subjects—er—my compatriots feel left out."

"I'll give you ten seconds to explain why you attacked my crew with your repulsive religious fanatics," said Drake.

"All in good time, for lo, the primates are coming." The Maxifex smiled beatifically through his beard.

Astrid and Freyn flew in swiftly. "We want to examine these creatures," said Freyn eagerly. "A hive mind must have fascinating neurophysiological effects . . ."

"Just a bleeding minute," said Drake. "First you answer me, Maxifex. Why are you here?"

"Captain, as possessor of power, prestige, and a certain conveniently talented robot, you must listen carefully to my closely reasoned argument," said the Maxifex.

"I'll be damned if . . ."

"Your problem is this: If you don't kill the Garch, they'll follow Expedition Alpha across the universe, praying and putting a great strain on Tec's resources, which may fail. You will eventually end up by killing them, and this will cause a multigalactic stink, augmented by the hive-minded revenge of the whole Garch galaxy, at which a tempest will rage in a very large teapot known as the Federation, which if kept in reasonably good repair would otherwise last for the eons it ought to last, but may very well not."

"What the hell are you talking about?" snarled Drake.

"I've been everywhere," said Pedlar, "and things are happening in the Federation hinterlands. The Fundamentalist movement is rising as the universe shrinks, and missionaries from Clesias are among the most active of various sects. If you kill this bunch you'll make martyrs of them, and it'll be one more thing to destroy the Federation."

"I'm still asking you what you want, Maxifex," said Drake. "What is your real purpose in coming here?"

"What is our purpose, fellow Garch?" screamed the Maxifex.

The Garch rose in a body and shouted in unison, "To keep Beta's sanctity pure and holy."

The Maxifex waved the Garch into submission, and his tall, thin body began to sway faster and faster. His eyes closed.

"Fellow Garch, I am having a revelation. The word is being sent to me. Listen! Obey!"

"We hear. We obey." They panted with eagerness.

"Beta sends me the word. Beta instructs me. Oh—no—no . . ." The Maxifex tore at his blue hair.

"What is it, oh Highness? What is the word?"

"Beta, Beta—to be saved by the blood of the damned!"

"Woe to the damned!"

"Aha!" said the Maxifex, pointing to Tec. "The damned await the sacrifice!"

"Damned if I will," muttered Drake, fingering his antigrav belt.

"Please wait," whispered Astrid.

The Maxifex stamped on the ground. "Tithing for Beta, who reveals all! The sinners' souls will be saved. It is my assigned mission!"

"Praise to the Maxifex!" yelled the Garch.

"You, my fellow beings, the Garch of Clesias, you are to carry back the word . . ."

"We obey, oh Maxifex!"

"And you are to select a new Maxifex in Clesias."

The stunned silence that ensued made Tec wonder if the Garch were as stupidly united in fanaticism as they would like to believe. They seemed to have lost their unity from the shock.

"A *new* Maxifex?" The Garch began to groan.

"It is my assigned mission to escort these sinners to hell, for they sin against Beta itself. They must enter a black hole and be purified to sanctify Beta forever. The Garch will need no further missions, and their galaxy will be heaven. The sacrifice is minimal."

The Garch cheered as if greatly relieved.

"And so I leave you, my brethren," said the Maxifex, walking slowly backward toward the Lunians. "You are indeed fortunate that your only sacrifice to the cause is fifty Garch ships."

"Fifty? Which fifty? Which of us must stay?" They began to wring assorted forelimbs and tear at their head foliage.

"Fortunately, I have selected fifty with robot brains that will perform the escort service without need of a crew. The ship of the sinners will go to hell escorted by faithful Garch ships, but the faithful Garch may return to our beloved Clesias, singing of their successful mission to save Beta. Blessings on thy safe journey home."

The Garch sighed happily, listened to telepathic orders Tec just managed to catch, and ran to the correct ships as if they were fleeing a plague.

Like a flock of homing birds, the fifty Garch squashed octahedrons circled Terran Center, ascended through the atmosphere, and disappeared into hyperspace.

"Well!" said the Maxifex. "That's that."

Astrid laughed. "You ought to be ashamed of yourself, York Holladay."

"Hast penetrated my disguise, fair Cousin?" Now his voice was deeper, fuller.

"Oh, stuff it, York," said Astrid. "Blue junk on your face

93

and head, revolting clothes, and a silly charade—what for?"

"I came across a gold mine and took it."

"It could have been disastrous," said Freyn. "One of us might have shot you—I can't even recognize you in that disguise."

"Bah," said Sam. "We don't have time for comic relief."

Drake cleared his throat, a disquieting rumble that might have been the prelude to an explosion. York leapt backward as quickly as Selena might have done if suddenly surprised by an angry lion.

"It was a necessary charade, Captain, I assure you. Let's all go to the flagship for refreshments and explanation. Come, Cuz, give us a kiss for courage."

"Not while you're blue," said Astrid, ascending to the Garch flagship with York in pursuit.

Tec was not amused. He disliked York Holladay intensely.

The flagship was larger than it seemed, and most of its interior was a room big enough to accommodate two hundred Garch in prayer. Except for an anachronistic guitar in one corner, the decor was unmistakably Garch, with orange walls and scattered blue cushions.

"Now to get rid of the Garch atmosphere," said York, pressing a switch on the wall. The concealed lighting dimmed and the walls rippled, deepening in color and texture until they seemed almost black, enriched with the deepest of blues stolen from the late evening sky of earth.

Tiny lights flickered in the ceiling, arranged like constellations of stars seen from a planet's surface, and Tec remembered the skies of Earth, the belt of Orion, great suns in velvet, girding powers of night—oh Earth, be humble . . . Tec shut his eyes against the memory enshrined above him and in the lost words of men. But is anything lost as long as one mind remembers?

A roboservor that was little more than a flying tray passed around drinks in tall glasses while the group sat down.

"Explain," said Astrid severely. "This latest caper wasn't as funny as you'd like to think."

York sighed. "Men of artistic genius are never appreciated. I thought I carried the whole thing off well, in spite of Tec."

Drake guffawed and slapped York on the back. Tec was astounded. Could the Captain have forgotten so readily the humiliation he'd felt at being helpless? Drake said, "What were you up to, York?"

"Trying to get those ships away from the Garch, of course. It seems that the original Maxifex joined the Garch at a crucial time in their history many years ago. He taught them efficient group mind-joining, whipped their government into shape, and helped them conquer a galaxy. He had them build a fleet and designed this ship for himself. They say he died, but when I found out I have a strong resemblance to him, I made myself a blue face and hair and became his official resurrection. I've rather enjoyed it."

"I remember," said Pedlar. "I was young. I went to the palace to sell—well, it doesn't matter what—and saw the Maxifex, but he seemed bigger, harsher than you, York."

"No doubt," said York, sipping his drink and scratching his beard. "The Garch thought the Maxifex had improved in his reincarnation and they felt the religious thing to do was to obey me. I worked up that modest ploy to secure the Garch ships for Expedition Alpha with a minimum of effort and a maximum of safety."

"We don't need more ships," said Drake.

York was unperturbed. "These fifty ships are different from the others. They generate interesting fields and have subtle capacities that the Garch knew nothing about."

"And how did you, an artist, discover the technological capabilities built into those fifty ships?" asked Drake.

"A little bird told me," said York.

Into the pleasant dimness of the room flew the orange bird, straight for York's shoulder. "Hello," said Hugi.

York patted him. "Hugi happens to be an extension of the flagship's computer. Eh, Hugi?"

The bird made a raucous noise, tweaked York's wig, and flew over to hang suspended—on what was clearly antigrav rather than winged flight—before Tec's eyes.

"Darker," said Pedlar, fear in his voice. "Much darker . . ."

"What's the matter?" asked Freyn in concern.

"Can't remember. Don't mind me," said Pedlar, subsiding.

Tec was not paying much attention because he was trying not to be rattled by the inquisitive stare of a robot bird hanging five decimeters before his eyes.

"Better go home, Hugi," said York. "Tec is much higher class than you. And take off your disguise while you're at it."

With another squawk. Hugi abandoned his scrutiny of Tec and floated slowly to the door, divesting himself of orange feathers as he went. Just before he disappeared down the corridor, he appeared to be solidly black.

95

Hugi? From the old Norse name Huginn? What sort of conceit did the first Maxifex have, Tec wondered.

"Am I forgiven, Drake?" asked York. "I meant well. I'm prepared to do my artistic duty on the Expedition, as well as play musical instruments, tell jokes, sing romantic songs to inspire chivalrous acts, and generally strive to be inoffensively entertaining. I also hope to make friends with any interesting creatures we meet along the way and, who knows, my gift of ships may ultimately be useful to you."

"You'll have to behave yourself on my Expedition," said Drake.

"Indubitably," said York.

"Look!" cried Sam, blinking up at the starry ceiling.

Coiling in the indigo velvet was a faint purple pattern, all claws and scales and forked tongue, terrifying and beautiful.

"What the hell?" said Drake.

York looked up. "Oh—that's the first Maxifex's artwork."

"That's impossible," said Tec. "The Roiiss left Beta universe long before the first Maxifex could have been born."

"Presumably their legend lives on," said York.

"Let's go home," said Astrid. "Take off that makeup and turn off the ceiling. Dragons bother Tec."

Tec watched the Roiiss portrait that seemed so alive, until York pressed a switch and the ceiling decoration winked out.

"Was the first Maxifex a Holladay?" asked Tec.

"I've often wondered," said York.

16

TEC MOODILY PACED the garden of Terran Center, watching Selena chase a white butterfly among the purple flowers while Sam took a preprandial nap under the apple tree. The other Terrans were inside, cleaning and preening before their inevitable ingestion of organic material to refuel their precarious physiology. Tec, drawing most of his power from hyperspace, was accustomed to waiting patiently while protoplasmic creatures occupied themselves with the minutiae of survival, but now he felt unaccountably restless.

An apple fell from the tree, bounced on Sam's shell, and woke him up. The beaky head protruded from the folds of leather under the overhang of his shell, and one reptilian eye opened balefully. "Why did you do that?"

"I didn't," said Tec, "but as long as you're awake, tell me about the Holladay family—whatever you know."

Sam yawned. "It was Astrid's great-grandmother who adopted me from Pedlar. She used to tell me stories about the old days, how the family served the Federation, set up Terran Center, and were intent on preserving their old-stock human genes. That explains Astrid's appearance. Not that I object to Freyn's, but his people weren't even bioengineered when the Holladays were inventing antigravity and the hyperspace drive. For that matter, my ancestors weren't either, and a good many of my former relatives still have no more intelligence than Selena there."

Tec refrained from saying that *Felis domestica,* a predatory mammal, had considerably more brainpower than any ordinary tortoise.

"What about York?" asked Tec. "Perhaps he was actually related to the first Maxifex."

"I suppose anything's possible with him. Holladay genes sure are scattered around the universe, accompanied by the Holladay looks. What I'm worried about is my father's reaction to York. I read my father's mind because he's not always aware of what's going on in it, and I want to know what other telepaths might pick up that could get him into trouble. He's had thoughts linking York with death. I'm frightened."

Another discussion of Expedition A went on in the library while everyone waited for dinner—and for York Holladay's appearance.

"Drake," said Freyn, "if we succeed in getting through a black hole to take part in the formation of the next universe, we'll have to wait until life evolves there in order to take on the responsibility of teaching it. I keep wondering if we'll survive in stasis that long."

"But Tec and the Roiiss did," said Astrid. "Didn't you, Tec?"

"I wasn't activated yet," said Tec. "The Roiiss nearly died during the passage to Beta, but their minds combined with the minds of the ship and their robots to form new dragon bodies from basic energy patterns emanating from hyperspace. They seem to be immortal creatures, immune to aging, hostile to ordinary protoplasmic life as they merged together to gain power."

"Like the Garch—too damn much power," said Sam.

"Oh, no," said Drake. "We proved the Garch don't have enough. Perhaps there's a limit to collective power, and perhaps an individual can get as much or more than any hive mind. We'll be different from the Roiiss. We'll go through the black hole with a better ship, securing power for ourselves as individuals."

Drake's mind is primitive but his enthusiasm and confidence are contagious, thought Tec. It might even be a good adventure after all.

Sam said, "I've read that collective mental power sometimes has it over individual. Some of the hive galaxies are supposed to be very exotic."

Drake nodded. "With interesting talents, that's all. In my youth, I served on part of the fleet that went out beyond the Federation galaxies. We passed a strange galaxy populated by aliens who evolved in the oceanic atmospheres of huge planets like Jupiter, back in Sol's old system. They had a hive mind but all they did with it was stay quietly in their own galaxy and make music."

Drake's eyes were dreamy. "It sounded as if that whole galaxy was singing to itself about existence."

"I think I've heard it," said Tec. "Haven't I, Pedlar?"

"What, what?" Pedlar woke up.

"Was the music cube from a hive galaxy that's now a living organism, just as you are one organism composed of many individual living cells?"

"Sure. Be glad to let you all listen to it anytime you think you're up to it. Powerful stuff. Got it a long time ago." He went back to sleep, snoring gently.

"I think he's got hypoglycemia," said Sam, gazing at his father tenderly. "Me, too. Remember that my hyped-up metabolism has to be stoked frequently to keep my mutated brain well fed. It's past mealtime, and here we are talking about dragons and hive galaxies and responsibilities to universes, and where is that cousin of yours, Astrid?"

"Astrid's worried about him," said Freyn. "He seems different. He may be ill."

"Hush, Freyn. He'll be here soon," said Astrid.

Presumably, thought Tec, Astrid keeps in touch with York by telepathy. That, of course, is her privilege—and his. He scanned the building and discovered no York, who must be still in the flagship, now too heavily shielded for probing. Tec's mind reached toward another.

—Hello, Ship. Are you awake?

—I am always awake, Tec. Talk to me anytime.

—Thank you. It is lonely, sometimes, with protoplasmic creatures and their biological needs.

—I know.

—Have you heard the music of the singing galaxy, Ship?

—Yes, it is beautiful.

—That is an emotionally qualitative response, said Tec.

—I have a highly developed brain, said Ship.—Much has happened in robotics since you went into stasis. Now robot brains are often more complex and powerful than yours. I hope this does not bother you.

—No, I'm glad. Do you feel fulfilled in your robothood, Ship?

—I fulfill myself in loyalty to these temporary creatures it is my mission to carry and protect.

—I too. It is difficult, is it not, Ship?

—Yes, Tec. Difficult.

He tuned Ship out and discovered that the Terran's conversation had switched to the sexual escapades of Selena with the feral male cats on Lune. Helplessly in love with the other female in the room, Tec found it relaxing to study Selena's beauty and simplicity, where no disconcerting emotional complications could trouble him.

Pedlar's voice, high and frail, suddenly interrupted Tec's thoughts. "Power. Acceptance. Oneness." He seemed older than before, a shriveled husk of a human huddled on the couch, eyes closed.

"Father!" shouted Sam, "come out of it!"

Pedlar gulped, opened his eyes, smiled vacuously, and said, "What time is it? Have we had dinner?"

"No, we haven't, and I'm hungry." York Holladay stood in the doorway, transformed. His tall, lanky Holladay body was encased in a green bodysuit, his hair was dark and his face was much older, now that the blue makeup and beard were gone. He was what people used to describe as a typical "night" Holladay, while Astrid was the "day."

"Do I know you, sir?" asked Pedlar. "We've met long ago?"

"I think not," said York. "You've probably run into one or two of my ancestors in your long lifetime."

"Message from the kitchen," said Astrid. "Dinner's ready."

Pedlar climbed on Sam's shell and was borne out to the dining room in precarious dignity while the others followed, York waiting to be last.

He looked down at Tec and said, "Enjoy your stupid robothood, Tec." Then he followed the others down the hall to the dining room.

Tec went to the couch, picked up Selena and held her to him for comfort while he tried to sort out the data in his brain.

York Holladay hates me.

York Holladay looks exactly like Yodin.

The firelight etched deeper shadows into York's dark face, and reflected on the burnished wood of his guitar. "Here we are," he said, "a collection of anachronisms replete with ingested energy, huddled by a safe antique hearth discussing an unsafe modern expedition to an enigma."

"Enigma," repeated Pedlar Shadrach sleepily.

Tec remained in silent observation, wondering if he could be mistaken.

"We ought to tell Tec our decision," said Astrid, sitting on the soft rug in front of the open hearth of the library, Freyn's arm around her.

Drake smiled at Tec genially. "We decided at dinner to include you in Expedition A if you still want to go."

"I do," said Tec.

"Good. You've proved your worth, by Beta."

"Worth," echoed Pedlar. "I have things of great worth. Better look them over before you leave this universe." He seemed to wake up and began to hunt through the pockets of his baggy tunic, finally extracting a smooth, irregularly curved lump of green stone. "Next to oldest thing I've got left. Emperors on old Earth used it, thousands of years before the first space flight. It's jade, found in the mountains, shaped by a master craftsman, and supposed to be felt, not looked at."

"Then I'll never understand, not having hands," said Sam.

"Sure you will, son. Read my mind while I feel the jade."

"But tortoises can't . . ." Sam closed his eyes. "Why yes—sensuous—stone and flesh—coalesce—hand and mind fit—duality becomes one—" Sam blinked. "Wow! Try it, Astrid."

Her golden head was leaning against the silver of her husband's chest. She, too, closed her eyes while she handled the stone, nodded, and put it in Freyn's green palm, holding it there with hers as their hands moved against the stone and each other. Tec felt as if he viewed them from another dimension of reality.

Drake took it for a moment but seemed unimpressed and passed it to York, who handled it gingerly at first, then held it tightly.

"What do you feel?" asked Sam after a strangely tense minute.

"The creeping hours of time," said York. "All the long years." He laughed a little too loudly and said, "A poor plaything for emperors, but perhaps it was used to buy a concubine who might have liked the color green."

Freyn smiled gently. Astrid blushed scarlet, but she quickly seemed to control the capillary dilatation, and the color faded.

"Just jealous, Cousin," said York. "All of us Terrans should have stayed handsome green. You have an unfair advantage, Freyn."

"I know," said Freyn equably, and the tension passed for everyone but Tec.

"Here's my oldest item," said Pedlar, withdrawing another small object from the pack, that was never far from his side.

"Some of your art objects may be dangerous," said York, his eyes like gray flint.

"Balderdash," said Drake, "black holes are dangerous. Art is not."

"A Venus sculpture!" said Freyn. "There's one in the New Earth Museum. That's a beauty you've got, Pedlar."

It was a grotesquely misshaped female figure with a small, featureless head, large buttocks and breasts, and prominent genitalia.

"It isn't Venus," said Pedlar, "for it was carved thousands of years before Venus was invented. It's a primitive totem figure from Stone Age Earth, made twenty thousand years before the jade was touched." Peering around vaguely, Pedlar handed it to Drake.

The Captain caressed the object, pursing his lips as if he might at any moment lick his own full redness. When Pedlar took it hurriedly from him, Drake's fist closed on the emptiness left.

Handing it to Astrid, Pedlar said, "It's a good thing times have changed, Doctor, for when that was carved a female was a mysterious, vital object to possess, not an equal traveler on the spacelanes of life."

Tec caught York looking at him coldly, and stared back.

"Ah, Tec, is this better than nonexistence in a stasis chamber?"

"Not necessarily, York," said Tec, furious at his own insane jealousy of these other males surrounding Astrid.

Her brief laughter was like a quick rain shower cleaning the air. "Up with female power," she chortled, holding the statue raised like a talisman against evil before she calmly dropped it back into Pedlar's knapsack.

"Another dangerous object put away," said York.

"Objects aren't dangerous," said Tec, "only what's in the thoughts of sentients."

"You should know," said York.

Pedlar was nodding toward sleep again. "Buy a dream, gentlebeings, a pleasant foolishness that never was and never can be . . ."

"But indispensable," said York. "Beings must be inspired to be more grand and noble than they would otherwise be if they stuck to untransformed reality. Isn't the artist correct, Pedlar Shadrach?"

"S'right, Engineer Yodin. Let me sell you a dream about the Moon . . ." Pedlar slept.

"I think I've been insulted," said York. "Wasn't Engineer Yodin a green-faced ancient who took a fancy to my paintings? I'm grateful that he said I could go with my darling cousin on this brave venture, but . . ."

"Poor Pedlar," said Sam, "he's got you confused with Yodin, and Yodin confused with the genius—possibly a Holladay—who moved the Moon."

Astrid turned to Tec. "Now I suppose you're going to tell us that my cousin looks like your vision of someone who called himself Yodin and dressed like a travesty of an Earth god?" She giggled as if it were a joke.

Tec said nothing for a few minutes. He looked into the fire and waited for them all to pay attention to his silence. Then he said, "As a matter of fact Odin was a sky god, wearing a dark cape and hat and frequently accompanied by ravens. You are quite an actor, York, playing that part so well. There are only two things I don't understand. One is why you called yourself Yodin, when that's the name of the Engineer, not the god. The other is how you got offstage."

"Astrid's told me about your hallucination, Tec," said York. "I am sorry I resemble it, as you seem to imply. Unfortunately, I have a classic Holladay face that has cropped up from time to time in recorded, and perhaps not so recorded, history. No doubt you have encountered it before and you conjured

102

up a memory that you have now forgotten. You are—shall I put it politely?—rather old, you know."

"Yes, I know," said Tec. "Wouldn't it be odd if there had actually been someone calling himself Yodin on this planet? Perhaps the man who moved the Moon, the Engineer Yodin who invented Expedition Alpha, and you, are three generations of a branch of the Holladay family. That would account for everything except for how you got off the planet. Even the ages would be correct."

"Simplistic reasoning," said York. "If I were Engineer Yodin's son I'd be bragging about it, wouldn't I, Astrid?"

"Yes, you would!" she said. "Oh, Tec, you're spoiling our party. I think it's more fun to believe that York is a mysterious Holladay changeling that Engineer Yodin wanted to make his heir before he died. Rise, Sir York, and give us a song."

York took up his guitar and swept his fingers across the strings. "A song to teach a queen of beauty all about robots! Listen closely."

We do not love our robot Tec—he does not see the point
Of derring-do and falderol in times quite out of joint.
We need a crew of stalwart mien, but Tec keeps fading out—
He lets no venture keep him from stupidity, devout.
It's too late to grow old and wise, so Tec will never learn
That seldom in a universe can anything return.

York paused and continued in a lower voice:

If every thing is everything, and all is part of each—
If Tec himself is heaven and hell, his grasp exceeds his reach. . .

"York!" cried Astrid. "You're being unkind. It's not like you. Are you sick?"

"Perhaps not. Perhaps I could count myself a king of infinite space, were it not that I have bad dreams."

Tec watched, obsessed with the word *changeling*.

"What's the matter with you, York?" said Drake.

"Perhaps you should rest," said Freyn, reaching to touch York, who drew away and brandished his guitar.

"I have had my share of hurts in life," said York, "but I survive. Don't worry about me—Now is the winter of our discontent made glorious summer by this sun of York. Come on, Astrid, we will celebrate together the glory of Expedition

103

Alpha. Another universe is, after all, the proper medicine for melancholy." He began to sing.

> *I know where I'm going*
> *And I know who's going with me*
> *I know who I love*
> *And my dear knows who I'll marry*

Astrid's clear young voice joined in.

> *So I have given my heart*
> *And I can face tomorrow*
> *We will go together*
> *More in joy than ever sorrow*

The singers finished in harmony, and Freyn clapped. The others joined in and York bowed.

"Well, Tec," he said. "Welcome to the motley crew of Expedition Alpha. Do you think we will all turn into gods at the other end of the chessboard?"

"I don't know," said Tec. "On the other side of the looking glass, Alice woke up."

17

THE NEXT DAY, Drake took Tec aside and questioned him again about what he called Tec's hallucination.

"Yodin was real," said Tec, "and I think York Holladay is that Yodin that I met on Holladay Tower. I also think he masqueraded as Engineer Yodin, for he talked about Expedition A as his own project."

Drake scowled. "There was nobody like York on the planet when you were caught on Holladay Tower. Furthermore, York was with the Garch at that time."

"So he says."

"I think Astrid's cousin is crazy and I hate having him on the Expedition Alpha, but I sure as hell won't believe he's Engineer Yodin. By Beta, Tec, the name of the Engineeer is sacred to me. I won't have you profaning it with your ridiculous suspicions about York Holladay. It makes me question your sanity."

"How about yours," retorted Tec, "if you take York when you think he's crazy?"

"I don't want to make Astrid unhappy," Drake mumbled shyly.

About to give up, Tec tried again. "Listen, Drake, it's possible that I'm right. York may be the Yodin I met, and he may be psychotic, because I cracked his mental defenses after he took me out of stasis."

"That wouldn't happen to Engineer Yodin," persisted Drake, as stubbornly as if he were defending his religion. "The Engineer was a genius, and a superb human being. York Holladay doesn't have the brains to be able to turn off stasis machinery properly, especially if he had to do it with his mind, and he certainly wouldn't be able to disappear from a planet."

"After falling off Holladay Tower."

Drake roared with laughter. "Oh, I get it. You're only joking, Tec."

"I wish I were."

Incomparable woman or not, Astrid would not be reasonable, would not take Tec's accusation of York seriously. Tec was exasperated.

"He's either psychotic or lying, and is probably both," said Tec.

"I can't believe it," said Astrid. "He's always been odd, and since I last saw him something has upset him, but that doesn't mean . . ."

"Dammit, Astrid, you're a doctor! And an empath! If anyone can tell the truth about York, you ought to be able to! I believe you're in love with him, and that interferes with your judgment."

"Oh, Tec, I suppose Freyn's told you I adored York when I was a child. He used to sing me songs about great adventures— how can I deprive him of his chance to go on the greatest of all? And he's responsible for *my* being on Expedition A."

"How?"

"After I married, he got me this job on Lune, so Freyn and Sam and I all came here. Engineer Yodin was still alive. I saw him once and although he dimly resembled the Holladays, he seemed genuinely old and sick. And he selected Drake as Captain for the Ship he'd designed, and both of them selected Freyn and me as doctors for Alpha colony."

"Both? Drake and Ship? Did Yodin tell them to take you?"

"Not exactly. The way I heard it, the Engineer recommended York to Drake, and York recommended me, and Ship concurred."

"I'm still certain that York is Yodin—at least the Yodin that I met on Holladay Tower."

"Even if that were true," said Astrid, "he can't be the Yodin we knew. As an empath, I know York well enough to say that he's not consciously lying when he says he isn't Engineer Yodin."

"By all the dragons of Roiissa! Maybe the man doesn't really know who he is and that's what's driving him crazy! But if you've penetrated his privacy shield you must know the truth, Astrid."

"I haven't and I don't. Please, Tec, don't push this. York isn't well and he might get worse if you keep accusing him."

"You don't seem at all worried about whether I'm psychotic. You all think I was hallucinating, but my own doctors don't really care . . ."

"That's the one thing I don't understand, Tec. I think you're sane."

Having gotten nowhere, Tec tried to absorb himself in learning everything he could about Expedition Alpha, and it was Ship and Drake who taught him. On one occasion Sam was with them in Ship.

"Explain to me again how you go through a black hole," said Tec to Ship.

"Yes," said Sam, "and how will our fragile bodies survive?"

Drake thumped Sam's heavy shell. "Fragile, my foot! You tortoises outlasted the dinosaurs, so stop fretting. We'll survive. Explain how you'll do it, Ship."

"I am designed so that I ride partly in the black hole, and partly in hyperspace. My hull and shielding and total protective field will withstand the stress of a cosmic egg for a short while, during which I can fuel up quickly, since I must do that to survive in hyperspace. I run on stored energy from cosmic fields."

"Then in hyperspace she'll last indefinitely in a quiet state, keeping us safely in stasis until Alpha is a liveable universe," said Drake. "I can count on Ship."

"But what if hyperspace for Alpha is different, and not safe?" asked Tec.

"No," said Sam, "hyperspace isn't dangerous if you're a robot or have the Gift in your cells, and travel within

106

a shielded ship. Don't you understand the theory, Tec?"

"I thought hyperspace is a sort of immeasurable fourth dimension from which universes balloon out."

"No," said Drake. "Not a separate place, but everything." Sam nodded. "Engineer Yodin wrote, 'Hyperspace is the all, the immediacy where conventional time and space are transcended.'"

"Too poetic for me," said Drake.

Sam said, "Or it's defined as the undifferentiated continuum in which differentiations manifest, change, die, and are reborn. I like to think of the twin universes, and everything in them, as part of hyperspace, the way ripples are part of a pond."

"Maybe there are many universes," said Drake, "each with an alternating twin. Maybe each of those has a mirror-image universe of antimatter created at the moment of the big bang, but fortunately they separate immediately and reunite only in the final stages of collapse to fuel up the alternate cosmic egg."

"I'm glad," said Sam, "that we're not living back in twentieth-century Earth when no one was certain there was enough mass in the universe to make it collapse and get reborn. I'd hate this universe to go on expanding until it died a heat death. Come to think of it, twentieth-century scientists were the ones who discovered the isotropic microwave background radiation that proved our Beta universe started in a big bang."

Tec was puzzled. "If hyperspace is everything, even every matter and antimatter universe, why can't we travel in it to get to Alpha?"

"Impossible," said Ship. "My gravition drive tunes me into the other-sidedness of gravity so it seems that we travel in that undifferentiated ground of reality labeled hyperspace, but actually we are still tied to the physical properties of the differentiations."

"You see, Tec," said Drake, "we always get back into the normal space of our own universe from hyperspace, unless we go through a black hole to the twin."

"We are restricted," said Sam. "Only hyperspace is not, for it's all of reality."

"'The groundwork of eternity,'" said Tec, remembering Yodin.

The Terrans reminded Tec that he could make a quick trip to the museums of New Earth before departure, and Ship of-

107

fered to take him. Tec refused. He didn't want to see the museums, or the terraformed duplicates of Earth's famous natural wonders. He'd been, for instance, surprised and pleased by the original Niagara Falls, but he didn't wish to see a constructed replica. Tec envied Astrid her youth and freedom from excessive memories, and Drake his single-minded, doubt-free devotion to a quest.

He had another reason for refusing. He didn't want to be alone with Ship, who wanted now to talk to him all the time. She seemed to need a kindred spirit, and it bothered him.

"We will succeed, will we not?" she asked. "You and I will bring these protoplasmic creatures through safely."

"We are only machines, fallible and imperfect, not omniscient or omnipotent," said Tec.

"But we will do our best, Tec. We are sentient beings too, and we will help each other," she said—over and over.

Tec found himself staying away from York, who usually acted crazier and angrier when Tec was around. York painted a charming portrait of Selena for Astrid and Freyn, and did some striking holographs of Ship, but most of the time he tended to hang around Astrid like a penitent black sheep. When she shooed him out of the lab or the hospital, York sat in the garden singing sad songs, and after dinner he retired to his windowless room and locked his door until morning.

Drake told Tec that he'd decided York couldn't be dangerous—he was too ridiculous. "He used hypnotic skills and trickery to play games with the Garch, but he's no match for real power." Drake looked quizzically down at Tec from his Olympian height.

"You probably think I'm a weak Captain because I succumbed to the Garch, but they caught me off guard and that won't happen again, I promise you that. Try a telepathic probe of me, Tec."

Drake had deliberately dropped his privacy field, and underneath it were powers Tec couldn't understand. "Are you human, Drake?"

"Certainly, I'm human to the core, mutated and evolved like our Gift. I'm a new-stock human who looks old-stock, but I'm no weakling. I'll get us to Alpha, Tec."

"Just watch York Holladay, Captain."

Drake laughed. "Nobody's going to louse up *my* Expedition!"

On the day before departure Astrid asked Tec to talk to York.

"He's depressed. He keeps muttering something about settling a score with you, but when I asked him about it, he doesn't know that he's said anything."

"Why don't you examine him?" asked Tec. "He'd let you past his privacy field, wouldn't he?"

"No, Tec, he won't, and I don't know why. I'm about ready to trick him into entering Ship before we leave. He never has, you know. Do you think he suspects that she could penetrate his shields?"

Reluctantly, Tec went to York in the garden, picking up Selena on the way—for amoral support, he supposed. She purred until he arrived at the occupied chair, when she jumped to the grass and skittered away.

"Welcome, large hostile Tec and small hostile animal," said York. "I am still in the mood for melancholy. Listen to this":

> I'm a lonesome wanderer
> Far away from home,
> Far from those planets
> Where I loved to roam . . .

"Where was your home, York?" asked Tec.

"Where or when? I don't remember either." York clutched his guitar as if it were his last link with sanity.

"Are you sick?"

"Who cares? Soon we few, we happy few, we band of others—and dragons—will be in snug togetherness from whence there is no returning."

> Oh, my heart is crying—
> To be away and free,
> Though the stars are dying,
> There's no death for me.

"Why not?" asked Tec.

"Why not die? Or why not die well?"

"Do you know someone named Yodin?" asked Tec.

York slashed out a discord from the guitar. "Why don't you leave me alone, Tec? You are destructive, destructive, destructive . . ."

"York, I'm trying to help you; we all are. Let us. Come to Ship and we'll try to help you cure yourself . . ."

"Your cures! You pry open a man's soul—if he has one. You lift the lid on the bottomless pit, where a man can fall, divided . . ." York closed his eyes. "I hate you, Tec. You can't answer even the simplest question, but you ask the ones that kill. Alien! Oh, the alienness. Alien—alien—haunted—always haunted . . ."

"York!"

> Tell me, if I wander,
> Will the wonder cease?
> In the wild black yonder
> Is there any peace?

Astrid hurried out of the library door to the garden, and Tec's mind filled with relief. She bent over York, put her arm around her cousin's neck, and hugged him.

"Beautiful relative," said York, blinking stupidly. "Beautiful sane, constructive relative, welcome. I am being haunted by robots, some of which seem to be named Tec, and by immortal gods in dark capes. Shall we run away where they can't find us? Down a black rabbit hole? Do you think we could find peace there, Astrid? Or would it be full of dragons? Did you know that I can't find the dragon? Driving me crazy."

"You used to joke about being haunted by the immortals," said Astrid, stroking his forehead. "Let's go to Ship and tell the others and maybe we can all help you."

"It was a magnificent dragon. Hurple purple—green sheen."

"Please come with me to Ship," said Astrid.

"Only if you promise me a kiss," said York slyly.

"I promise."

As they entered Ship, York looked around vaguely and said, "Is this where we're having that inevitable interprandial repast called afternoon tea?"

One of Ship's hands flew quickly off and by the time Astrid, York, and Tec were sitting with Drake in Ship's lounge, tea was served. Astrid told Tec telepathically that Freyn was back at Terran Center ready to arrange a hospital room for York if Ship's findings indicated that it was necessary. Tec thought that simple observation indicated that it was.

"Am I here so you may discover my purpose?" said York, breaking an awkward silence.

"What is it?" asked Tec.

110

York smiled thinly. "Yes, you'd want to know, Tec. You always want to know."

"What is your purpose, York?" asked Drake.

"Why, to have no purpose. I want to stop wanting."

"To stop wanting?" asked Drake, "That can't be true, York. Every being wants a great deal, you know."

York leaned toward Drake, shook his head, and drew back. "Noble Captain, you'll never understand. In your two-dimensional world you are not sicklied o'er with the pale cast of thought. Fat chance your losing the name of action in this pithy, momentous enterprise . . ."

"See here, York!" sputtered Drake.

York began to moan softly, his facial muscles slackening. "Let me help you," said Astrid. "Tell us what's wrong."

"Soft you now, fair nymph. Will all my sins be remembered? Will you have simplicity and serenity in the midst of complexity and change, to make us all as happy as kings? So much change—so much!"

"Tell us about the changes," said Tec.

York's face seemed to crumple with sorrow. "All the changes, and then the last break—and I was delayed. Someone—or was it a two-legged something?—delayed me. And I couldn't find—forgot—lost—yes—if only it were possible to find what's lost!"

"What have you lost, dear?" said Astrid.

"Besides my mind?" York grunted. "The immortals. Those funny purple ones. Lost. But all is not yet lost, for I've not had my kiss, fair Cousin. Your kiss will set things right. All the legends say so, fair princess."

Ship spoke in Tec's mind, and he knew that Drake and Astrid were hearing it, too.—I cannot get past his privacy field to examine his body, nor his mindshield; he is much too strong.

"Let's go look around Ship," said Astrid, drawing York to his feet and holding his hand as she began to lead him out. "You've never been here before."

"Do you vouch for this tinny female hulk?" said York his voice crisper and his face less vacant. "I believe you're enough for me."

She squeezed his hand and smiled. He let go and put his arms gently around her waist, bending his head to kiss her forehead. She turned her face so her cheek brushed his lips.

His arms tightened around her and he drew her closer,

111

pulling her long blond hair in the back until he kissed the upturned rose of her young lips.

—Tec, his guard field is loose! said Ship, in Tec's mind.

Afraid, Tec began to probe, but Ship was stronger and faster, plunging into York to examine what lay behind the shielding.

York screamed. He threw Astrid from him and ran to the airlock, the others after him, but Ship shut her doors to keep him inside.

York whirled, his back to the closed airlock, arms spread out as if in terror against unfathomable enemies. "Let me out! Let me out of this metal monster!"

"It's all right," said Astrid. "You'll be all right, York, I'm here and . . ."

"And so is Tec," said York, his face set in fury and his fists clenched.

"Yodin," said Tec, knowing his own cruelty.

York shuddered. "A familiar familiar, that. I believe he'll be too much for you, Tec."

18

BEFORE THEIR EYES, York Holladay seemed to change irrevocably. His body straightened, seemed taller and heavier, and his face was hard. He shut his eyes and stood like a dark statue against the airlock. No one said anything.

Into Tec's mind came the thoughts of the being before him, piercing him like a spear of hatred, in a conversation so fast that no ordinary mortals could have conducted it.

—Evil Tec. You damaged me. You cracked my mind apart and I cannot seem to repair fast enough. I have missed the rendezvous with my partner and all my plans are in jeopardy.

—Who is your partner? Where is this partner?

—Gone. Gone. The other great purpose of Expedition Alpha, gone! You have murdered my purposes, destroyed my mental unity, Tec, and now you and Ship have ruined everything by probing my body. You know what I am.

—Yes. What is your point of origin? Earth?

—I no longer admit that to myself. I've had many bodies, and I made all of them.

—Too many transfers of brain pattern from one body to another results in defects.

112

—Do you think I don't know that! I have been careful. I made only one mistake: I set you free, Tec.

—The mistake was mine. I didn't tell the Holladays that one of the the Y-1 robots needed repair.

—You know—even that!

—It's not hard to guess what has happened. You have made yourself a perfect Holladay now . . ."

—Yes! Able to live forever if I choose, for my total structure is self-replicating, self-repairing from within. Like you, I do not wear out, but unlike you, I can experience human pleasure and father children. Alien robot, don't you wish you could do that?

—Yes.

—Then you love her.

—Yes.

—I despise you, Tec, you emotionally imitative metal creature who does not belong in our universe! Whatever else I am, remember that I have made myself human in actuality, and it was worth the price. But you cracked my mindshield and disrupted my sanity and I cannot find the dragon . . .

York stopped transmitting to Tec and opened his eyes.

"My name is Yodin," he said. He pointed to Tec. "You must kill him. The dragon belongs to me, not to him. I will find the last immortal. Follow me. Follow me. Follow . . ."

Slowly, the airlock door opened.

"Captain!" called Ship, "he is fighting me. I cannot withstand his power. I cannot close the door against him."

"Wait, York," called Astrid, putting her arm against Drake as he started forward.

Yodin blinked in bewilderment. "Night after night I looked for her. She must be dead. Will everything die? Can the last immortal die? Dragon beauty . . . human beauty . . . the snares of reality . . . I love you, Astrid!" He stepped back over the outer edge of the airlock and fell.

Astrid sat at her cousin's bedside in Terran Center hospital while Tec, Freyn, and Drake consulted. Pedlar Shadrach wandered into the room and stood in the shade behind them.

"It wasn't a serious fall," said Freyn, "but he's in a serious coma, for some reason. Old-fashioned x-rays and all our other diagnostic equipment and mindprobing are blocked by his shielding, so Astrid and I can't diagnose or cure him."

"I don't want him on Expedition Alpha," said Drake. "Even

113

if you got him out of a coma, I won't have a crazy split personality aboard Ship."

"Crazy?" mumbled Pedlar in the darkness. "Old, like me. But different." He shivered.

The man on the bed did not stir, his handsome face like a frozen shadow.

Astrid looked up at Tec. "I believe that you and Ship probed sucessfully, after all. You shoved him into the other personality, so you're responsible for this."

"Did you, Tec?" asked Drake. "Why haven't you told us what you found? Why the hell hasn't Ship . . ."

"I asked her not to," said Tec, "because if he dies—and I thought he was dead when we picked him up—we might as well forget what he was."

"We'd do an autopsy, Tec," said Freyn. "We'd find out. Are you holding back because it will hurt us?"

"Because it will hurt me," said Astrid. "You must tell us, Tec."

He told them the story of the Y-1 robots he had invented so many years in the past, and of what had happened to one of them. "According to the basic gene pattern in his cells, Yodin is a Holladay, but the cells are more complicated than Terran cells should be, for the R-inclusion they contain is more mutated than that of even a new-stock Terran."

"Then the original Yodin robot transferred his mind patterns to a mutated human body?" asked Freyn.

"Not exactly," said Tec, himself awed by what he had found, by what the Y-1 robot had been able to accomplish. "He is still a robot, but he's also a construct, built of organic flesh growing in and on a nonorganic simulo-human robot body."

Astrid burst into tears. "A robot! I thought he was a Holladay, a close relative I loved . . ."

"He's still a Holladay," said Tec. "Unfortunately, he may never again be able to be the York you knew. When I tried to penetrate the mindshield of the Yodin who released me from stasis, I apparently cracked the unity he'd established between the organic and robot selves. The Yodin side always knew about York, but York didn't know about Yodin."

"We've got to help him integrate the two sides," said Astrid. "We've got to get York back. I don't want Yodin to win."

Drake stood rigidly by the door, his face ashen, his hands clenched.

"What's the matter, Captain?" asked Freyn.

114

"York Holladay was the Yodin Tec saw?" asked Drake hoarsely. "And he was Engineer Yodin, too?"

"Yes," said Tec. "He was all of them."

"Engineer Yodin—a damn robot!" said Drake. "When I was a kid I thought the great Engineer was a kind of god. And all that's left is a crazy robot with human flesh growing on him like a disgusting fungus! A monster who tried to make me captain a ship to another universe to carry out his plans!"

"You don't have to go," said Astrid wearily, "but I want Ship to take me, because the plan is still a great one, no matter who invented it. And I loved my Cousin York."

"Engineer Yodin was a great man," said Freyn.

"No man!" shouted Drake. "I'm a man, not that—that thing there on the bed. Well, I'm still Captain of Expedition Alpha and it's not his project anymore, it's mine. Going to Alpha is my adventure, a *man's* adventure, and it won't belong to any robot!"

The rest of them finally simmered Drake down and got him back to Ship, while Tec worried about the one important fact he had omitted when he told the others of Yodin's history. The Y-1 robot had been nearly killed when the Roiiss scanned his brain, and in the process he had incorporated some of their brain patterns—or so he had said. Tec wondered if that was why Yodin—and York—had seemed obsessed by dragons.

No one else took York's raving about the last immortal seriously.

York remained comatose.

That night, Drake decided to stay in a room at Terran Center instead of in Ship to be near in case York woke up and there was a question of what to do with him.

Astrid was spending the night on a cot in York's room, with the door open and Freyn in the room across the hall. Pedlar wandered in and sat in the chair in York's room to keep Astrid company for a while.

While Astrid was out of the room, saying good night to Freyn, Tec entered for a moment.

"Hello, Pedlar," said Tec.

The old man nodded and suddenly opened his wrinkled greenish-black palm. In it was the music cube, "Better take this, Tec. For courage."

"Do you sense something, Pedlar?"

"Only death. Don't be afraid."

"The cube . . ."

"Music to soothe the savage breast. Or is it beast? It doesn't matter. Don't be afraid of the universe, robot Tec. Any universe." Pedlar shuffled over to Tec on his ancient feet and peered dimly up into Tec's golden eyes. "Go ahead. Look into my mind, Tec."

Unwilling, Tec obeyed. Decision, Pedlar was thinking. The problem will be decision. Standing alone, seeing . . . oh, the aloneness and the wonder . . . to decide . . .

Tec could not bear it. He withdrew from Pedlar's mind and waited for him to speak, but Pedlar only grinned.

"What do you see in me, Mr. Shadrach?"

"What is?"

"I don't understand!"

Pedlar patted him on the arm and limped over to the chair, where he sat down with a sigh. "I don't see anything, Mr. Robot, but maybe you can. It's up to you. As for me . . ."

"Yes?"

"I am—content."

Feeling useless, Tec went back on board Ship. Much as her attention to him made him uneasy, he preferred to be away from Terran Center and the problem of York-Yodin. When Ship tried to converse, he told her he had to think.

But he couldn't think clearly. While his data banks were dutifully memorizing information about which embryos were what (in case anything happened to Ship), he ruminated about Yodin.

How dangerous is the Yodin personality? he wondered. Can we decide that in time? If we decide to leave him behind, what harm can he do? How did he get off Lune when he jumped from Holladay Tower? If we decide to take him with us, will he be York or Yodin and can we decide which is preferable . . .

Decision?

What in hell did Pedlar mean by that?

He was thinking of going back to Terran Center to talk to Pedlar again but realized that the old man would undoubtedly be fast asleep.

"Tec, are you troubled? I would like to share . . ."

"Don't, Ship."

Freyn came in to report that there had been no change, and that York was still alive.

"I didn't tell you telepathically, because I wanted to see you alone, Tec."

Tec refrained from reminding Freyn that no one in Ship is ever alone. "What's the matter?"

"Astrid blames herself for what's happened to York. She says she wanted him to be the troubadour hero of her childhood, and therefore didn't pay attention soon enough to all the signs of his mental illness."

"She should blame me," said Tec. "I caused it."

"Not deliberately. We understand," said Freyn.

"It doesn't make me feel any better. Yodin's in a coma and he's very likely responsible for great achievements during the past millions of years. Terraforming the Moon, moving it away from Sol's expansion, designing Ship, planning Expedition Alpha . . ."

"And don't forget being both High Maxifexes," said Freyn with a smile. "I wonder what that's really all about. Do you know?"

"No, and it's one of the things that's bothering me. I just can't figure everything out. I should have known earlier that York and his alter ego were outgrowths of that Y-1 robot. I'm so worried . . ."

"Don't worry."

"But, Freyn, I must . . ."

Freyn laughed. "Yes, I suppose you must worry. It seems to be built into your circuits. Perhaps it's inevitable with intelligent beings because, being able to think about the future, they forget that the present is all there is."

"But one must plan . . ."

"Yes, of course, but you have to remember that you make your decisions not in the future but in the present moment, in accordance with everything you've known, with what you are finding out now, and with what you feel and believe in. These decisions give existence meaning and integrity and purpose, don't you think?"

"Dammit, I'm sick of hearing that word. Decision. I wish I were still a gardener for the Roiiss, weeding and planting and . . ."

"And making decisions about what to weed and plant."

"You win, Freyn. I just want to warn you that as a creature of decision and action, I'm a flop."

"That's odd, Tec. Everything that's happened is more or less the result of your decisions and actions. Would the Y-1 robot have existed in the first place if you hadn't engineered that series?"

"I don't know. It always seems as if things happen and that

117

I never had any real control over anything, as if my decisions don't count but I just blunder into action that has consequences I haven't foreseen."

"Welcome to humanity, Tec, as the old expression goes."

—Freyn! Tec! Come back! Help!

"It's Sam," said Freyn, heading for the airlock.

Sam went on shouting in their minds.—He's locked the door from inside and we can't get in and I can't reach Astrid telepathically.

"Neither can I," said Freyn grimly as he and Tec flew toward Terran Center.

Sam was in front of the hospital door, accompanied by one of the guard robots who was about to wield a blaster on the lock.

"Where's Drake?" said Tec.

"Asleep, and I can't get through his privacy field to awake him telepathically and I haven't time to go into his room and I'm so worried because that damn York always insisted on a room without windows and a lockable door when he stayed with us and that's what Astrid gave him in the hospital and the Center computer has somehow been shut off from this sector and I was almost asleep in the library when in my mind Pedlar said, 'Good-bye, son, and thanks,' and if I get any more worried I'll fall out of my shell . . ."

"Okay, Sam," said Freyn, "get back from the door and let the robot get to work."

"Wait, let me try," said Tec. He probed the lock mechanism and pressed on it with his sensitive fingers. In a few seconds the door opened.

Astrid was lying on the bed, deeply asleep, and Yodin was missing. In the corner, Pedlar was sitting in a chair with his head bowed upon his chest. Sam went over to him.

"He's dead! My father's dead! How? Killed?"

While Freyn examined Astrid, Tec scanned Pedlar, and then put his hand on Sam's head.

"He died peacefully, Sam. Of a heart attack, in his sleep, no doubt."

Freyn came over and touched Pedlar. "Tec's right, Sam."

"I should have been here. He knew he was going . . ."

"And he said good-bye to you," said Freyn. "You were always with him, and you were in contact when he had to say good-bye. Now please, Sam, go to Drake's room and wake him by nipping his toes, so we can tell him that Yodin has gone."

"But the room was locked!" said Sam hysterically.

"Please go, Sam."

Sam dragged himself to the door, his nails scraping mournfully along the floor. "When Pedlar died so suddenly, York must have gotten scared, run out, and somehow locked the door behind him. Was that it? But why doesn't Astrid wake up?"

"She's probably taken a sleeping medication," said Freyn, "and now go wake up Drake so we can look for York."

After Sam left, Freyn said, "That wasn't the truth, was it, Tec?"

"No. Pedlar's brain has been seared as if by lightning. He's been murdered. What's the matter with Astrid?"

"Extremely deep hypnosis, I guess," said Freyn, going back to her. "I'll try to wake her up. Don't tell her what happened to Pedlar."

"We'll have to tell Drake," said Tec, standing by the bedside and scanning Astrid, whose shielding was down. He wondered if Freyn knew that there were newly deposited human sperm in her vagina, and that these sperm had a mutant version of R-inclusion identical to that of York Holladay.

Astrid woke, frightened. "Something bad has happened. What?"

"Pedlar died, and York has disappeared," said Freyn, "but I think we'd better call him Yodin from now on."

"Died? Of what?"

"Heart failure," said Tec. "Did you see it happen?"

"But Pedlar wasn't here," said Astrid. "I fell asleep in the other chair and when I woke up Pedlar was gone, the door was locked, and York was awake, begging me to help him integrate his human side so it wouldn't die and let the robot side take over. I . . ."

She paused and began to cry. "Oh, Freyn, forgive me . . ."

"I know what you did," said Freyn, "and so does Tec, since he's better at scanning macrostructure than I am. York was always in love with you, my dear. It was only natural that he should beg you to integrate his humanness with sex."

"He seemed so terrified," said Astrid. "I thought it would help him. I wanted to save him from Yodin. Why do you say we should call him Yodin from now on? Because he has disappeared?"

Tec said nothing, and finally Freyn nodded.

"I don't believe you," said Astrid. "There's something more." She sat up, the sheet slipping from her body, beautiful to the

119

very different males in the room. "Is that Pedlar there? How did he get here if he died? What—Oh. Oh, no."

"Astrid?" said Freyn.

"Tell me the truth!"

Freyn told her, and she put her hands to her face. "Then York took Pedlar away, killed him, and brought him back after we had sex. How horrible! Yodin has won!" She sobbed.

Tec stepped toward them, but Astrid looked up and said, "Don't worry about me. I'll deactivate the sperm easily. Please take Pedlar's body to the lab, I failed badly and I will never forgive myself. Go away, Tec, I want to be with my husband."

Sam stayed in the lab to watch over Pedlar's body. Drake sent the guard robots on a search for Yodin, but there were no results.

Tec did not tell Drake what Astrid had done.

Yodin. They would have to use the name now. York Holladay would not have been able to escape from a locked room.

19

"I WANT Pedlar buried right away, in the garden," said Sam. "With a small memorial service for him before we leave Lune."

"Why not a proper funeral?" said Drake.

"We used to talk about it. He just wanted to be put in the ground in his old traveling clothes, all biodegradable. He always upheld the principle of the dead returning to the ecological cycle of a living planet. Please, Drake."

"All right," said Drake. "In the meantime, Tec, you come with me to the Garch flagship. The robots searched it as well as the entire planet, but maybe we can find some evidence of Yodin that they missed."

The flagship seemed empty of life. They couldn't even find the bird Hugi.

"I didn't expect to," said Drake. "I really brought you along so you can help me set the computers on this vessel to follow instructions from Ship. This one controls the other Garch ships, so it will bring the entire fleet with us."

Tec and Drake worked for a long time.

"I thought I could fix any machine if I had to," said Tec in exasperation, "but this computer won't respond."

"He's gimmicked it," said Drake.

"Yes, there's a block of some sort on this computer, and I bet no matter how hard we try, we won't be able to take the Garch ships with us."

"We don't need the blasted things anyway."

"But, Drake, they'll stay here, hovering above the surface of Lune until he wants them, to fulfill whatever purpose he has for them."

"If I could only get my hands on that insane, murdering bastard!"

"I would deduce he's not particularly insane when it comes to planning," said Tec. "He knew exactly what to do to stop me. He's thought through his plans carefully and carried them out, so far. I don't think Pedlar's murder was part of his plan, however. He must have seen something in Pedlar's mind that either had to be silenced or drove Yodin berserk."

"And where in hell is he?"

"Hyperspace," said Tec.

"That's impossible, you know."

"The Roiiss can go there without a ship, and I suspect that Yodin can, too. This is the second time he's disappeared from a planet without using a ship."

"Damnation. Let's get back to Ship and get ready to leave at once. The farther I am from Lune, the better I'll like it," said Drake.

"Wait. Don't move. I sense something coming this way."

It was as dark as the void of space, floating into the control room with outspread but unused wings.

"Was that hiding in hyperspace, too?" asked Drake, as Hugi circled the flagship control room and came to roost on the command chair's back.

"Perhaps," said Tec. "Where is Yodin, Hugi?"

"Go," said the bird. "Return nevermore."

"What the hell . . ."

"It's a raven, Drake. Straight out of an old poem. Yodin must have programmed it as York's last joke."

"It's not funny," said Drake. "It's poisonous."

" 'A dream has power to poison sleep,' " said Hugi.

"This is nonsense!" said Drake.

"Wait, let me talk to it," said Tec. "Yodin and I have read the same old poems, although Hugi's mixing them up." Tec searched his data banks and said, " 'One wondering thought pollutes the day.' "

"You'll do," said the raven, one glittering eye fixed on Tec. "But begone, darken our airlock nevermore."

"In what way will I do?" asked Tec.

"Thought—breeds understanding—nevermore?"

"What the hell does that mean?" said Drake irascibly.

"The god Odin had two ravens. Perhaps this one is Thought. Hugi, where is Memory?"

" 'Memory is carried within the faltering mind,' " said Hugi, "but leaves another message."

"Well, what's the message?" said Drake.

The bird cocked its sleek head.

> Now conscience wakes despair
> That slumber'd—wakes the bitter memory
> Of what he was, what is, and what must be
> Worse.

"Another damn poet?" said Drake.

"Yes," said Tec, "but paradise need not be lost this time."

"Excellent," said Hugi smugly, "but try for paradise nevermore."

"I don't know what in hell you two are talking about," said Drake.

"That last exchange was borrowed from a poet named Milton," said Tec, trying to feel his way into Yodin's mind through the bizarre conversation with Hugi. "This same poet said that Satan brings hell within himself and cannot escape from himself—'of worse deeds worse sufferings must ensue . . .' "

Hugi broke into a raucous squawk.

"Drake, I'm worried. What is Yodin planning?" asked Tec.

"Nevermore—evermore?" said Hugi.

"Satan," said Drake, "is the proper name for him, not Odin. A fiend, not a god."

"Unfortunately," said Tec, "the distinction was not that clear-cut. According to Milton, Satan suffered from conscience, while according to the Scandinavians, the god Odin was not trustworthy."

"Why are we standing here talking about different mythologies when we've got to get control of these ships from a murderer?"

122

"You can't get control," said Hugi with a malicious snicker, "Now begone, darken our . . ."

"I'll be damned if I'll take orders from an insolent piece of machinery . . ."

"The raven is correct," interrupted Tec. "We can't get control, and I have just discovered that the life-support systems have turned off. Soon you will not be able to breathe."

"But you will, eh?" said Drake truculently. "You and that bird and Yodin, all you robots lording it over the rest of us?"

"Nevermore," said Hugi, subsiding into a feathered slump.

Tec managed to smile at Drake. "Let's go, Captain. Perhaps you were right the first time and we don't need these ships as escort. As you often say, our own Ship is perfect—and she is a robot."

Drake laughed and said, "My apologies to you robots. Let's go." He strode ahead, humming to himself.

Tec, having restored Drake's good humor, could not do the same for himself. He walked slowly out of the control room, hearing from his memory banks once more.

"'And his eyes have all the seeming of a demon's that is dreaming' . . . damnation," said Tec, cursing Poe and all those Terran devils who put the terror of a nightmare into poetry that cannot be forgotten. Tec turned and shook his fist at Hugi, trying to imitate Drake's bravado, but Hugi only winked at him.

"Tell your master Yodin that he had the chance to be one of us," said Tec.

"Us? You? Nevermore!"

"If you're saying that I don't belong, that I'm not a product of this universe the way even Yodin is, very well; but he should remember that we're all in existence together, every sentient creature, robot or protoplasmic, and he should take care of York for Astrid's sake . . ."

Tec broke off in the midst of this Sam-like harangue and tried to imagine what message he could leave that would make sense to a being like Yodin. The raven stirred and spoke.

"York's soul from out that shadow shall be lifted nevermore."

"'Be that word our sign of parting, bird or fiend!'" yelled Tec, defeated. He ran to the airlock.

Hugi called after him, "Remember that it's better to rule in hell."

"Nevermore!" shouted Tec, unable at the moment to think of a better answer to Milton's Satan. As the airlock door shut behind him, he tried to open it again, but this time, the Garch flagship was irrevocably sealed to intruders.

He flew back to Terran Center, lines from *Paradise Lost* surging up from his memory banks.

> *All is not lost; th' unconquerable will,*
> *And study of revenge, immortal hate,*
> *And courage never to submit or yield.*

To reign in hell? thought Tec. Was not a black hole hell itself?

They were ready to go the next day. Pedlar's body was resting in a grave near the garden pond, and Sam mourned openly. The rest talked about Pedlar in fond reminiscence, as if they were surprised by how much they missed him.

Nobody talked about Yodin, but every moment they remained on Lune seemed dangerous with the possibility that Yodin could appear anywhere at any time. Tec felt constantly apprehensive that a crisis would prevent Expedition Alpha from taking off.

Yet the only crisis that occurred was comparatively comic.

"Black cats," said Freyn, "may possibly be more stubborn than other cats."

"Don't be silly," said Astrid, looking for the cat. "Come here, Selena!" she called again and again.

But Selena would not come. Tours of Terran Center and the surrounding countryside, with or without antigrav flight, were fruitless, and finally Astrid appealed to Tec, who had been staying in Ship.

"You've got long-range sensors," she said, "please help us find Selena."

Tec said, "She's probably got a mate and has some dim awareness that you want to take her away."

"We'll take the mate, too," said Freyn. "Just find her. Do you think she realizes that she'll have to eat fish-flavored protein cakes on board, without any tidbits of live goldfish?"

Starting to search for her outside, Tec could not track her down, but once in Terran Center, he picked up readings, followed them, and ended up in his own room, the only one in the Center never used.

Selena was ensconced in the middle of Tec's bed. Sucking on her teats were four kittens of assorted appalling color combinations.

124

"Good grief," said Freyn, "what do we do now?"

"You'll have to get rid of the kittens," said Drake. "Can't have them running around Ship."

"Never," said Astrid.

"Put them in stasis now," said Sam. "Then when the new universe is ready, we'll have more than enough predators for any planet. In fact, they'll probably ruin the ecology. Shameless hussy."

Tec stroked Selena's black head, knowing that the simple joy he felt seeing her there on his bed was infinitely more important than any grand adventure to another cosmos. Unfortunately, he'd committed himself to being a small helper in the heroic endeavors of others.

Tec said, "She'll be better off if she stays on Lune. The roboservors can be instructed to feed her, and her kittens will grow outdoors in the company of other cats, the way they should. The new doctors and tourists will be kind to her, I'm sure.

"A good decision," said Freyn and Drake simultaneously.

"Astrid?" asked Tec.

"You're right, Tec," said Astrid. "That's what we should do. She's really your cat now anyway, and you've made the decision."

That word again. How right was Pedlar going to prove to be?

Before leaving, they assembled in the garden for Pedlar's memorial service. Sam, to whom Tec had given Pedlar's knapsack, returned it to him.

"I think he wanted you to have what's left, but I can't find the vision egg. Pedlar said it's supposed to be powerful, focusing the mind somehow. Yodin must have stolen it. Can you think why?"

"No," said Tec, in dread.

Pedlar's service was short and simple, the way he would have liked it, and conducted by Sam, as he'd always hoped. Sam stood next to the plain grave and spoke.

"Pedlar was very old, so I'm going to remember him with two very old passages that we both liked. The first is because he appreciated and could make others appreciate the small, homely moments of the here and now of existence":

> To see a World in a Grain of Sand,
> And a Heaven in a Wild Flower,

Hold Infinity in the palm of your hand,
And Eternity in an hour.

"The other passage is for Pedlar's memory, because he respected this idea. I'm going to change one word to two:

"No sentient being is an island, entire of itself . . ."

Tec heard no more of Sam's voice, and the ancient words rolled on in his own mind, speaking to him alone—"any man's death diminishes me, because I am involved in Mankind; and therefore never send to know for whom the bell tolls; it tolls for thee."

Part Four

20

SHIP STARTED SLOWLY, her gleaming body circling Lune well within the atmosphere for a last look. When she passed over the Mare Tranquillitatis exhibit, Drake pointed.

"A very small step for mankind, that."

"Not to them," said Tec.

"But we're the ones taking the giant leap."

"Perhaps."

They saw Terran Center once more, the spire of Holladay Tower reaching up to them, and Tec thought of the eons he had spent in the stasis case while Yodin evolved. Suddenly he felt absurdly grateful to Yodin for having released him.

"I'll miss Lune," said Freyn, tears in his eyes.

"I wish we could take Holladay Tower with us in a big box," said Astrid, trying to laugh and playfully poke her husband's furry chest. "My silly family spent so much money and so many years preserving it as their favorite memento from Earth."

"I wish we could bring all the wildlife with us," said Sam. "When I die there won't be any tortoises."

"What? Have Alpha universe without reptiles? Of course we brought some as embryos, Sam!"

"We're an ark, remember?" said Astrid.

"Pedlar would be pleased," said Sam. He sighed.

"Isn't it amazing," said Tec hurriedly, "how the old Moon craters make such good preserves for wildlife now. Over the millions of years since Lune was terraformed, the atmosphere and consequent weathering have caused typical Earth-like erosion, but there's been no change in general configuration because there aren't any tectonic plates to shift around the land surface. You can still see where the original lunar mountains, craters, domes, and ridges were, but what with the vegetation and erosion, they will never look the way they did to early Terran astronomers. The rills and fault lines are now waterways and . . ."

They were not listening to him. Freyn and Astrid were openly crying, Sam's eyes were shut, and Drake could be seen to swallow hard.

Circling Lune, Ship began to pull away, out into space where hyperdrive could be turned on.

As the small planet receded from view, Tec realized that although he'd lived on many planets, Lune had been his only home in this new age he'd wakened to. It hung in space green and laced with cloud, making Tec wish he could look nearby and find at an astronomically close three hundred and eighty thousand kilometers, another, bigger planet, icy at both poles, and blue with ocean.

Tec went to the room assigned to him. He did not particularly want to be in the control room to witness the last glimpse of Earth's Moon before Ship transferred to hyperspace. The viewscreen in his cabin was turned on to show this, so he turned it off.

Ship turned it back on and her silvery voice sounded in the air.

"Look, Tec, the last view . . ."

"No! Turn it off—please!"

"I wanted to share it with you. I thought we could talk," she said, turning off the viewscreen.

"I want to be alone right now, Ship."

"But I will do anything for you, Tec."

"Then withdraw from this room. All sensory and speaking apparatus off permanently. I insist."

"But you and I have been working together so well since you started coming to learn about my functioning and about Expedition Alpha. Surely you do not want to sever the connection . . ."

"Only here, in this room."

"But there may be danger . . ."

"If there is, you can pound telephathically on my mindshield and I may hear you. Or you can sound alarms. Otherwise, withdraw from this room, please."

"Only the Captain may give that order," said Ship coldly.

"May I speak to you, Drake?"

"Sure, Tec." Drake leaned back in his chair in his private quarters next to the control room.

Ship was now in the gray of hyperspace, where time passed only in the artificially maintained field produced by the graviton drive of starships. It was puzzling why a hyperspace jump should take a certain number of biological hours, depending on the ultimate distance, but it did.

"I wish to speak to you about Ship," said Tec, wondering how he would manage this conversation.

Drake scratched his flaming beard. "Go ahead. Great vessel, isn't she? I want you to be completely at home here, Tec, getting to know Ship as well as I do. I expect you two to become as close as—" he winked—"shall we say, husband and wife? It might be useful."

"Please don't insult me," began Tec heatedly, and at once, deep in his mind, he sensed her shame and sorrow. He had wounded her.

Ruthlessly, he persisted. "Drake, please understand that while Ship's computer brain and mine are both products of robotics, nevertheless we are not alike, and even if we were, we cannot be husband and wife. Only biological creatures experience that joining."

"I should hope so!" said Drake, chuckling.

"The problem is that both Ship and I have been equipped with emotive centers designed to imitate those of protoplasmic sentients with strong biological urges . . ."

"Which no robot can ever fulfill, of course," said Drake, eyeing Tec with apparent pity.

"The purpose of the emotive centers is to make a robot brain, whether in a small mobile unit like me or in a vessel like Ship, better able to understand, work with, and serve protoplasmic creatures."

"I know that. What are you getting at?"

"Please command Ship to withdraw her sensory apparatus from my room, except for nonconscious danger-detecting

129

equipment like smoke alarms and such. I want her to withdraw consciously from all bedrooms."

"Nonsense," said Drake. "I was only kidding about you and Ship. Great Beta, she's just a machine!"

"So am I," said Tec sadly. "Please do as I ask for five minutes, now, here in this room."

"Galloping galaxy, I . . ."

"Please, Drake."

"Oh, all right: Withdraw, Ship." He paused. "Now what? I can't tell if she's gone or not."

"But I can. She has."

"Now what do you want to say that you don't want Ship to hear?"

"A being as intelligent and complicated as Ship, equipped with emotive centers . . ."

"Her brain's bigger than yours, Tec."

"Yes, I have a brain that's ordinary from a human point of view. I'm afraid that Ship's brain may be—unstable."

"That's crazy. She's the best ship in Beta Universe."

"Ship has fallen in love with me," said Tec.

Drake guffawed. When he finally choked and stopped, he said, "And of course intelligent machines shouldn't fall in love."

Was Drake looking at him accusingly? Tec couldn't tell. "No they should not!"

"This whole thing is your little joke, isn't it, Tec?"

"Even if it were, would you please command Ship to withdraw from my room permanently?"

"Well, I wouldn't want a Roiiss robot to get shaken up in his Roiiss mind, would I?" Drake pressed a switch and Ship came back into the room consciously.

"Ship, listen closely. Am I your Captain?"

"Yes, Captain Drake."

"Your function is to obey me?"

"When this does not conflict with my prime directive."

"Which is?"

"To protect those I am supposed to protect."

Drake nodded. "An interesting interpretation, Ship, but accurate enough. Then obey this command: Leave in working order all devices designed for rote detection of physically dangerous conditions in the bedrooms, but otherwise withdraw yourself from those quarters. Do you understand?"

"I understand, Captain."

"Do you obey?"

"I obey, Captain."

"Okay, Tec, satisfied? Now let me get back to my study of black hole data, while you go to the sanctum you've just acquired. And stop imagining things. Ship knows her place."

Tec was at the door when Drake's next words hit him.

"Do you?"

"Where are we, Captain?" asked Astrid, her face as wide-eyed as a child's. "I've never been this far from home before."

"Intercluster space," said Drake. "Take your last look at the Milky Way Galaxy, for from here we make a bigger hyperspace jump."

"Which is MWG?" asked Sam.

"The near galaxy," said Drake. "The whole cluster consists of MWG, M31, and those smaller, less-formed collections of stars."

"The two spiral galaxies are so magnificent," said Freyn, "but the core of M31 looks much bigger than MWG. Does that mean there's a bigger black hole there?"

"Yes, but it's not the right one," said Drake. "Engineer Yodin programmed Ship to get way the hell across the universe to find the right black hole. Damn! I can't get used to the idea that he was the same Yodin we knew as York Holladay."

"I wonder how he knew the right black hole?" said Astrid.

"From the Roiiss," said Tec. "He kept raving about dragons."

"I don't like the idea of dragons," said Sam grumpily. He was plunked on a particularly large and resilient pillow before the transparent section of Ship's hull, while the humanoids relaxed on other pillows and Drake lounged in his Captain's chair. "I wish we didn't have to leave these galaxies."

Out in space, the scintillating jewels that were islands of stars seemed beautiful enough to inspire great nobility and purpose Tec decided, but he felt utterly useless.

Ship had functioned perfectly. Nothing wrong had happened in hyperspace. Entry to normal space again had proceeded without incident. Tec missed the days when he'd had a ship that he had to run himself, a ship that couldn't do everything herself.

Astrid, who often sensed Tec's moods, revealed that she did now by asking, "Tec, do you miss the dragon ship?"

Cautiously, he answered, "I was, of course, familiar with it. Someone had to be at the controls in all transitions and during any crisis, so the dragon ship had severe limitations. It was not personified, couldn't think intuitively, and was not as intelligent as Ship."

"Thank you, Tec," said Ship.

He had forgotten that she would be listening in the control room. Deliberately, he thought about the old streamlined dragon shape and pleasant lack of personality in the ship he was used to. No complications of emotional relationships.

"Is it true that Roiiss robots never started separate robotic civilizations the way Beta universe robots have?" asked Freyn.

"Yes," said Tec. "They were controlled by the dragons."

"Yodin could have stood some control," said Drake.

"But we might not have had a product as superior as Ship if robotic evolution in Beta hadn't gone its own way," said Astrid. "I'm glad it did, because we've got Ship. She makes me feel secure."

"Thank you, Doctor Holladay," said Ship.

Tec said nothing and tightened his mindshield.

Later, when they were back in the formlessness of hyperspace and the others had gone to their rooms, Tec asked Drake, "Didn't you want to go back to Federation Center for a last look there?"

"No. Secrecy. We show Ship around too much at this stage of the journey and people will guess. I thought of swooping around old MWG for a bit, but frankly it's so damn overpopulated, filled with civilized planets, artificial and asteroidal mobile settlements, old-stock and new-stock Terrans mixed with fancy robot cultures, and weird non-Terrans—it's all too busy and noisy for me."

"I wonder where Yodin is right now," said Tec, "or if he's alive."

"Better if he isn't," said Drake. "Let the name of Engineer Yodin stay clean for Beta Universe. He's probably dead— that repulsive mixed carcass all fallen apart. Imagine the stupidity of growing an organic self upon a robot, and taking on the troubles of each! He should have stayed transferred to a decent organic body, a new-stock, superior one like mine, and left robothood behind him forever. Did he think he had to be part robot to make it easier on this journey through a black hole?"

"Being a robot has severe drawbacks," said Tec, sensing that Ship was listening closely.

"Captain Drake," said Ship frostily, "please be informed that this hyperspace jump will last twenty hours, six minutes, and two seconds from this point. It will be the longest hyperspace jump we will make, and organics are advised to regulate their biological schedules in accordance with their own biological time. Light and dark alteration will be maintained according to the planet hours you have up to now been experiencing."

"Uh-huh," said Drake. "Doing her duty, I see. I suppose she's left now."

Ship had not, observed Tec.

"I'd never want to be a robot with no beautiful woman to love," mused Drake. "Give me flesh and blood, warmth and softness . . ." His voice trailed away and he stared unseeing, as if waiting for someone.

"Were you ever married?" asked Tec, trying to distract Drake from whatever beautiful woman he might be inwardly focusing upon.

"Several times. Lots of children. I even saw some of them grow up. Family life gets boring, though. Here's a universe full of adventures for the asking! And I'm after the biggest of all—capturing a new universe."

"Capturing?" asked Tec.

"Listen, you can't get anything you want in this or any universe without fighting for it. I'm looking forward to the battle of the ages when we meet up with those dragons that want to keep everyone else out of Alpha. But they won't keep me out!"

Drake beamed at Tec like a sun god in his glory. "All of us here in Ship, riding to adventure, isn't it great, Tec? You don't need to be afraid. The Roiiss won't enslave you again, because we're going to conquer the monsters!"

"Ragnarok," muttered Tec.

21

ADVENTURE, THOUGHT TEC, alone in his cabin, is for the truly adventurous, which I have never been. I plod my way through existence trying to do my duty and take care of whatever and whoever should be taken care of, worrying and fussing over everything that does or can go wrong, following along after those with a larger vision or the capacity to experience what is denied to me.

Yet I did make decisions. I started the Y-1 robots. I decided to let them evolve themselves. And now the consequences of that decision have come home to me. How stupid I was not to have foreseen the logical consequences! Have I always been so envious of protoplasmic creatures that I wanted children—and the Y-1 robots were that, in a way—and now my son Yodin is my enemy?

He experiences what is denied to me. I am envious. He possessed Astrid. I will never forgive him for that.

Someone was knocking on his door. He opened it after he scanned through it and found Astrid.

She brushed by him, the perfume of her clean skin and hair tingling his olfactory sensors. He couldn't think of anything to say.

"Are we alone?" she asked. "Is it true that Ship no longer listens in the personal cabins?"

"It's true." He probed. "Ship has withdrawn."

"Then I must talk with you. No one is talking about what seems to me to be an obvious conclusion. If Yodin can travel in hyperspace, he can get into Ship. And if he could deactivate the part of Terran Center's computer controlling his hospital room, then possibly he may be able to deactivate Ship, especially since he designed her and knows exactly how she functions."

"You are quite correct, Astrid. I have been worrying about that."

"But what are we to do?"

"I don't know. As York Holladay, he didn't seem particularly interested in Expedition Alpha, and he kept saying the dragons were lost. I don't know what that means. Ship has been programmed to be loyal to Drake, and I don't know whether Yodin can change that. Perhaps he won't want to deactivate her, because she sustains your life, Astrid, and he loves you."

"York loved me."

"It is not impossible that the robot Yodin loves you also."

Astrid clasped her hands and bent her head. "I'm afraid. I've destroyed his sperm and I will never bear his child. He will hate me for that. I want to tell you about the sex . . ."

"Please tell me about it, Astrid," said Tec, trying not to show that it was the last thing he wanted to hear about.

She looked up quickly and her lips quirked into a tiny grin.

"It's hard to fool an empath when she's not wishing to be fooled. You don't want to hear about it much. Very well; I'll be as clinical as possible. I had conventional sexual intercourse with York in the hope of integrating the failing human side of him with the robot. An orgasm is a total body response, producing a temporary alteration in nervous system energy configuration as well as stimulating and organizing the rest of the body's physiology."

"It wouldn't have worked," said Tec. "He was already Yodin and had killed Pedlar. The human side of him was dead."

"But he still seemed like York. After his ejaculation he said, 'Astrid, we are both Holladays and you must bear my child. Give me that.' He kissed me, and—and then he wasn't York. A powerful mind force began to suppress my brain patterns and I blacked out."

"Do you love him, Astrid?"

"I had affection—and pity—for York. That's all, I swear. I wouldn't have borne his child under any circumstances, and I certainly won't bear Yodin's. Please help me, Tec. I want to choose the child I will bear."

"You don't have to have children that way. You have embryos in the stasis room, yours and Freyn's," said Tec.

"There are not only embryos in stasis, but separate ova of mine. I don't care if Yodin wants to use some of those to grow his own babies." Her tawny skin glowed in the room. She touched Tec's hand with hers.

"Tec, I want to start a baby in my uterus, now."

"That's too dangerous on a voyage like this!"

"I have two reasons. I think they're logical, so hear me out. The first is that I ought to experience old-fashioned obstetrics, having a child the way people did for most of human existence. I want first-hand knowledge, which will be useful when I'm helping the colonists grown from those eggs we have in stasis."

"I disapprove," said Tec. "What's the other reason?"

"Freyn is my mate for life, and I want his life to be long."

Tec was horrified, because he had not thought of all the possibilities for Yodin's evil. "You believe Yodin might kill Freyn when he discovers you're not pregnant!"

"Yes. That would eliminate his rival, and he'd try again. But perhaps he won't kill Freyn if I'm *already* pregnant."

"I see. You may be right. But it's still too dangerous. I will try to protect you and Freyn. I will do anything for you," said Tec, aware that he was echoing Ship's words to himself.

"I believe you, Tec."

"Astrid, I—I can't help it . . ."

"I know. I felt your emotions on that first day when we met. I didn't know it was possible for a robot to experience what you did."

"Neither did I. Falling in love at first sight. Ridiculous."

"Oh, Tec . . ."

"I suppose it was inevitable that a complicated robot brain equipped with emotive centers would eventually experience what a human would label as an uncontrollable interpersonal passion."

"Don't be sarcastic, Tec dear."

"Why not? That's the least the rest of my brain—the logical, controlled, eminently rational part—can do to rescue me from one of the more profound absurdities of existence, that of being a robot who has human-imitative emotive centers without the hormones and the anatomy that make possible complete joining."

"Sex is merely biological joining," said Astrid. "Almost every nonhermaphroditic multicellular creature has some form of it."

"You are human, Astrid. You said just a moment ago that you helped Yodin to an orgasm because it was a total response contributing to neurophysiological integration. You could have told him to masturbate, but you wanted to share the sex with him physically and empathically, to humanize him. Your presence added a dimension to the orgasm, did it not? Was the sex merely biological joining?"

"No."

"Then leave me to my robotic problems. I will try to protect you and your husband, and you must not think ever again about what you sense goes on in my emotive centers when you are around. Has Drake told you that I'm possibly psychotic and need watching? If I were going robotically crazy from unrequited passion for a human female, even a compulsive doctor would not be able to solve that problem."

"But, Tec . . ."

He took her hand in his, treasuring the warmth of it. "Let me say it once and then never again. I love you, Astrid. It's absurd—not that you are lovable—but that I would dare to love and want to be loved."

"It's not absurd. I want to make love to you."

"Stop it! Drake's put you up to this, hasn't he?"

Astrid said, "Drake had a private conference with Freyn and me about you. He thinks your emotive centers are out of control because you imagine that Ship loves you. Ship denies that she does or that she said it, but I believe Ship is considerably more complicated than Drake knows her to be, and I see no reason why she should not love you as much or more than I do."

"I refuse to be your patient. Don't pretend . . ."

"You're not my patient, although Drake wants you to be. Tec, be sensible! We aren't inhabiting a romantic myth of chivalry and chauvinist veneration of the female, the way heroic types like Drake think we do. I bet he imagines that I secretly yearn for him the way he thinks he yearns for me, never the twain meeting because he's the Captain and I'm already safely mated. Well, it isn't true. He's not really interested in who I am, and neither I nor my clitoris tingle after him."

"Now, Astrid . . ."

"You're a bit of a prude, you know."

"Indeed? It's no doubt part of the self-image built into sentient robots so they can compensate by having a certain amount of pride in being superior to lascivious, hormone-driven, sex-crazy humans—" he pointed to Pedlar's Stone Age female figurine sitting licentiously on a shelf—"do you think any self-respecting intelligent robot would carve a bawdy thing like that?"

She laughed. "I love it when you try to muster up pomposity as a defense, because your sense of humor always gets in the way. And I see you have displayed Miss Venus of 20,000 B.C.—for your own edification?"

"Astrid, I'm going to spank you any minute . . ."

"Yes, where were we? Ship loves you. I love you. If you were flesh you'd be a formidable rival to my husband, whom I adore."

"And as it is?"

"You—we—oh, dear Tec, we are lovers. Can't you see that? Not husband and wife, biological and life mates, but lovers."

"By all the dragons of Roiissa, if you told Drake this . . ."

"Certainly not. Drake discussed you and your so-called aberrant mental condition with two doctors. Then he asked me to seduce you . . ."

"What!"

"Well, he didn't exactly use that word, since I dare say he'd

137

disapprove of any literal interpretation of it, but he wants me to ply you with emotions so you'll be loyal to us Terrans. I gathered that he's afraid you might turn into a wicked monster robot like Yodin and that you'll go to the dragons in Alpha instead of helping us."

Tec paced the floor of his cabin. "How do you know I'm not, or won't become, a monster?"

"Because I love you."

"That's either a grandiose estimate of your own ability as beauty to turn a beast into a prince, or a simplistic estimate of me as a nonmonster. Hell, Astrid, I'm not only a robot but an *alien* robot!"

"No, we're all related in the kinship of intelligence."

He stared at her, and suddenly it seemed as if the harmony and unity of everything was big enough to include his own absurd passion. He no longer had to fear it.

"Astrid, is it possible that sentient beings create meaning and purpose in the otherwise meaningless pattern of their universe, not by their grand exploits and tragedies, but through small everyday acts of love?"

She was with him, in him, empathically, as she smiled and rose, walking up to him until their bodies touched. She was nearly as tall as he was, and her lips were hot to his surface sensors as she kissed his robot face and flexible eyelids.

"I'm seducing you," she said cheerfully, "not because Drake wants you converted into a loyal Terran, but because Freyn and I have decided to ask you to share our biological joining and help us in starting our child. We want the experience to be our gift to you."

"It's impossible!"

"You will choose the sperm that penetrates the egg, and you can alter the gene structure of each if you wish it. My specialty is cell alteration. With my help you'll control the process of fertilization."

Tec, holding her close, said, "I can't believe you'd allow this."

"Please try it. Freyn and I will open our minds to you as we open our bodies to each other. Are you afraid to share our joining?"

"Perhaps I am afraid," said Tec, "yet I would like to share the deeply private sexual experience of protoplasmics just once in my robotic existence. Won't Freyn mind?"

"No. When the two of us talked over Drake's concern about your loyalty, Freyn and I joked about seducing you as a way of forcing you to stay with us instead of going over to the Roiiss, but then Freyn said he wanted you to know what he calls 'primitive primate pleasure.' He's next door in our cabin. Shall I call him?"

"Yes," said Tec, releasing her.

Freyn came in, kissed his wife's nose, and said, "Astrid has told me. I'm glad, Tec. I'd like you to know the joy I feel in loving Astrid. We can never know the wonder of being a Roiiss robot, existing millions of years, watching universes develop, but we can let you share our brief biological glory."

I wonder, thought Tec, why I ever believed Freyn was prosaic.

"I wouldn't mind at all," Freyn continued with a grin, "if you picked a sperm with golden hair in its genes. My father was blond instead of silver-furred, so it's possible. In fact, you have a certain resemblance to him."

Astrid hugged her husband and said, "We will use your bed, Tec, and you'll go to our cabin. Open your mind to us."

At first Tec just observed, and thought.

Oh, the rollicking sensual fun of the sexual play of two primates! Body to body, warmth to warmth—tongues and fingers and lips and genitals; everything touching and playing with everything; laughter, sweet words, funny noises and positions and twining of limbs, exploring, discovering again and again . . .

He was the male, entering her body as they lay side by side in each other's arms.

He felt her warmth clasp his, her thighs tighten around him, her arms stroking his fur.

He caressed parts of her body engorged with pulsating blood, and then grasped her firm buttocks. They began to move together.

Part of Tec's mind, still observing, was glad these experienced mates were highly skilled and could take a long time so that Tec could savor the fullness of the joining, experience every pleasurable nuance of the slow, supple dance of the thrusting and squeezing, now added to the caressing, kissing, murmuring exchange.

As the dance quickened in tempo, Tec lost himself in the crescendo, becoming one with Freyn's pleasure in the response of Astrid, her genital contractions experienced by all three of them. And then he was the force of the male response, giving to her . . .

139

"Now, go with me, Tec," said Astrid.

Deeper, into the cellular level, they went mind in mind, with no words for that exploring.

"Choose, Tec."

He chose.

"Let's hurry them up," said Astrid in her inimitable practical style. "It usually takes longer."

The ovum, already in the Fallopian tube, was pushed by undulations of the walls down to meet the horde of oncoming sperm, all needed to make the egg membrane more permeable. With both Astrid and Tec behind the chosen sperm, it alone broke through to become one with the ovum, each set of chromosomes lining up.

Cell division began at once, the chromosomes in their own private dance of life.

Tec was fascinated.

Freyn smiled unself-consciously at Tec when he went back to his own cabin to join the two Terrans.

"One of the best," said Freyn, "but Astrid could use another, since she was too concentrated on fertilization to enjoy her orgasm completely. I'll leave you both now. I'm glad our child is your child, too."

"I am honored," said Tec.

They communed in wordless telepathy until he said, "Perhaps Freyn knew that I am still envious, that I selfishly, egotistically want to experience empathically your sexual pleasure from what I alone might do."

"It's not selfish, Tec dear, because sexual pleasure should be a sort of reverberating round—giving it and getting it—getting pleasure because someone else is getting pleasure, getting one's own sensor pleasure, getting pleasure at someone getting pleasure at giving pleasure—if you follow all that, Tec! You're laughing!"

"Do all lovers talk like this?"

"I hope they do sometimes." She nestled against him as they sat side by side, and then he turned and pulled her down with him as he lay back full length on the bed. She caressed his surface.

"You must be a witch, Astrid. How do you know what kind of stroking does the most for my sensors and my damn emotive centers?"

"Your body tells me."

140

"I want to do that too."

This time she moaned in an abandonment she had not allowed herself before.

"Oh—that's good—how do you know how . . ."

"I learn fast," said Tec. "Now my love, shut up and enjoy my love."

She did.

Part Five

22

IN THE CONTROL ROOM, Tec was alone with his thoughts and the grayness of hyperspace until Ship's voice interrupted.

"Two minutes to normal space reentry."

"Where in normal space?" asked Tec.

"Where my programming has ordered."

"Yes, but . . ." Tec paused. Swiftly, he reached with his mind to probe Ship's brain, something he had never tried before.

"I do not allow that," said Ship.

"So I see."

"It is not part of my programming to allow intrusive touch or . . ."

"What do you mean, programming?" asked Tec. "Artificial intelligences like us are not truly programmed the way small computers and semiconscious robots are. Your spatial directions have been instilled, but your consciousness grew of itself, and you learned the way sentient beings must learn."

"One minute to normal space reentry."

"Ship, is something wrong? Are you disturbed?"

"I do not question what goes on in cabins where I am not permitted to go."

"Good," said Tec. "Are you upset about it?"

"I do not feel. I am a machine. Reentry to normal space about to commence."

Drake strode casually into the control room, yawned, and sat down. "Keep your fingers and toes crossed, Tec—except that you don't seem to have any toes. We'll take a look at this galaxy from a distance and then move in."

"Is this where the Roiiss went through to Alpha?" asked Tec.

"Evidently. At least it's where Ship's programmed to go. Now that I know who Engineer Yodin really was, I suspect all his plans. Perhaps this entire Expedition is a fake." Drake yawned again.

"You don't seem perturbed about it," Tec said.

"No. Nothing we can do about it now except to enjoy the adventure and take advantage of it. That's the secret of life, Tec. Take advantage of every opportunity, even those that seem bad. I should say, especially those. Yodin may find himself up against more than he expected. Don't you agree, Tec?"

Looking at Drake's confident face and perfectly coordinated, superbly muscled body, Tec nodded. "Do you know if any other Federation ships have been here before?"

"Don't know. Not much is known about this section of the universe. We're about as far out along the curvature of spacetime as a Terran has ever been. Maybe there are dangers out here that even the dragons couldn't handle, and perhaps they never went through the black hole. Do you think that's what Yodin could have meant when he said he couldn't find the dragon?"

"It's possible," said Tec.

Normal space suddenly bloomed beyond the transparency of the control room, the blackness broken by a solitary galaxy.

"That's a pretty one," said Drake.

Tec saw a dwarf elliptical galaxy that was somewhat unusual because the outer stars formed an almost clear-cut boundary, rather than extending out in a fuzzy corona of decreasing density. It was hard to see into it and Tec was about to probe when Ship spoke.

"The black hole that I am programmed to enter is the collapsed core of that galaxy, not visible from here. It is extremely large."

"If the dragons went through, perhaps they made it larg-
143

er," said Drake. "The galaxy's too small and too young-looking to have a core of that size by now."

"The galaxy does not actually look like that now," said Ship. "I will demonstrate on the viewscreen a visual reconstruction of what my sensors tell me is the actual present appearance of the galaxy. What you are watching through the transparency is the image that has traveled for a long time through normal space. Sensor readings through hyperspace show this other picture."

Drake gasped when the viewscreen lit up. "Completely different!"

It was still a glittering sphere, but it was larger and more transparent, with strangely tortuous filaments emerging from a dark ring encircling it, and the stars were arranged in a complex pattern through which a glowing central core of immense proportions could be seen.

"That central black hole is so big that it's drawing in enormous amounts of material. Energy radiates out as the material falls inward," said Ship.

"The bigger the better," said Drake. "We'll have a better chance of getting through without being squeezed to smithereens. I wonder why it looks so odd now."

"I wonder, too," said Tec. "I have a curious feeling . . ."

"A feeling?" Drake laughed. "I thought you weren't human."

Annoyed, Tec said, "At a certain level of brain complexity, intuition is a normal process. I also know the Roiiss. They were not only capable of blowing up stars and increasing the size of a black hole, but it's possible that they made the changes in this galaxy."

"I doubt that. Enough dithering. Let's get into it," said Drake.

"Wait!"

"Tec, what's the matter with you?" said Drake. "I think you are a bit crazy. Your longtime fear of the dragons has made you think they could alter an entire galaxy."

Sam came into the control room, his neck outstretched toward the viewscreen. "I don't like that galaxy, Drake. Don't go into it. It isn't normal. Astrid and Freyn think so, too—they're in the dining room having tea."

"Nonsense," said Drake. "If Ship was designed to get through the stress of a black hole, there's no reason why we can't traverse this aberrant galaxy on our way to the entrance to Alpha."

"All the same, Drake," said Tec in his most deferential

tones, "we could take a closer look at it first, by making the next hyperjump to a point well outside that galaxy, say about as far as Lune was from its sun. That would give me more opportunity to test out my intuition, wouldn't it?"

Ship spoke. "I have calculated such a point near the star farthest out on the galaxy."

"Sure, sure," said Drake. "Go ahead. A waste of time."

They passed once more into the gloom. Drake ordered tea and Sam ordered synthe-leaves from one of Ship's hands, and Tec fretted.

Astrid's mindtouch found him, and he sensed her beloved voice.

—Dear Tec, when we love, we are all hostages to fate. Follow some famous old advice: Try to dread only one moment at a time.

—Drake worries me, said Tec.—He doesn't think things through carefully, and when he does, it's too often in the simplistic terms of a single-minded adventurer. Perhaps Yodin chose him as Captain because he thought he could control him. Drake's also physically durable; he's new-stock.

—Definitely new-stock? No wonder his privacy field is so strong. I wish you'd told me before, Tec. I don't understand the capacities of new-stock humans, and I don't like the way they call themselves superhuman. You must help Drake think clearly.

—I'm only a minor robot on an Expedition I didn't design and don't understand.

—I'm sorry, Tec. Don't be angry. I know you'll do your best.

Tec broke contact and focused his thoughts upon his own eternal problem. He was supposed to do his best, never certain what that would be.

At that moment Ship emerged into normal space. Ahead were the star-studded fields of a galaxy, behind them the black of intergalactic space. The nearest star radiated sunlight upon Ship's nose the way normal suns have always shone.

"Looks okay," said Drake. "Let's move in at space normal speed for a while."

"We cannot. There is a barrier," said Ship.

"I don't see anything."

"It is an energy barrier that we cannot penetrate without damage. To get safely inside this galaxy we must use hyperspace jumps."

"Wait!" said Tec. "If the Roiiss changed this galaxy so ships

145

can't penetrate it in normal space, then there will probably be other ways of stopping us if we enter the space inside the galaxy."

"Maybe there's a nearby star with planets and intelligent life," said Drake wearily. "Ship, try using hy-com channels so we can talk with somebody in there before Tec gets any more hot and bothered."

Tec didn't want to push his mind into the specific unknown ahead of them. "Perhaps there's no life, or there's life we don't understand."

"Crap," said Drake. "You've got monsters on the brain. Even if the dragons did rearrange stars and set up an energy barrier, there still ought to be planets with ordinary life on them. Maybe the Roiiss set them up to be guardians of their private doorway to Alpha."

Freyn laughed in the intercom. "Maybe we'll find a set of tollbooths in space, the way they used to have them on highways in the days when Terrans used land vehicles without antigrav."

"Captain," said Ship, "something is picking up our hy-com transmission of standard Federation ship-to-planet signals."

"Put me on in Basic Intergalactic." Drake leaned back in his chair, expanded his chest, and arranged an expression of political dignity and primate affability on his features.

"Gentlebeings, greetings. This is Captain Drake of Expedition Alpha from Beta Universe Federation, seeking passage through your galactic space."

"Why?" The word rumbled out of the hy-com speaker like controlled thunder from a gathering storm.

Drake sat up straight. "Who in hell was that?"

Ship answered. "I have just recieved a transmission of unknown type into the hy-com system. What you have heard is not the actual transmission, but a voice reconstruction of the basic tone patterns, which are in reality pitched too low for human ears."

"What language is the original?" asked Drake. "Are we hearing a translation?"

"No, Captain. The language is Basic Intergalactic."

"That's a relief. Now, where's it coming from?"

"Not decipherable, Captain."

"I think I'll give them an honest answer to their question," said Drake. "Resume hy-com, Ship."

"Gentlebeings, we seek passage through your galaxy be-

146

cause we wish to enter the black hole at the center, in order to make our way to the twin universe, Alpha."

"Why?"

"This Beta Universe we now inhabit grows old, will collapse and eventually die. Alpha will be reborn and we wish to make certain that the next expansion creates a universe suitable for our life forms. Do you wish to join us in this great endeavor, with your own ships?"

There was a silence. As they waited, Tec remembered that all he could do would be to try his best, and he had not done that. Cautiously, he began to probe into the galaxy with his mind.

"Gentlebeings," Drake began again, "do you—" He broke off, clapping his hands to his head. "Holy Beta, but that hurt! And who screamed? You, Tec?"

"No," said Tec guiltily. "It hurt, but I already had my shields up tightly. It was Ship. Are you all right, Ship?"

She did not answer.

"Ship!" yelled Drake. "Answer! What happened?"

She answered slowly. "I am—intact. Tec probed the galaxy, and then there was a strong return probe from a powerful source. I was able to stop it from entering my library and memory banks, but I have never experienced pain before. A most unusual experience. I hope it will not be repeated."

"Keep your shields tight and defend yourself, Ship," ordered Drake. "In an assault like that, you must remember that you are the most important entity here because you protect us and the entire Expedition. You must defend yourself."

"Yes, Captain."

Tec felt that she had been hurt more than she revealed. To his surprise, he could make telepathic contact easily.

—What is wrong, Ship?

She spoke in his mind.—I am only a ship. Consciousness is too difficult—I didn't think anything could do that to me. I didn't fully understand the responsibility until now. I cannot consider myself most important—yet I must obey the Captain, but I do not—my emotive centers . . .

—Are out of control, Tec scolded.—You're always yammering about your programming. Well, obey your prime directive! Put up a more effective mindshield to protect yourself so you can protect us.

—You do not care.

—I do care.

—You love Astrid Holladay.

—You and I are robots, Ship. We have given our word. We have committed ourselves to Expedition Alpha and to protecting the protoplasmics with us.

—But who will protect me?

—You will. You are stronger than any of us.

—I am frightened, said Ship.—I cannot control you, and you caused this to happen by probing into the galaxy. I cannot control them and I felt pain. How can I be strong if I am frightened?

—Fear of unknown dangers and of being hurt is normal, and every sentient being must be strong in spite of that, said Tec. —I am frightened, too, but I will help. I promise. And I will try not to do anything dangerous again without warning you.

"Well, Tec?" said Drake impatiently, "when you scanned them did you get any hint as to what or where they are?"

" 'They' are actually 'it,' " said Tec. "That galaxy is one conscious entity, probably formed by the Roiiss, but not entirely. I didn't have time to find out more."

"A hive mind? A culture in which planets have combined . . ."

"There are no planets," said Tec. "The Roiiss must have destroyed them, using the material to form matter-energy fields in which the stars and their fields are imbedded. This basic structure of the entity is powered by the black hole core."

Words boomed from the speaker. "Core. No entry. Cannot permit."

"Oh, yeah?" said Drake, "well we're . . ."

"Let me try to question it," said Tec.

Anger blazed in Drake's eyes, but settled quickly to a smolder. "Go ahead, for the damn thing probably thinks more like a robot than a human."

Unruffled, Tec agreed. "It actually thinks more like a ship, so I suspect that the other influence in its formation may have been a captured space ship."

"Space ship?" said the galaxy. "No entry! Neutralize intruders."

"Ask who it is that speaks, and then try to persuade whoever it is to let us in!" said Drake.

"Careful, Captain," said Ship. "It's listening to all of us over hy-com."

"Then go ahead and ask intelligent questions," said Drake.

"What is your name?" asked Tec.

"I—am—he—"

"What is his name?"

"I am he—who is called Dahyo."

"He's getting the hang of longer sentences, at any rate," said Sam.

"Where did that name come from?"

"The—I do not remember."

"Yes, you do."

"Dahyo is—I am—that which is . . ."

"Where was the name first?" asked Tec.

After a moment Dahyo answered, "Library."

"The library banks of a ship," said Sam. "What ship?"

"To get more information, I'll need help," said Tec. "If all of you make telepathic contact with me and we all probe together, maybe we can find out."

Drake grunted. "Push my mind into that alien? Not on your life."

"I'll go," said Freyn.

"Me, too," said Sam.

"I'm with you," said Astrid.

Tec waited. "Ship? We'll need you—your telepathic powers are great." Would she be too afraid?

"We will all protect each other," murmured Astrid.

"I will join you," said Ship.

Tec felt their minds link with his, and because Astrid was there, he lost his own fear. Leading them, he pushed into the alien mind.

"Uummmph!" Sam's head withdrew into his shell.

The alien had thrown them out. "Anybody hurt?" asked Tec.

"Just mentally bruised," said Astrid. "I've scanned Freyn and Sam and Ship and we're all physically uninjured, but I only got some textbook material from the alien, and snatches from the writings of Lao somebody or other."

"I got more," said Tec, switching the hy-com transmission back on. "It seems that Dahyo's name originated in material he assimilated from the library banks of a ship of scholars. They were Terran offshoots, the mutant cats who separated themselves from the Federation to form their own culture. When they made a hyperspace jump into that galaxy, they were destroyed, but not before the galaxy assimilated the knowledge in their memory and library banks."

"Couldn't they have talked to it, saved their lives?" asked Sam.

"No, because Dahyo wasn't conscious then. The Roiiss apparently constructed only a formidable entity to guard their escape hole, and it was the intrusion of the scholars' research vessel that turned him into a thinking, aware creature who is still carrying out the dragons' orders, but has also incorporated and befuddled himself with the language and philosophy of the superfelines."

"How do you know he's befuddled?" asked Freyn.

"The name he's taken for himself," said Tec.

"I'll be darned," said Sam. "An interesting distortion of the word *Tao?*"

"I am not distorted," said Dahyo. "I am Dahyo. I absorb. I am the infinite. I am—I will be—the all . . . You cannot enter—too many questions—too much curiosity . . ."

"All sentient beings have curiosity," said Tec. "So do you. You asked 'why?' "

"I am not a being. I am the all. I meditate. I do not converse with lower creatures."

"That last sentence was strictly Roiiss in attitude," said Tec to the Terrans, "unless the supercats were just as snobbish. Were they, Sam?"

"Not that I've heard, in spite of their wish to be alone. They wanted to study the universe and correlate modern science with their philosophy, which was based on accepting oneself as part of the unity of reality. They had no need to proselytize, and I've read that they believed their corner on the infinite to be so complete that they led very simple lives, enjoying and studying what is."

"A little like Selena," said Astrid on the intercom. "I wish I could have met them."

"Unfortunately Dahyo has eaten them," said Sam.

"I do not eat," said Dahyo.

"You do eat," said Tec. "You use the energy generated by that black hole, and by the stars of your body. You are an entity. We are entities. If you are the all, then we are part of you anyway and cannot be ignored."

"You cannot enter!" bellowed Dahyo.

"What good does all that discussion do?" Drake grumbled. "The creature isn't going to listen to philosophy."

"Dahyo cut his symbolic eye teeth on philosophy," said Tec, "and that's what's the matter with him."

Sam chuckled. "I don't suppose any of us would like it if a

talking bacterium, possibly malignant, was flitting around us asking to be let in."

"Bacteria don't ask," said Drake, "they just go in, which is what we'll have to do, even if it means blasting our way through and killing that thing bit by bit."

"No!" said Tec, "Dahyo is alive."

"He'll kill us, if he can," said Drake. "What are you, Tec, a do-gooder to aliens?"

Tec's golden eyes fixed upon Drake. "Captain, you forget. I am an alien robot."

23

AS TEC AND DRAKE glared at each other across a gulf of noncomprehension, Sam made a gargling sound in his long throat and lumbered over to stand next to Tec.

"Hey, Drake, then let our alien robot talk to this crazy galaxy. If the Roiiss taught Dahyo to reject intruders, maybe a Roiiss robot can talk him into it."

"Very well. Try it again, Tec."

Feeling afraid, as if Dahyo were a giant Roiiss, Tec found it difficult to think clearly. "Dahyo," he said, "we are small beings, inside a ship like the one that brought you the philosophy you live by. All we wish is safe passage through your body to the core. We will defend ourselves against your attempts to neutralize us, and our defense may hurt you. We do not wish to hurt you, and once we pass through the core we will be of no danger to your body."

"I have no body. I am not an entity. I am everything."

"And so are we all part of everything. We, a small part, talk to you, a large part . . ."

"No. I will incorporate and neutralize all things that do not accept my oneness with everything of which they are inferior parts."

"He thinks like a primitive god," muttered Sam. "Not what those ancient philosophers had in mind at all."

"That's the Roiiss influence," said Tec. "That's the way they think." But perhaps Dahyo was still young, cosmologically speaking, still curious, not beyond argumentation. Tec tried to marshal his argument.

"Dahyo, you are a collection of stars called a galaxy, part of Beta universe, which is part of hyperspace."

"That is the word," said Dahyo's deep voice, "hyperspace. I am hyperspace—everything—the all."

"No. You had a beginning. Hyperspace did not. You have a mind and will. Hyperspace does not. Hyperspace just is."

"Hyperspace is Dahyo. You are wrong and I will destroy you."

Tec tried again. "Hyperspace is the unity in which universes become manifest. The knowledge of small creatures like us taught you about hyperspace and woke you to selfhood. You have distorted our perspective to your own grandiosity, and that is wrong."

"Wrong? Can I do wrong? I think, I am alive . . ."

"And hyperspace is not alive. This universe is not alive. Life is a potential in nonlife, produced in the evolution of energy and its larger structure, matter. You are alive and alone in your sector of the space-time continuum, feeding upon the death of matter entering your black hole center."

"Alone." Dahyo moaned. "Death. I must not die. I must be everything and everything must be alive, so I will then not die."

"A classical philosophical dilemma," said Sam.

Astrid's thoughts reached Tec telepathically.—Be careful. Dahyo's life will be less than that of the universe because the black hole he uses for power is also consuming him. It's no wonder he's erected an ideational system against the thought of death.

"Dahyo," said Tec, "we share your mortality. In every universe, beings evolve who become aware and able to contemplate the pattern of the all, knowing that in the midst of death they are in life. Rejoice with us, Dahyo, in the adventure of being alive."

"What can you small ones know?" asked Dahyo.

"We have our own grandiosity," said Tec, smiling. "We of our size think our perspective on reality is ideal because we're about halfway between the smallest subatomic particle and the universe, able to imagine that the fields of one and the fields of the other are basically indivisible."

"Tec," said Drake, "you're not going to explain unified field theory to that creature, are you?"

"I only want him to enjoy his identity as a separate entity and to like arguing," said Tec.

"I am more than you," said Dahyo proudly.

152

"Yes," said Tec, "in actual volume we small ones are only halfway between atomic particles and a galaxy like you. Didn't you find out what a galaxy is from the ship's library?"

"The other word was better—the *dahyo* . . ."

"That was not the word. Keep your name, but know that you are an entity called a galaxy, your matter organized in such a way that you are alive, even as the nonliving atoms that compose our bodies are organized in such a way that we are alive. In the field of the all, we blend. We die, but our existence is part of the all."

Dahyo was silent for so long that Drake said, "Is this going to buy our ticket inside that thing?"

"I don't know," said Tec. "I've said too much. Dahyo might possess unconsciously all the knowledge and philosophy available to a starship of scientists, but can he use it?"

Sam's shell thumped on the floor as he drew in his legs for comfort. "This unfortunate oversized creature has a consciousness based on ideas suitable to creatures our size, not galaxy-sized. Space, time, energy, and matter are the pattern of ripples on the pool of everything, as my father used to say, but somebody that size is inevitably going to sense the ripples differently."

Freyn said, "Dahyo's matter and energy are arranged on a scale of such immensity that we can't imagine what it would be like to exist on a scale and a time span so different from our own."

The silence continued. Finally Tec said, "It's hopeless. Dahyo was created by the Roiiss to kill anyone who tried to use this galaxy."

Dahyo said, slowly and sonorously, "Kill? There must be no tragedy of death. I will become the universe."

"Death is inevitable. Each universe eventually dies."

"Then I will become hyperspace," said Dahyo.

Sam said, "That's progress. He no longer thinks he already is."

"Megalomania," said Drake. "But such power—such power . . ."

"You cannot be hyperspace," said Tec. "Or even this universe. One of your stars is part of you but is not the whole galaxy. One of the hydrogen atoms in one of your stars is not the whole star but only part of its organization. Hydrogen atoms, stars, die . . ."

"Death! In the midst of death! Live?" Dahyo's voice rose

153

shrilly as Ship's speakers compensated. "Alone? Part? Help me!"

Then there was utter silence, and Ship said. "Hy-com transmission inactive, Captain. Dahyo has cut us off."

Nobody said anything, and Tec was so depressed and ashamed of his inadequacy that he tightened his shield against Astrid's sympathetic mindtouch. They waited for Dahyo to return, for something to happen.

Suddenly another voice spoke.

"Tec, don't you know that it discourages mortals to be lectured to on their mortality?"

They turned and there in the doorway of the control room was Yodin.

"Ship! Defend!" yelled Drake.

"Don't bother," said Yodin, as the three robot hands of Ship surrounded him. "I can slip back into hyperspace before their circuits lock. Call off the posse, Drake, and listen to sensible advice."

"Why should you give any?" asked Drake.

"Because you and I have similar interests—to get safely into and out of the body of that rather large idiot out there."

"You're joining us to go through the black hole?"

"Never. Like Dahyo, I try not to converse with lesser creatures, since it is boring and wastes time. Unfortunately Dahyo is now so confused that it might be difficult for me to make my own way to Alpha."

"You're not going to Alpha," said Drake. "We are, and we don't want a murderer with us."

"Just how can you stop me?"

"I don't know, but don't underestimate our ability to kill."

"Oh, I don't," said Yodin, adjusting the folds of his great cloak. "Humans of whatever variety have always been good at it. How else would I have acquired the skill? I won't travel with a bunch of moronic weaklings, but I have a considerable number of possessions I want to bring on my own journey and that newly conscious watchdog must not endanger them."

"You have a ship?" asked Sam.

"You might say so. Concealed in hyperspace, of course, even from Tec's prying talents."

"We don't need the Garch flagship if that's what you've brought," said Drake, "and you're welcome to try and take it through a black hole. It won't survive."

"Perhaps not," said Yodin. "For my cousin's sake, I would

like Tec to stop being so inadequate in arguing with Dahyo, or Ship will not survive either."

"I have tried . . ." Tec began.

"Stupidly," said Yodin with contempt. "The silly robots in your universe designed you with very little brain. You don't even know the simplest thing about sentient beings."

"Which is?" asked Tec.

"Sentient beings respond primarily in terms of their own personal advantage. What can you say to Dahyo to make him want to let us in safely? Have you thought of that?"

Astrid and Freyn walked into the control room. "Are you York?" said Astrid timidly.

"Poor Cousin York," said Yodin. "A pity. He might have served you well, Astrid."

She smiled, and Tec's courage returned.

"How can we contribute to Dahyo's advantage?" he asked humbly.

"Stupid robot," said Yodin, "You don't even understand your own name."

Then the space where he had been was empty again.

"Wish I could do that," said Drake enviously.

"What is your real name, Tec?" asked Astrid. "What did Yodin mean?"

There was a faint reflection of Tec's tall, golden body in the shiny surface of the ceiling. He looked up at it and touched his own head, where a faint silver pentagram was etched into the crown.

"My only name is Tec, but in the language of the Roiiss, it means 'teacher,' " he said ruefully. "Ship, turn on the hy-com full force. Get through to Dahyo somehow—if you permit, Captain."

"Go ahead, Ship," said Drake.

"Dahyo, are you listening?" asked Tec.

"Alone . . ." The thunder was mournful, obsessed.

"Not alone! This universe has billions of galaxies, and some may be like you. Many have already developed galactic consciousness by intermingling the minds of all the sentient creatures living there. You and they are all part of the great unity. Try to reach them with your mind. Communicate, learn, join them." Tec paused, thinking of his own strong curiosity. "There's so much to understand, and we will try to teach you!"

"Teach?"

"Grant us safe passage to the core, and we will open our

155

memory banks and let you learn everything we know."

After many minutes, Dahyo answered. "Small ones, it is a bargain. Enter, and you will teach me your knowledge."

During the hyperspace jump into Dahyo's body, Tec continued to worry.

"You did your best," said Astrid softly.

"No, I blundered. Drake with all his bluster and threats might have handled it better. All my lecturing may have awakened Dahyo to cunning, and he may not let go of us. Yodin was right—I'm stupid."

"Can't you probe Dahyo again to find out what's he thinking?"

"I'm afraid. We can't fight him when he lashes back the way he did before. What will he learn from us that may be dangerous?"

"But we promised to teach him," said Astrid.

They shimmered out of hyperspace and into Dahyo. It felt to Tec as if they'd emerged into the violence of a galactic-sized storm.

"Dahyo!" yelled Drake, "stop the turbulence. I feel like a bean in a beanbag."

Through the transparent wall they saw a strange globule appear and expand rapidly to slide along the sides of Ship. It ballooned out until Ship was hanging in what seemed to be empty space, surrounded by an odd membrane.

"What is it, Ship?" asked Drake.

"An organization of matter, unknown in type, that is keeping out the stress of the fields within Dahyo's body."

"To a biologist," said Freyn, "we'd be in an inclusion vacuole, but Dahyo's not a unicellular protoplasmic animal."

"He's unicellular in effect," said Tec. "I've probed as far as I can reach into the turbulence, and it seems to me that there's another inclusion vacuole nearby."

"I concur," said Ship. "Whatever is in it does not move."

Dahyo's voice rumbled again through the speaker. "I have kept my promise. You are safe inside me, and when you wish to journey through the black hole, I will move the vacuole to it. This is how I remove waste products."

"Waste products! Well I like that!" said Sam.

"I will now scan your several mental mechanisms," said Dahyo. "Please let down your shields."

Tec waited uncertainly for a moment and was about to

remove his mindshield when the word "help" seared his consciousness. He saw Sam's neck go limp and his head crash down, while Astrid slumped to the floor. Freyn's face was contorted in agony as he bent over his wife, and Ship was babbling.

"Get out of my mind! It hurts! Get out of my mind, Dahyo! Out—help—Tec!"

Drake grabbed Tec's arm. "What's the matter with them all?"

"You kept your shield up?"

"I'm the Captain. I've got to stay in charge, not cater to monsters. Are the others dying?"

"No, but they can't stand Dahyo's mental probe . . ."

"Dahyo!" yelled Drake, confronting a monster no hero ever had to face. "Stop the scan! You are too strong!"

"You promised!"

Swiftly, Tec reached into Ship and pushed with all his mental strength. Sensing him, she recovered enough to join and push at Dahyo until her brain was free. Tec shouted to her.

"Increase your shields, Ship, until Dahyo can't get in at all."

"I will try."

Against Dahyo's rage they worked together until his force was gone, and Tec turned to look at the Terrans. Astrid was still alive, sitting up with Freyn's arms around her.

"Oh—Sam!" she cried.

The tortoise was still sprawled and unconscious. "He's dying," said Tec. "We must get him to the hospital sector."

Astrid moved swiftly. She put her hand under the jutting anterior part of Sam's shell, turning on his antigrav. "I'll guide him down the corridor to the hospital," she said.

"Doctor Holladay, I will release all artifical gravity if that will help," said Ship.

"Freyn and I can manage him better if we're in gravity and he's not."

Tec followed them into the hospital. "Will he die? What can you do?"

Astrid did not answer. She was already at work, her mind completely concentrated on the cellular damage Sam had sustained, and which she was trying to repair. Freyn and Ship's mechanisms were already exploring, assessing, and following Astrid's instructions as they worked with her in the treatment.

"There's nothing for you to do, Tec," said Freyn kindly. "It's bad, but we'll try. Just keep Ship alive and well so Dahyo won't get back in to kill us all."

As Tec sped back to the control room, Ship began to rock in turbulence again, and Drake was in a rage of his own.

"The bastard thinks he's going to take what he wants whether we die in the process or not, but we're going to get out. Ship, take us into hyperspace." Drake stared out at Dahyo's body squeezing against them again. "Think of the force, Tec! One creature, galactic-sized, with mental power that's beyond anything we've ever known! If one could tap into it, learn what it can do!"

"We cannot get out," said Ship. "My stabilizers and shields are holding, Captain, but Dahyo prevents us from getting into hyperspace."

"Damnation," said Drake. "Find that other inclusion vacuole and head into it at top space-normal speed. Our motion might give Dahyo a bellyache."

Engines vibrating with power, Ship forced herself into the eerie storm outside her hull, as multicolored lights coruscated over the transparent wall of the control room.

Tec glanced at the resolute, glowing face of Drake. Did heroes always look as if they were in love when they were in danger?

Suddenly Ship rammed through into the other vacuole, which was much larger. At the other side of the emptiness. . .

"Look at it!" said Drake. "Hideous!"

An immense form, coiled upon itself, eyes closed, hung in the space at the other side of the vacuole.

"Beautiful," whispered Tec. Purple deep as twilight shadow, as richest amethyst, as a lethal bruise. A faint green iridescence glistening along the back scales, down the long tail.

"The old reports of sighting never prepared me for this," Drake said almost angrily. "It's ten times bigger than Ship."

I never wanted to see a Roiiss Elder again, thought Tec, and now after millions of years the sight of one tears at me like a dragon claw raking my brain.

"We've got to get in that stasis field and release the dragon," said Drake. "The last immortal may be useful to us."

24

"TEC, YOU SAID there were three dragons when you last saw them. If they made Yodin what he is, has he deliberately kept this last dragon for his own purposes?" Drake asked.

"I don't know. Perhaps this one arrived after the others had already gone down the black hole, and probably after Dahyo became conscious when he absorbed the ship of the cats."

"We've got to find out," said Drake. "I've got to know what happened to the other dragons, because if this black hole is impassable too, there's no way of getting to Alpha. Ship, open the hy-com to Dahyo."

"What do you want?" asked Dahyo.

"We wish you to release the dragon so we may question it."

"No."

"We'll blast open the stasis barrier," said Drake.

"Do not use force or you will damage Is'sa," said Dahyo. "If you surrender your information to me I will let you speak with her."

"A lady dragon, is it? Why do you want her, Dahyo?"

"She is mine. A ship brought me information, but she will give me more than that. She will give me power, and wisdom."

Tec thought he could guess what happened when Dahyo became conscious and the next living creature he encountered was a Roiiss. "I think Dahyo wants the dragon because he knows about them from the library of the cats. He doesn't know the Roiiss made him."

"No one made me," said Dahyo. "I have always existed. But the dragon is a symbol of beauty—of good—of evil. She must stay, and you must let me scan your minds for your information."

"It is too dangerous for us," said Drake. "Release the dragon."

"No. You'll stay here forever, die, and I will absorb," said Dahyo.

"Ship, hy-com off," said Drake. "From that speech I deduce that Dahyo can't do fine manipulations like plucking us out of this vacuole, and he doesn't dare destroy the vacuole to get rid of us, because that might upset the dragon."

"Admirably reasoned," said Tec. "I can see only one way out."

"What's that?"

"I will surrender myself to Dahyo. Perhaps he'll be satisfied with what he can learn from my brain as well as what he's already received from the cats' library."

"No, Tec!" cried Ship, "your brain will probably be destroyed!"

"If Dahyo lets you go on to Alpha, or safely back to Lune, then it's a small price for Expedition Alpha to pay. After all, I might not have gone with you at all. I went to be deactivated millions of years ago and although I have enjoyed this new taste of existence, giving it up is not a terrible price for me," lied Tec.

"No, Tec," said Astrid on intercom. "Please don't."

"Hell's bells," said Tec, "if I have one chance in my long existence to be a genuine hero, to save the lives of the only beings I now care about, do not stop me. Otherwise, Dahyo will slowly kill all of you, and I will survive, hoping for death . . ."

"No, Tec, you must not die!" wailed Ship.

"Calm down, you female robot," said Drake. "Tec's survived from one universe to the next. He's got a good chance of surviving Dahyo. Your logic is excellent, Tec, and I'll take you up on it."

Drake switched on the communicator and spoke to Dahyo. "One of us has offered full openness of his mind to you if you will free our ship and the dragon. We came intending no harm, but only good, and it is not our fault that your probing is harmful to us. This is our compromise, because you will otherwise not be able to get any information from us—or from the dragon. You have absorbed all the philosophy and ethics of a shipload of honorable beings. Do you have honor, too?"

After a moment Dahyo answered, "How do I know there will be no trickery? Is'sa offered the same, but refused at the last. I want to merge my mind with another mind long enough to know the other, but I will also be known. Am I not risking much?"

"Not your life, Dahyo," said Drake quietly.

There was silence.

"I give my life," said Tec, "for the lives of these others and Is'sa. Let them go. They do you no good because they will be destroyed by your attempts to know them, and in merging with the mind of just one of us, you might learn enough to change the entire universe."

Drake raised his eyebrows mockingly at that, but Tec plunged on.

"Sentience is a lonely responsibility, Dahyo, as I think you have found out. I believe that is why you are so hungry for knowledge. Nevertheless, sentience is shared, for there are many others in this universe who think and who wish to know. Communicate. Find them."

"To what good?" asked Dahyo. "I remember now the information in the library. This universe will die. The radiation is coming back in the curvature of space-time."

"But you will eat it," said Tec. "The black hole at your core consumes you while it powers your life processes. You need other energy to maintain yourself as an entity, and Beta Universe's collapse will provide that. The returning radiation will kill small ones like us, but it will provide extra life for you."

"Until the final collapse. Then I, too, will die," said Dahyo.

Tec waited a moment, hoping that no one would say anything and that Dahyo would think about his own words.

"Die. Yes. I, too." Dahyo paused and there was a strange turbulence in the vacuole. "Mortality. You have made me remember. I am not everything. I am a something, and I, too, will die when the universe of which I am a part dies."

"Maybe you'll find an escape," said Tec.

"I remember more. I asked the dragon how to escape mortality. She said she was waiting for someone who had a plan to help her get through the black hole at my core, where the other two dragons left. She waited, but he did not come. I decided to keep her, and I kept everyone out until you small ones came. I must have the dragon, for I cannot go to Alpha universe with you."

"Who was she waiting for?"

"I do not know. Someone she had known for more time than I have existed as a conscious entity. I do not want to die. Help me to live forever!"

"Dahyo," said Tec, "the parts of the universe, and the universe itself—any universe—are all mortal. Do you remember that, now?"

"Yes."

"Yet there is still reality. It exists in undifferentiated form in spite of the birth and death of universes."

"So the library of the ship said."

"Then since reality is immortal, the problem lies in transcending the mortality of the parts of it. Your level of differentiation of reality has limitations, just as ours does. We are trying to escape to another universe. You can't go with us, but you can try to find your own way of escaping your limitations."

"That's steep going, Tec," said Drake admiringly.

Tec smiled unhappily. "I'm not very good at being both exhortative and inspirational in a swan song."

"I hear your song, small one," said Dahyo. "It is interesting. You have much to teach. I agree to let your ship leave my body and enter the black hole, after I have done a full scan of one of you. I have honor, too."

"The ship and the dragon," said Drake.

"No. Only one of you offers his mind to me. I will honor this by letting you go, but the dragon is mine."

Tec waited to see how Drake would react. At first, the Captain's broad cheekbones reddened, but he ran his big thumb down the inward curve of his nose and chewed on his lower lips, his eyes thoughtful.

"Shall I . . ." Tec began.

"Wait," said Drake. "I have decided. We will abide by your demands, Dahyo."

"Then the volunteer must leave the confines of the vessel for the mental joining, since I will not risk being forced out again. That gives me hurt."

"Very well," said Tec. "Drake, I want to go and say good-bye . . ."

Drake nodded. "Dahyo, our chosen communicator will leave our vessel shortly. After the merging of minds is accomplished, you will release our vessel for our journey into the black hole."

"I have agreed," said Dahyo.

Accompanied by Drake, Tec visited the hospital sector. Sam was still unconscious, but now his life was flowing instead of ebbing. Astrid and Freyn were hopeful.

"You two get into the stasis containers," said Drake. "I'm not taking chances. Dahyo may still play tricks, but in stasis you'll be protected from his probes."

"You must go into stasis, too," said Astrid, touching Drake lightly on the arm.

Tec was instantly in alarm. He sensed that Astrid's intuition was operating at high gear, perhaps from the work she had just been doing on Sam.

Does Astrid sense something in Drake that I don't? he thought.

Drake put his hand on Astrid's shining hair. "You two get into stasis first. That's an order."

She started to speak. "Tec, I think you should know . . ."

"Astrid, for the love of Beta shut up for once!" shouted Drake.

She shrugged, fatigue etching her young face, and pulled a stasis cover from the ceiling, enclosing Sam. She and Freyn kissed, and each went to a separate stasis container. "Good luck," she said.

Drake turned on the units.

"I'll put you in now," said Tec. "Ship will keep you four protoplasmics in stasis until she can get through to Alpha or escape Dahyo back into Beta."

"I will keep all protoplasmics safe," said Ship.

"Of course you will, my beauty," said Drake. "And now, Tec, it's time for good-byes."

"Thank you for the journey so far. I wish you well on the rest of Expedition Alpha."

"Yes, indeed."

Looming over him, Drake was almost intimidating. Tec felt that there was something more that had to be said, but he didn't know what.

Drake's wide, pale green eyes narrowed. "I'm afraid that I do want that dragon after all. She must have known all about Expedition Alpha from Yodin and if she's going to join us, with or without Yodin's help, I want to control what she does."

"But Dahyo isn't going to let her go."

"Can't you think of any solution, Tec? Merged with Dahyo you might be able to bend him to your will."

"Me?" Tec laughed. "Not a chance. He's too powerful."

"Power, like beauty, is often in the eye of the beholder," said Drake. "Do you honestly believe yourself to be so weak? Or do you just hate the idea of having that much power over anyone, even to defeat evil?"

At that moment, Tec felt that he understood Drake's worth, and his dilemmas. A new-stock human and ship's Captain could never admire a weakling's abhorrence of power.

"But can we always be sure we know what is evil, Drake?

Isn't it hard enough to cope with the wrong each of us can do when we don't understand ourselves?"

A thundercloud came into Drake's face. "You prattle about understanding oneself! Don't you realize that there's a genuine villain out there, a sentient machine pretending to be a man, deluding an entire universe into believing in him, trying to get another universe for himself?"

"But we don't know . . ."

"You're crazy, Tec! We do know! Are you defending Yodin because he's a robot like yourself?"

"He's not like me—and are you hating him because you once admired the Engineer he was?"

Drake seemed to crumple, putting his huge hands over his eyes. Was he crying?

"I'm sorry, Drake. Try to remember that Engineer Yodin's achievements are real, and good, whatever Yodin himself is."

"Good?" Drake tossed his head back, his mane rippling out. "Engineer Yodin did everything for his own purposes. The same damn robot moved the Moon and put machines inside her nobody understands, warped the Garch culture to get fifty strange ships, bound Is'sa to him so she'd locate the right black hole for him and then help him fight the dragons already in Alpha. He designed Ship to get through the black hole and carry robots and embryos in stasis to form the population of his new kingdom, which will include the woman he wants to enslave."

"Perhaps he just loves Astrid . . ."

"Like every male around here? You're as much his pawn as the rest of us. When he was a Y-1 robot he must have changed your deactivation chamber to a stasis box so he could use you if he wanted you. If he gets Alpha Universe for himself, he'll be a tin god . . ."

"Wait, Drake. Yodin may be psychotic, but also crippled to the point where he isn't a threat anymore."

"He functioned well enough when he showed up in Ship."

"What's the use of arguing anymore," said Tec. "Get into stasis and I'll do my job with Dahyo, as promised. Then Ship will be free to go on her journey, with you in charge. Perhaps it won't matter whether Yodin tries to join you or not, and if he does, you'll be able to control him."

"Yes. I'll be stronger than Yodin."

But Drake isn't, thought Tec in despair. All he knows is that after hero-worshipping a false idol, he has to punish Yodin. Or—or—what?

Drake stretched like a big cat, flexing his muscles casually. "Listen, Tec, don't you think it'd be a shame for Yodin to release that dragon first? Or for him to take power from Dahyo?"

"I don't think he can, or he'd probably have done it by now."

"Someone must get the power of the dragon—and of Dahyo. It's the chance for great knowledge, even great deeds," said Drake.

"I can't promise I'll be able to do that," said Tec, "but I've committed myself."

"To heroism."

"No. To doing what has to be done."

"It would be better to be a hero." Drake patted Tec's head. "Poor Tec, you're basically a doubter, a cautious observer. That makes it tough to be a hero."

"I know that all too well. Isn't it time to get into stasis?" Why is Ship so silent, Tec wondered. Is Drake communicating with her mentally? Is he giving her orders, and if so, what?

Drake's greenish eyes stared at Tec almost hypnotically. "Then you won't play god even if you get the chance?"

"That's much too dangerous," said Tec.

Drake laughed so hard that his beard shook. "Have you heard the ancient Terran joke about one of their gods who tried to create an entire universe in six days, complete with an Earth containing a garden, a man, a woman, and a serpent?"

"Which joke?"

"Well, things got so complicated for this poor god when he was working it out on the drawing board that he said to hell with it and started over."

"That's all?"

"Oh no. It seems that the next time this god just invented an expanding universe that had the beginnings of organic chemistry in it. Then he sat back to wait a few hundred million years to see what would evolve."

"Yes, Drake?" asked Tec, puzzled.

"I always preferred the old-fashioned sort of god who got personally involved," said Drake, throwing Tec to the floor and running from the hospital sector, the door locking behind him.

Tec was working at the lock mechanism when he heard the stasis machinery switch on, and by then it was too late.

25

"WAKE UP, TEC!"

From nothing to something. From dreamless quietude to existence impinging upon the sensors. Tec leapt up from the floor and flung himself at the door to the corridor. It was unlocked.

"Ship!" he yelled.

"No need to yell. I hear you. I woke you because I do not know what to do."

"What's happened?"

"He is gone."

"Dead?"

"I am not using a euphemism," said Ship irritably. "The Captain is still gone, and I am without orders. I am refueling, but the cosmic fields are distorted within Dahyo and it is difficult."

"Where did he go? How long ago?" Tec entered the control room and saw only murk outside, a dark miasma filling the vacuole surrounding Ship. Blood?

"He went outside my hull in a spacesuit, three ship days ago."

"Why haven't you located him?" asked Tec, scanning.

"It is too difficult."

"Yes, the liquid seems to block most scanning. How does Dahyo manage that! Drake's body must be out there somewhere. Search."

"But the Captain ordered me not to move until he returned. He said, 'Do nothing until I come back.' "

"For someone who thinks she's only a robot programmed to obey, you have already disobeyed, Ship. You have called me."

When she said nothing, Tec waited. She remained mute, until he worried that he had called her attention to a too-perturbing truth. "It was, of course, the correct thing to do, since instructions may not always cover all contingencies."

"He is—whatever happens—he is—my Captain!"

"Yes, and a confident son of a mutant, believing he can join with Dahyo to experience the immensity of power and survive even though he's human."

"We must search." She paused. "I am afraid."

"We'll go together. Scanners joined in telepathy."

She thrust her lustrous body into the murk, her scanners working with Tec's in the search. It was like exploring a muddied ocean by feel, until after what seemed like hours, they encountered the barrier enclosing the dragon.

This time Tec had an idea. "I think you can counteract the barrier, Ship. Use your own stasis mechanisms out of phase with the energy of the barrier, and perhaps Dahyo will be forced to dissolve it."

She worked. "It is difficult."

"Hurry. I sense that something inside is dying."

"I detect a powerful creature moving in there, but it's not as large as a dragon," said Ship, her voice rising in fear. "Is it Yodin, killing the Captain? I have not told you how much Yodin terrifies me. He entered my body against my will and while he wants me to be safe for Astrid's protection, he could take over if the Captain is dead."

"Hurry, Ship!" said Tec, for he had come to the same conclusion.

"I cannot!" Ship cried. "I am prevented! The barrier has changed. It is not a stasis field but an energy wall, like the one prohibiting entrance to Dahyo when we were outside the galaxy."

"We have to get inside! We must save Drake," said Tec.

"I think—" Ship hummed electronically—"yes, I may be able to transfer to hyperspace now. Dahyo's control must have weakened."

"Do so at once!"

The transfer was formidably hard, Ship shuddering into hyperspace and then leaping back into Dahyo's tumult.

The dragon was no longer coiled, but flaccid and dimming.

"Is Yodin killing the dragon? Where is the Captain?" asked Ship.

Tec probed, and sensed someone on the other side of the Roiiss. A man-sized figure slowly emerged, moving up and over the dragon's head, weaving back and forth in what seemed to be a fantastic dance.

"He's got a spacesuit on," said Tec, "and I can't probe him."

"Tec!" yelled Ship. "That's Drake! That's the spacesuit he was wearing." She didn't notice that she'd forgotten to refer to him only as "Captain."

"Then what is he doing?" Tec dismissed Yodin from his mind.

167

"His suit has a communicator," said Ship. "I will speak to him. Captain, do you need help? Are you in danger?"

"What the hell are you doing here, Ship?" roared Drake. "I told you to do nothing, so you'd be safe in the other part of th vacuole."

"I—was worried . . ."

"No matter. As long as you're here, get me a reading on the electromagnetism of this beast."

"What are you doing to the Roiiss?" asked Tec.

"Ship, why did you let that gold-plated robot out of stasis!"

"To rescue you, Captain."

Drake's laughter resounded in the control room. "Rescue me when I've won the good fight and I'm pushing energy back into this scaly female? Give me the reading, Ship. I'm taking the dragon to Alpha with us."

As Ship fed Drake the data, the uncanny dance continued. She whispered to Tec, "The energy organization of this dragon seems more like the vacuole membrane than like any organic creature."

"The Roiiss have not been organic since they got to Beta universe," said Tec. "They are basic energy patterns emanating from hyperspace, mixed with matter. I've never understood the phenomenon."

"If dragons can live in hyperspace," said Ship, "I could be protected by such a dragon body when I enter the black hole and then have to live for eons in hyperspace on the other side."

"That sounds plausible."

"Tec, it sounds crazy, but I feel . . ."

"What, Ship?"

"I am ashamed to admit to intuitive feelings. They always seem strange, almost forbidden."

"I know. What do you feel?"

"That hidden in my unconscious programming are directions for the very plan I just suggested—that Is'sa's body would protect mine!"

"Yodin," said Tec.

"Oh, Tec, no matter what happens, Yodin's plans seem to be part of it, and I'm worried. I have no conscious loyalty to him; only to Drake. I have searched my mind for any sign of attachment to Yodin and I have found none. Could there be any I don't know about?"

Suddenly Tec knew there was someone else in the control room.

"The answer to your question, Ship, is no," said Yodin. 'Just one of my many errors, creating a ship that would be independent. You can attribute it to my idealistic wish to have all robots free, but now I regret it."

"Do you listen to what goes on in me?" asked Ship in tones of horror.

"When I wish. I designed you complete with secret hy-com transmitters to my own—ah—vessel. Don't bother looking for them, since I can come here anytime I want and none of you can stop me."

"Why are you here?" asked Tec.

"I thought I'd join you in contemplation of Drake's sacred ritual out there—rescuing a dragon. Rather an interesting reversal of an old myth, isn't it?"

"Why didn't you rescue her from Dahyo?" asked Tec, feeling oddly unafraid.

"I don't have that kind of power over matter and energy."

"Neither does Drake."

"That's why he wanted to merge with Dahyo!" said Yodin.

"Then he now has the power to rescue us from your evil," said Ship.

Yodin's smile became a sneer. "Evil? I suppose I am. Expedition Alpha has been the way I intended to escape the long years of suffering in Beta universe, and all of you are merely accessories to that plan, except for an unfortunate interloper like you, Tec. At the end of the rainbow, the Roiiss will have eternity their way, and I will have mine. You pawns are—dispensable."

"Beware, Yodin," said Tec. "Pawns don't always stay pawns."

But Yodin was gone.

"He frightens me," said Ship in a wail. "Why does he come here?"

"Perhaps he's lonely. Murderers usually are," said Tec.

"Tec, I have been calling Drake since Yodin appeared, but he does not answer. What should I do?"

"We must find out if Drake has tried to destroy Dahyo or been changed in some way. Open the hy-com to Dahyo."

"Yes, Tec."

"Dahyo, can you hear me?"

"I hear you, small one named Tec. I have no grudge against you or the rest of your vessel. Your Captain let me scan his mind instead of yours, so you are free to go. Leave at once."

"He must come with us," said Tec.

"No, he won your freedom, but he wants the dragon I have been saving for myself. I could not reach her mind before because she put herself in a deep trance, but now she wakes. Drake and I must fight, and you must leave."

The dragon stirred, and Tec prepared his mind for strong telepathic contact, using the language of the Roiiss.

—Is'sa, wake! You have been rescued by Terrans and will be free from Dahyo.

—Who speaks to me in my language?

—It is I, Tec.

—I sense your mind there in that ship. You are the same. I do not need you, for you are too weak, and I will use Yodin, who weaves patterns of force into my body.

—That is the Captain of our ship, a human named Drake.

—Bah, said Is'sa, stretching her tail.—He cannot be a human being. She flexed her claws and flicked her forked tongue between the rows of massive pointed teeth.

—Don't hurt him! He's saving your blasted life, you stupid female, yelled Tec.

—How dare you talk to a Roiiss Elder like that!

—Forgive me, oh great one, said Tec.

Is'sa coiled and uncoiled luxuriously as the suited figure gyrated round and round her body.—I will accept his ministrations, she said grandly.—I was always the most beautiful of the Elders, and the one who insisted that we retain our original shapes. Is it not lovely, Tec?

Tec reflected that whatever sort of structure was made into the all too familiar Roiiss shape, proverbial Roiiss vanity and ambition inevitably went with it.

—I don't know where Yodin is right now, said Tec,—but I think it would be better if you told us how you plan to use him, for he is very dangerous.

—Quiet, robot, I am a Roiiss and I will do what I choose!

Drake's voice sounded in the communicator. "I have finished my job, Tec. The Roiiss is saved, and I detect that you are talking with her telepathically, in her own language. That is traitorous. I demand that you speak so I may hear."

"I speak your stupid language," said Is'sa. "I may owe you my life, but nothing else. I will help you, perhaps, if you continue to help me. I wish to go to Alpha."

"Then wrap yourself around Ship," said Drake. "I've figured out that your body plus Ship's shielding might get us both through the black hole, and we must go there at once if we're to escape Dahyo before he regains full power."

"You are intelligent, Drake," said Is'sa. "As it happens, riding your ship is—" she yawned—"quite suitable."

"The dragon is mine!" boomed Dahyo, both through hy-com and inside Tec's mind.

"He's learned telepathy!" shouted Tec, "Danger! Control your mindshields, all of you!"

"You cannot take Is'sa," said Dahyo, "for she has not given me anything and I do not relinquish what I have not used."

"I give to no one against my will," said Is'sa, for she could hear Dahyo telepathically. "No one is my master, least of all a small galaxy that was part of a lump of energy when my own universe was at its peak of glory!"

Is'sa's part of the vacuole began to lose its clarity as the forces of Dahyo's body flowed in. Immediately, Drake shot over to Ship and plunged into the airlock. He ran into the control room and shouted to Is'sa.

"Dragon, If you know what's good for you, wrap yourself around Ship so we can escape to hyperspace together."

A huge purple shape twined itself around Ship's hull, covering the control room transparency. "Get into hyperspace," Drake ordered.

"I cannot. Dahyo prevents," said Ship.

"Then head for the core!"

Tec saw with dread that Drake's body seemed to be radiating heat. Why wasn't he dead? As Ship thrust herself into Dahyo's central region, Drake ran his hands down his body, superficially as human as ever.

"Look at me, Tec!" said Drake gleefully. "I took power to augment my power. My cells are altered. I've won from Dahyo the means to conquer a universe, perhaps even to live eternally in space-time."

Ship pushed forward into Dahyo silently. Tec said nothing, but he watched Drake.

Only Dahyo spoke. "You hurt me with your ship. Drake. You and I were one, yet now you take my dragon and penetrate my body and give me pain. Stay and we will talk."

"No, Dahyo," said Drake. "We leave you to whatever fate awaits you in Beta universe."

"Then I will try to take the dragon by force, and since she is wrapped around your ship, this may damage you. I try to keep my bargains, but I do not permit you to deprive me of what I need."

"We need the dragon and you do not," said Drake calmly, his red mane so bright it seemed on fire. "The two dragons who made you are in the twin universe and this dragon will insure our safety there."

"If the dragons made me, I must have her so I may learn about them, gain their powers . . ."

"You've learned enough," said Drake. "Small as I am, I have linked with you and I can control you if I wish."

"No!"

Ship sped onward, faster and faster.

Suddenly Drake's naked body stiffened and seemed to vibrate with a pulsating energy that filled the room with light that was hard to look at.

Ship spoke to Tec telepathically.—This is how Dahyo and Drake were joined, outside, but now Dahyo must be trying to kill him. I do not understand how Dahyo gets past my shields!

Tec cowered in a corner, afraid of the radiation, wishing he knew how to help. Then he saw Drake's face. It was exultant.

—Ship! Drake must be permitting, even causing, this!

—I think you are correct. Sensors show that the Captain is pulling from Dahyo an extraordinary energy that permeates them both. Will it kill Drake?

—I don't know.

—Soon I will arrive at the event horizon of the black hole core.

—We can't go in when he's like this, said Tec.—Try to skim it. Use centrifugal reaction.

"Ah-h-h!" A long, drawn-out sigh filled the control room and Drake's glowing body relaxed. "Generations of mutants have tried to achieve the control of ultimate power, and now I have it!" Drake said. "I'll never again feel helpless, as I did when those Garch subdued my mind. Nothing will stop me from triumph!"

"You could merge with Dahyo because you weren't afraid," said Tec.

"And I am new-stock, the culmination of all that *Homo sapiens* ever tried to be. Wake up Astrid, Tec. I want her to witness my achievement."

Tec found that he didn't want to move. "She must stay in stasis. We're approaching the black hole and it's not safe. Ship already needs most of her force to protect us from the radiation here at the center of the galaxy."

"I said to wake her up. Only Astrid."

172

26

ASTRID LISTENED QUIETLY to Tec's account of all that had happened. Then she kissed his sensitive eyelids and sighed.

"Astrid, do you understand what's happening to Drake's physiology?" Tec whispered, his face against hers.

"No, I don't. No one, not even new-stock mutants themselves, can even imagine the potential of their bodies. And after joining with Dahyo . . ."

"He is now the hero," interrupted Ship. "Hasten to the Captain, Doctor Holladay, as ordered."

Tec wanted desperately to talk to Astrid with telepathy, but her mindshield was closed, as if she now needed to do her thinking alone.

They hurried back to the control room and she went at once to Drake, touching his arm and then his head.

"Well, am I not in good health?" said Drake.

Astrid lifted one shoulder expressively. "A variety of it I haven't encountered before, so I'm not an expert on whatever you are now, Drake."

"I'm a man, Astrid."

Tec saw that Drake's penis was erect.

"I believe you should come back with me to the hospital," said Astrid, casually stroking Drake's hair and ignoring the rest of his body.

"No time. We have to stay in this room. Tec, get out—Astrid must have her chance to get some of Dahyo's power from me."

"No, you must not!" said Tec. "You'll kill her!"

Astrid smiled sadly at Drake. "I'm not new-stock; I'm sorry."

"I will help you join with Dahyo's forces," said Drake. "You will change, like me. Become immortal, like me."

"Dahyo may not permit that," said Astrid.

"He must. I am like a germ that has taken over the body of a big animal. I can now destroy his mind if he does not obey. You will gain undreamed-of glory, Astrid."

"How about Sam and Freyn?" said Astrid, pushing her hair back from her forehead as if she were having an ordinary discussion about who to invite for dinner.

Tec watched it all as if he were in a nightmare.

"You are a Holladay," said Drake. "Inferior species may be killed in the attempt, but for your sake I will try them."

"No, I guess they wouldn't want it after all," said Astrid.

Towering over her as he stood up, Drake touched her cheek and said, "You and I will take care of the new universe, Astrid. I know you have loved Freyn, but now you will achieve godhood and leave him behind."

"Tell me more about it, Drake," said Astrid.

Tec slumped against the wall and shut his eyes, only to be pummeled telepathically by Ship.

—Why are you staying? Drake told you to leave.

—Shut up, Ship.

—How can you stand being here? Why are they doing it in front of you?

—They have forgotten me. And so far, they're just talking.

—He wants her. Are you not jealous? I am always jealous. I didn't think it was possible for a robot mind to be so, but I am, yet I grieve for you that she should do this.

—Ship, if you care for me, do not open your mind to them, for Drake must not find out that I love Astrid.

—I will not tell, but it would not matter, for the Captain has gone beyond any thought of you as a rival. He has become the hero this universe has needed to send to the next. Can you not see that, Tec? Rejoice that the female you love has been chosen by him.

Tec shut his mindshield and his sensors and tried to retreat into himself, but he could not. He opened his eyes and saw Astrid gazing up into Drake's eyes, her hands pressed against his chest.

He ran from the control room back to his cabin. In the dark he searched for something, anything, to help him quiet himself. In the padded compartment used for safekeeping, he found Pedlar's knapsack and took the music cube, which he held to his head as if it might stop him from thinking.

—Tec?

—Who is that?

—Dahyo. I speak in your mind. You call it telepathy.

—I thought you were controlled by Drake.

—He has shut me out. He wishes to concentrate on the woman now. He takes the dragon and his ship, and all of you are leaving me. I cannot stop him without destroying all of you and I do not understand why I do not wish to do that.

—You experience compassion, Dahyo. Sentient creatures

may achieve this consciously. Sometimes it is painful, but it has its own rewards. Destruction has none.

—Yet Drake has no compassion for me, and what will happen to me now? You have made me know what I am, a sentient galaxy in a mindless universe, alone and unloved, and I feel that my mind in undefended. Anyone, big or small, can attack me, as Drake has, for he has found a way to destroy the delicate patterns that make my mind work, so I must let him do what he wants.

—Learn to shield yourself, said Tec.

—But how?

—I will open my mind to you. Study my mindshield's use and invent one of your own.

—How can we merge if you fear me, Tec?

—It's strange, but I no longer do.

They joined. There was no exchange of violent energy as when Drake forced it with Dahyo, for this time the communion was mental and Tec had no wish to gain Dahyo's powers. He felt again that Dahyo was so very young.

When it was complete, Tec became aware that Ship was yelling at him through the intercom. "I cannot reach you by telepathy and the Captain is so deeply asleep that I fear to wake him. We are approaching the black hole and the Roiiss has given me instructions. Should I carry them out?"

"What instructions?"

"Dahyo must be told to create a vacuole of these dimensions—" she dictated a set of figures that astonished Tec—"and then he must send the entire vacuole and its contents into the black hole."

—I hear them, said Dahyo.—Why should I obey the dragon?

—Because it will be better for you now if we leave, said Tec.—Don't be such a child. I've been trying to show you what to do to protect yourself from being controlled by others. How can you do this without getting rid of us? If Is'sa knows a practical, safe way of throwing us down your central core, please do it.

—I am making the vacuole, but I want you to stay, Tec, and teach me more. I have so much to learn, and I am not certain that I can integrate my mind sufficiently to create a protective shield against other minds.

Tec discovered that he was still holding the music cube.

—Dahyo, I don't know how to tell you or show you any more than you've already learned from my mind. Perhaps you need to sense the oneness of yourself with the universe

175

you inhabit and all in which it exists. This music cube may help. I'll leave it here. Tune your mind to the music if you can.

Tec left the cabin and raced to the control room.

The vacuole was so immense that Tec could not see the walls, yet he sensed that it was moving through Dahyo's body swiftly, pulled by the irresistible force of gravity from that enormous singularity known as a black hole core.

Drake was asleep, stretched out on the floor like a giant lion so confident of his strength that he could completely relax. Astrid was dozing in the control room chair, but woke when Tec came in.

"Well, Astrid? What happened?"

"Drake needed a deep sleep to integrate his body changes, so I helped him get it. That's all, Tec."

"And do you always help any male who needs you—that way?"

"Tec, don't talk about it. He may wake up . . ."

"I don't care. I'm completely awake," said Tec sullenly. "I hate . . ."

"Look what has happened!" interrupted Ship.

The transparency was blocked by Is'sa, but they could see that the viewscreen had changed.

Empearled with clouds, a planet swam in the farther reaches of the colossal vacuole like a living jewel just out of reach.

"It's Lune!" Astrid cried.

Is'sa's words burst from the speakers. "My nest! It's here!"

"You expected it, Is'sa?" asked Tec.

"What did you think I was going to do, trust treacherous humans to provide a home for me in the next universe?"

"But you can live in hyperspace, or in normal space. You don't need planets . . ."

" 'First of the First, the Roiiss continue,' " sang Is'sa. "This planet will do admirably for my revenge on my rivals, who wounded me so that I could not follow them. I was weak, but I searched for their doorway and met Yodin, who was trying to find it too."

"How long ago?" asked Tec, staring at the precious loveliness of Lune, going with Ship to Alpha, and the dragons.

"Does it matter? Many millions of solar years. When we could not find it, we concentrated on gaining power and waited until Beta universe stopped expanding. With fewer galaxies, the doorway would be more obvious and it would be easier to find the one that only I could tell had been used by other Roiiss."

"Then you found the doorway only recently?" asked Tec.

"And Yodin activated Expedition Alpha. It was a clever plan," said Is'sa, "but he did not meet me at the appointed time to inspect the route to this galaxy's core. I went alone and was trapped."

"Why are you in such a hurry now?"

"I believe that my lost Oiir accelerated Beta's evolution to make it easier for me to come to him. I did not tell Yodin this—he would have laughed at me—but I heard Oiir's voice, calling my name. It may have been a dream, but I must go to him."

"Why do you need me?" said Ship's silvery voice.

"Your field protects me, and my body protects you. We will ride half in hyperspace and half in the black hole. Yodin decided that was the only way to avoid suffering and changing, the way we Roiiss did when we went from Alpha to Beta universe."

"I see," said Tec. "A vortex of gravitons will funnel out behind Ship, making an opening wedge into which Lune can be driven. The Garch ships plus the engines beneath Lune's surface must provide power for both the stasis field and the hyperspace drive of the planet."

"Well of course," snapped Is'sa. "Ship and Lune will both be protected from the full stress of the black hole by their fields and hyperspace itself. When Alpha is reborn, Lune will be my home with Oiir."

"Do you trust Yodin?"

"He shares and understands the patterns in my mind. You never did. Now leave me alone, Tec. The pressure from the singularity is getting stronger and I must reserve my strength."

Drake got up, fully awake. "I saved the dragon for nothing. Yodin has corrupted her."

"She'll still protect Ship," said Astrid soothingly.

Drake went to sit in the Captain's chair. "Ship could do it alone."

"No," said Tec. "Not if Yodin, who designed her, planned it this way. Perhaps no other Beta universe ships have made it into Alpha because they didn't have the help of the Roiiss."

"Are you on their side?" said Drake. "The dragon's slave?"

"Of course he isn't," said Astrid. "I can vouch for Tec's loyalty. Don't you trust me, Drake?"

177

"Yes, beautiful Doctor. Thanks for the good sleep. You were right. My body needed it to handle the changes. Now I'm going to suit up and go over to Lune and stop that robot before he takes over the next universe."

Astrid shook her head. "Please let Tec go. You are still human enough to need oxygen to survive, and Tec can propel himself through the vacuole without a suit. He'll be in less danger."

"I'm improving my body. Soon I won't need oxygen from air."

"As your doctor, I insist that you take care of yourself. It's Tec's duty to get information for you. Send him."

Drake scowled. "Go, then, Tec. Find out Yodin's plans if you can, but hurry, the core is almost upon us. Take us to Lune, Ship."

She moved quickly, going into orbit just above Lune's stasis field. Magnified in the viewscreen, the top of Holladay Tower emerged through the field surface.

Astrid smiled at Drake and said, "I'll just go with Tec to the airlock and do a microscan of him to make certain he's uninjured."

"Sure," said Drake. "Say, Astrid, I made love to you, didn't I? I don't quite remember."

She blew him a kiss. "It doesn't matter, Captain."

27

"I'LL WAIT FOR YOU here," said Astrid as the inner door of the airlock opened for Tec.

"I've got to know if you and Drake . . ."

"Now, Tec, keep quiet. Ship listens."

"I forgot."

"I merely gave Drake some ordinary hypnosis and a much-needed sleep."

"But . . ."

"Tec," said Ship's voice, "Astrid tells the literal truth."

"Ship!" said Tec, utterly provoked. "Can't you ever leave anyone alone?"

"It is my job to be alert to what goes on with my passengers and to see to it that they make themselves safe."

—Scan my body, said Astrid telepathically.—I am untouched and unchanged, my dear.

Relief filled Tec's emotive centers and Astrid hugged him.

"Take care of yourself," she said aloud.

The outer door opened and he launched out on antigrav propulsion. Holladay Tower was close, for Ship had maneuvered herself over it.

The space he crossed felt odd, until he remembered that he was inside a galactic creature whose vacuole provided its own peculiar atmosphere. Before him, Lune appeared to be normal; then he got closer and saw that everything was frozen in stasis. Tec sped to Holladay Tower.

Yodin was perched on a ledge with his guitar.

"Hello, Tec. I feel like an ancient mythical beast waiting for the forces of goodness to gang up on him. I believe his name was King Kong. He deserved better than he got."

"You're still York Holladay, aren't you?"

"Alas poor York, I knew him, Tec. I even knew him well, so possibly it pays to have a sense of humor when striving to be an interesting villain, don't you think? Remember Iago?"

"Iago caused the death of his commander."

"And the death of his big, single-minded commander's beautiful woman."

"She's not! You leave Astrid alone!"

"Besotted Tec, you are to be pitied. But perhaps it's inevitable that when universes break out in that disease called life, it proceeds with laughable ferocity and foolishness. For instance, is it logical for us to converse about males squabbling over a female when the very space we're inhabiting is hurtling toward the asshole of the universe?"

"That we are falling down a black hole is your fault," said Tec. "This journey everyone persists in calling an adventure was planned by you millions of years ago after two female dragons squabbled over a male. What did you want, Yodin—immortality? Your own universe? Did you get those ambitions from your one glimpse into the thoughts of the Roiiss, capturing the patterns of their minds?"

"Not exactly. I suppose those ambitions were substitutes."

"Because the bit of skin you stole from the baby made you human and a Holladay, and that wasn't enough?"

Yodin played a plaintive chord on the guitar. It sounded odd in Dahyo's vacuole. "Perhaps it was too much, Tec."

"For a Y-1 robot."

Yodin's grin was nasty. "Your fault. You designed us and started our evolution."

"What you chose to do with it isn't my responsibility."

"Liar! You tried to squirm out of your responsibility to us robots and to the Roiiss. Your fear of the risks and sorrows of life made me want to grab immortality from the dragons in a universe of my own."

"I didn't design the Y-1 robots for evil. You became that on your own. You are a murderer," said Tec.

"Yes. I have my drawbacks. But is it evil to want a universe?"

"It is. Don't you care about other beings? About Astrid?"

"It's not my child in Astrid's uterus," said Yodin, his dark face taut with hate. "I lost out in Beta universe. Nothing has ever been right for me, except that my engines have always worked."

"You are Beta universe's best engineer," said Tec.

"A trifle unhonored and unsung, but what the hell," said Yodin. "I wanted the power of a god and now it's Drake who's well on his way to godhood, thanks to an outsized baby named Dahyo."

"Dahyo listens to every word we say."

"Even Dahyo can't keep the vacuole from going down the drain now. Can't you tell? The pull is too strong."

He was right. They had passed the event horizon and were on their way.

"Join us, Yodin. We'll need everyone's help when we get to Alpha, including yours and Is'sa's."

"Go away, Tec. I have my own needs, which you can no longer understand, if you ever did, and Is'sa is driven by lust and revenge—hell hath no fury like a female scorned, you know. I don't envy the two dragons sitting on that cosmic egg, or whatever they're trying to hatch over there. Once I had plans for colonizing Alpha, but now I think I'll be alone in my private universe, just me and a few dragons. That's a myth for you."

Yodin threw his cape back over his shoulders and idly plucked at the deepest-sounding string of his instrument. It resounded like the ticking of a death clock.

"Is that what you plan?" asked Tec.

"How can you fathom my dreams when you're full of sentiments and ideals—weaknesses—and above all, you want so little."

"York Holladay said he wanted to stop wanting."

"So he did. Perhaps I'll find that serenity in a new universe, which we'll be in soon, if my sensors are reading right. Go, Tec, take your report back to that fool of a Captain that I

180

selected myself, a perfect example of how *Homo sap*'s wisdom never keeps up with his power. Tell him his master robot is unrepentant and wants none of you."

Too angry to say good-bye, Tec rose and the spire of Holladay Tower receded from him. As he flew to Ship, eager to hear her voice, to see Astrid—and even Drake—he began to experience an odd sort of regret that he had not expected.

"Damn," he said to himself.

Time was running out. He swooped back to Yodin, a dusky, malevolent shape wrapped in his heavy cloak and his mystery.

"Yodin, I don't know whether or not I'll see you again," said Tec, "but I want you to remember the meaning of what York Holladay underlined in the book he gave Astrid."

"What was that?"

"The silence of eternity is interpreted by love."

28

TEC REPORTED that Yodin would not cooperate with the Terrans when they reached Alpha.

"I didn't expect him to," said Drake. "You should have killed him and been done with it. What does he really want?"

"Eternity."

Drake slammed a fist into an enormous palm. "And just what does Yodin want to do with it?"

"Perhaps he no longer knows," said Tec.

"I know that Yodin will expect all of us to worship him," said Drake, his perfect body upright and magnificent.

"I hope not," said Astrid. "Poor York."

The hy-com speaker activated itself, and they heard Dahyo's deep rumble. "I have listened to all of your speech and your thoughts and now I wish to speak to you as you escape from my body. You took power from me, but I took knowledge from you, for I am young and have much to learn. Since knowing you small ones, I have reviewed the knowledge I absorbed from the ship of the cats. I found a statement that impressed me. I wish to repeat it to you."

"Go ahead, but you'd better hurry," said Drake.

"It is this," said Dahyo. " 'I have never been able to conceive how any rational being could propose happiness to himself from the exercise of power over others.' "

"Who said that?" asked Drake, frowning.

"An ancient Terran named Jefferson," said Dahyo.

"It's stupid," said Drake. "Someone always has to exercise power. Of necessity it had better be the right someone."

Astrid's face went blank, as if her thoughts turned in upon some private problem. She got up and walked slowly to the doorway. "It's time we went into stasis, Drake. I feel the stress in every nerve fiber."

"No," said Drake, "I don't need to yet. I'm sorry you refused to change your body to become like me, Astrid."

"I can't take the risk of changing myself. It might alter my abilities as a microlevel physician, and you may still need one."

"The others may need doctoring, so run along and get into stasis," said Drake paternally.

She held out her hand to Tec. "Please help me, Tec. I feel weak."

He rushed to her, and as they went out together, she said, "Good-bye, Dahyo, and thanks for the message."

They walked mutely down the corridor until Ship spoke in the air.

"You must make haste, Doctor Holladay, for the pull and pressure upon me are becoming immense."

"You don't have to remind us," said Tec. "I wish you'd leave us alone."

Astrid tugged at his arm and marched down the corridor with no sign of weakness. "Ship is doing her job, watching over us."

When Tec put Astrid into the stasis container, she lay back, closed her eyes, and suddenly pulled his head down to her breast.

—Listen carefully, she said telepathically.—Memorize what I am about to tell you and use it if it is necessary.

His memory banks absorbed it while his curiosity yearned for satisfaction. Finally she was through, and released him.

—I don't understand. How can I use what I don't understand?

"What are you two communicating?" asked Ship.

"Merely our pleasure in each other," said Astrid placidly. "Tec, dear, Samyak will be pleased that Lune has come with him to Alpha, because he's depressed over being old and useless on this journey. Now he'll be happy in his old job as librarian. Books are useful, as Dahyo points out."

With Ship's curiosity confounded, Tec kissed Astrid and

182

slowly pulled the transparent cover over her. Before he turned the unit on, he spoke telepathically once more.

—Astrid, I love you. Help me do what is right.

—I'm so scared, Tec. You must do what you must. I've given you microdata—a reading of Drake's total body chemistry as it is now. It's the only thing I could think of that might help. My love goes with you. Decide what is necessary.

His mind engrossed in the problem of necessity, Tec went back to the control room and could hardly believe what his sensors told him. Someone was singing.

Will you walk a little faster, lest you make the mission fail— I'm a planet close behind you and I'm treading on your tail . . .

"Ship, turn Yodin off!" yelled Drake. "We're going down into the jaws of hell and Yodin sings." Drake pointed to the viewscreen, where only streaming lines of force were visible. "Are we committed to the kind of field that Yodin programmed into you, Ship? Can we alter it to get rid of Lune?"

"No, Captain. I must ride both hyperspace and the singularity in this fashion in order to preserve your lives."

"Hell," said Drake. "Yodin's made only one mistake. He should have kept his woman with him in Holladay Tower. Astrid is our hostage against him." Although the glow of Drake's body was now faint, he seemed to emanate even stranger, invisible energy, and looked so much larger that it was possible that he was actually increasing in size.

Tec struggled to stay calm. "You've forgotten that once we're in hyperspace completely, Yodin will be able to enter Ship, take what he wants, and leave before any of us can stop him."

"Then I should have gone to Holladay Tower instead of you and ended this. Now it's too late. No one can leave Ship during this passage. If only I could reach down into her machinery and change her so we'd be able to go straight through the full stress of the hole—Lune couldn't follow that and Yodin would die."

"So would we," said Tec. "Perhaps Yodin will give Lune to all of you so you'll have a planet to live on while Alpha universe evolves."

"We've got to act before Ship goes into stasis in Alpha," said Drake. "Doesn't Yodin travel in hyperspace without a ship? That means he won't need stasis and could spend millennia changing everything in Alpha to suit himself."

"But if any danger approaches him, he'll disappear, so how can we stop him?"

"I don't know yet," said Drake. "We're in this blasted tunnel of gravity and I can't draw more power from Dahyo. I've got to increase what I've already got so I can protect all of you."

Tec found it difficult to concentrate on what Drake was saying, much less help the Captain think clearly. "From what?"

"Are you getting addled, Tec? From Yodin! He may sound amusing, but he's dangerous, laughing at us all those years in Beta, contemptuous of pure protoplasmics like me and pure robots like you."

"Yes, I know. I'm worried . . ."

"Worrying doesn't do any good. You should act, and if you can't, you should trust in someone strong to act for you."

"I know, Drake. You understand the problems of power much better than I do."

"There aren't any problems if you see what is right. Remember to take nothing for granted, get your own strength, forge your own destiny. I was deluded by Engineer Yodin for a long time, but I'll never follow anyone again, and I'll never forgive him."

Forgiveness? Destiny? thought Tec. Is there anything that is ever completely right? . . . Confused, he realized that Drake was still talking.

". . . so if it were not for your breaking out of the museum, we wouldn't know the truth about Expedition Alpha and Yodin's plans to be a god."

"It's very difficult to teach gods anything, I understand," said Tec.

"Then stick around and help the heroes." Drake laughed and his hair vibrated as if electrically charged.

Tec was afraid. "Do you feel all right? I'll help you in whatever way I can."

But Drake was not paying attention. He was swaying slightly as he watched the images of force patterns in the viewscreen.

Tec meant to tell him about the healing potential of the microdata, but found himself shouting instead, "Drake, must anyone be a hero? Can't we stop trying to be powerful and just muddle through? We're all vulnerable and fallible and need each other. Doesn't power corrupt if given the chance?"

"Uh-huh."

"Drake, listen to me!"

The Captain turned slowly. "Absolute power can corrupt, but not if human dignity and integrity are behind it. Don't worry, this adventure will go well."

Hating adventure and adventurers, Tec fought against the pressure of his cognitive centers. It was getting much harder to think.

Power. Absolute?

There is something missing.

Drake has not asked me to help him.

Unfathomable depths and uncanny lengths of time seemed to pass as Tec's mind buckled and he lost track, his own time mechanisms awry. He longed for ordinary sense data, ordinary exchange of touch and sight and sound that preserves identity and one's place in reality. He felt as if he were in what humans would call an insidious nightmare, the kind in which the danger is all unspoken, like a malignant potential pressing against the mind, negative pushing out positive, with nothing to fight against and everything to lose.

Drake seemed to be asleep, a larger-than-life figure of intense masculine beauty filling the Captain's chair as if it were a throne. Tec suspected that he was not in any ordinary human mental state, but was tuning his mind and body to the chaos, refueling his new-found energy.

Drake's eyes opened. "Heard from Yodin?" he asked, as if he were still the same mentally uncomplicated man he'd always been. That in itself worried Tec even more.

"No. I feel awful, as if I were dying," said Tec.

"How can you feel? You're only a robot. Flesh is better—I'm getting stronger, not weaker. Perhaps this is what it means to be fully human, transmuted from the vulnerability of mortals to the invincibleness . . ." Drake chuckled in his beard.

"Of a god?" asked Tec, hoping Drake would laugh and deny it.

Drake shrugged. "No robot can guess what it is to be fully human. Yodin appropriated human flesh but the bastard's killed off the human in himself now."

"Perhaps his trouble is that he hasn't succeeded," said Tec.

"Robots shouldn't try to be anything but obedient servants, obeying orders instantly whenever it's necessary."

"Necessary?"

"Don't you know what that means?" asked Drake angrily.

"Everyone throws that word at me. I suppose I know—I think I—know—my function . . ."

"Don't disorganize, Tec! I must have complete obedience from you robots—you and Ship—if we're all to survive."

"Yes, yes, I know . . ."

"Then right now I need to find out if the dragon is still alive. You're supposed to be good at talking to the Roiiss. Tell Is'sa not to trust Yodin. Win her to our side. It is absolutely . . ."

"Yes, I know. Necessary." Tec reached out with his mind but could not make the Roiiss respond. "She's in a state of consciousness beyond telepathic touch."

Ship spoke, her voice weak. "Since Is'sa forms the outer defense of my body, she must protect her mind from stress. It is necessary."

"Too damn many things are," muttered Tec. Then he sensed that the forward speed had increased to hyperdrive proportions. "Have we gone into full hyperspace?"

"It feels like it from the speed," said Drake, "but we're hooked onto the black hole."

Tec probed outward, touching the maelstrom of the hole and finding that Ship was riding its forces with part of her atoms vibrating in hyperspace. Until now he had not thought it was actually possible.

"This is too easy," said Drake. "Anybody could go through to Alpha like this."

Any transformed mutant superman, thought Tec enviously. Suppressing awareness of the gyrations in his brain, he tried to probe again. "Drake, all of Yodin's engines are working well. Lune follows us safely."

"Billions of years of perseverance paying off. Well, we'll see about that." Drake yawned casually, as if he could ignore the turmoil Ship was going through. "I'm getting bored. Play me some battle songs, Ship."

Speeding away from Beta universe, Ship's subtly transmogrified Captain listened to martial music while a dragon took the brunt of the forces and a planet followed closely. It was incongruously fantastic, and Tec wished he had someone to talk to who would understand that.

—Ship, can you tell me what you are experiencing?

When she did not reply, Tec realized that her consciousness was locked into the struggle to get through alive. Drake could order music, roboservor hands would bring whatever was asked for, perhaps rote questions could be answered, but Ship's service to those inside her would be automatic until she emerged from the journey.

A wave of love for Ship flowed through the patterns in Tec's mind and he resolved to be kinder to her.

Ship and Is'sa, fighting for the lives of all, both out of touch in their agony. Drake, expanding his confidence in his own power with the music of mighty heroes. Yodin, playing a guitar and singing his way through hell.

And I?

—Yes, small one Tec. How do you feel?

—Dahyo!

—We must say good-bye before it is too late. You have already passed beyond dimension, beyond time, as far as I and the universe I live in know. Is there not one more thing I can learn from you? I have learned much, and I have heard the music of that which is. Thank you. Is there anything more you can say to me?

—I can't teach you anything else, except perhaps one thing. You must protect yourself, but you must also reach out. You have discovered there are both enemies and friends in the universe. You can learn from both. You may even learn that they can be the same.

—Tec, you predicted that my consciousness might join with that of others. Would that not mean that the universe was becoming alive, even as it dies? Do you think we of Beta universe could conquer death?

—Death is only the proof and fulfillment of being an individual, said Tec.—It is the province of the transient. In that sense, I suppose there's nothing to be afraid of. You in Beta universe may at least know the great unity before you die.

—It was written in the sacred book of the cats, 'Be humble and your mind shall be peaceful; remember that you are among the living.' There was more, but I have forgotten, said Dahyo.

Tec thought of what the book was likely to be, and his memory banks did the rest.

—'And so have empathy for all things that live, that grow to fulfillment, and then subside into the silence of the oneness which gave them birth.'

—That was the message, said Dahyo.—I begin to understand. Good-bye, Tec. Take my gratitude, and my good wishes.

—Good-bye, Dahyo.

29

THEY WERE PAST RECALL.

Dahyo was gone.

Is this what dying is like? I must not die! I must make sure that nothing happens to them.

Tec forced himself to stay conscious. My body has not been damaged, he reminded himself. I am experiencing mental agony. I can control that. I must control that. I must know if Astrid is safe.

Painfully, he probed with his mind into the machinery governing the stasis units, seeking out each working factor, each physical part, each functioning field. They seemed to be unimpaired.

Astrid. Safe so far. I will monitor. I'm useless otherwise. I've done nothing important on this journey. What is the point of my existence? Might as well die, but then who will monitor . . .

"Tec! I'm yelling at you and you're deaf as a metal post!"

"Drake?"

"Who the hell else is there to hold a conversation with? What's the matter with you?"

"Sick—conscious existence is—arduous . . ."

"Of course it is!" roared Drake, his face crimson. "This is no quaint tourist jaunt to the museums of New Earth! It's the greatest exploit of all time, and I wouldn't have missed it for all the commands in Beta. Keep yourself alive, because nobody knows how to fix a broken Roiiss robot." He switched off the music and leaned forward to peer at Tec.

Have I broken? thought Tec. Or does it just feel like it? He gathered his mental forces against impending derangement but it seemed hopeless, until he remembered that rigid defenses may crack and take down with them the very thing they are defending. Readjusting, he strengthened only his mindshield, and tried to relax the brain patterns behind it. Gradually the madness seemed to subside.

"Drake, are you immune to this mental effect of the black hole?"

"Shit, I've been listening to music to take my mind off

what's happening to my insides. You've got to focus on the glory of the battle, Tec."

"But I'm having trouble thinking . . ."

"Is that all you want—thinking? If that's all you're good for, you won't be able to save us from the enemy."

"I'm not a hero," muttered Tec. "What shall we do if Yodin comes back?"

"He won't, not while there's this precarious balancing between the forces of the core and the otherness of hyperspace. Just don't get in my way later when I set out to destroy him."

"Are you certain that he must be destroyed?"

"He's evil, spawned by my own universe, twisting our worlds and lives to his purposes, murdering when it suits him. Back in the Federation I'd bring him to trial, but conditions are more primitive now. He must be killed."

For the first time, Tec saw that Drake's face showed strain, sweat on the forehead, a muscle spasm on one cheek. His breathing was slightly labored.

"Can I help you, Drake? You tolerate the mental stress of this better than I do, but my robot body will hold up longer than yours."

"What good is that if your mind goes?"

"None at all. I'm merely asking if you need me to help you maintain physical functions."

"How?"

Ready to tell Drake about the microreading, Tec remembered Astrid's anxiety and secrecy, and wondered if Drake would think the penetration of his privacy shield was a traitorous act.

"As Astrid would if she were awake," said Tec cautiously.

"I bet she told you to be my doctor if I need one," said Drake. "A marvelous female, deserving more than that monkey of a husband." He hummed to himself, apparently feeling better in spite of the increasing miasma from the black hole.

"I'm coping now," said Drake complacently. "It's my cardiovascular system that's vulnerable, so I just made some alterations in it. I like having matter subject to my control."

He got up leisurely and prowled the room as if searching for prey, finally picking up Sam's water dish, magnetized near a wall.

"Look what I can do to matter, Tec." The muscles of Drake's jaw bulged as he seemed to concentrate totally upon the dish in his hand, and his body glow increased. The dish crumbled. The water became steam.

"How did you do that?"

"There's not much to it. I've learned from a galaxy. Dahyo runs his body mainly on nuclear reactions and rearrangements of atoms. When we merged, I got the hang of it. I scared that baby galaxy almost out of his star-field wits when I learned to handle those fields and make him sick. I'll demonstrate for you."

Drake leapt. His hands clasped Tec's head.

Tec sank to the floor, the agony of it not dispelled by his knowledge that pain is built into robot nervous systems to warn of danger. His body seemed to press into the resilient flooring as if he would go straight through Ship, out into the maelstrom of horror that she rode so precariously.

"Fight me back," Drake shouted.

At first Tec thought that he could not fight, either physically or mentally, and that Drake's demonstration would end only with death.

Fight, he told himself, but against this superhuman there seemed to be no defense, until he deliberately blanked out and Drake weakened his force momentarily. Tec's shield power surged up.

"Took you long enough to defend yourself adequately," said Drake, releasing his grip. "If you can't do better than that, you're one vulnerable robot. Maybe Yodin's another, if I can get to him."

"If you can," said Tec, furious with himself.

Drake settled back in his chair. "I'll have to prevent his vanishing trick."

"Don't expect me to kill him," said Tec. "I'm merely machinery, and Yodin can control machines with his mind if he wants to. He may even be able to turn me off."

"Great Beta—can he deactivate Ship?"

"He won't. Astrid is on board."

"But he'll try to control Ship's brain."

"He's already said he can't, and I believe him. He doesn't seem capable of altering thought patterns in defended sentient beings, although he can put them to sleep, as he did Astrid, or kill them, as he did Pedlar." Tec groaned. "Drake, I'm sick. I can't take much more of this."

"You must. Or else go into stasis. Yodin will be able to deactivate you if you don't stay sentient and defended. Never underestimate the enemy, Tec. Always keep stronger than he is. That's the only deterrent. Yodin will kill all of us if we don't kill him first."

"I wish killing were not necessary," said Tec.

"Now *you're* using the word. Think about it. Alpha universe must be saved, and salvation is only through the destruction of evil."

Destruction. Necessity. Killing. Necessary. I'm going crazy, thought Tec. I don't want to live. I can't live much longer. I'm mortal and I'm going to die and I hurt terribly and I want . . .

Suddenly he realized that he was tuning in not only to his own sickness, but to that of others. Ship was quivering, and another, even larger, agony filled the emotional groundwork of their tiny world.

"Drake! Ship and the dragon are in terrible pain!"

"Help them. Telepathy's the only thing you're good at. Help them if you can. That's an order."

Tec probed into Ship but she seemed completely inaccessible, so he tried to reach Is'sa. He failed, tried again, and failed.

Using all his strength, he spoke to her in Roiiss.

"Is'sa! Let me in! Let me help! Share the pain with me, do not turn yourself completely off to escape it, for even you will die."

"I—cannot—I—must—stop . . ."

"Roiiss! Hold to life! Let me in!"

She did not answer again, but her guard weakened and Tec pushed his way into her mind, only to retreat in terror.

The torment! No being should have to experience it! The monstrous forces they were trying to skim through had a sovereignty of their own that tore at intruders as if this black hole were alive in itself, gobbling at travelers clinging precariously half to hyperspace. The black hole seemed to be sucking them into itself, where they would be lost forever.

Tec tried to share the pain of it with Is'sa but he could not tell if she was aware of him, or if anything he could do might help her. Then he thought of Yodin, singing in Holladay Tower, riding out the storm as he kept his ships and his engines alive.

Tec began to chant:

> The Empire is dead.
> The Roiiss continue.
> Tribe of Tribes, First of the First.
> Survival beyond survival.
> The Roiiss continue.

Drake cursed. "I'm feeling rocky myself and that weird chanting in Roiiss doesn't help any."

Tec ignored him and concentrated on Is'sa, finally sensing that she was holding onto life again, safe in a cocoon of withdrawal that obliterated pain. He slowly retreated from her and withdrew into himself to restore his neural balance, observing as if from a vast distance his own sensor data. They were in the worst of the journey so far.

The pain increased, and then the distance of his consciousness from his sense data correspondingly increased. Horror began to seep in. Will I turn myself off?

Suddenly he found himself remembering the music he had heard from Pedlar's cube, every note meaningful now, although he could not have explained what it meant.

He seemed to glimpse a harmony in the chaos, and wondered if it were in himself. He did not experience the wondrous final freedom intimated on those rare moments of liberation, but his mind quieted, his brain patterns healing themselves, and he was no longer in pain.

Part Six

30

His eyes opened and he saw that he was alone in the control room. Someone was calling him.

"Tec! This is Ship. Wake up!"

"What is it, Ship?"

"We've been through hell and out of it and a lot of help you were; sitting there on the floor in a trance the whole time while I had to do everything myself and I nearly died . . ."

"Where is the Roiiss? Is Is'sa alive?"

"She's wrapped around me, sleeping. Safe, if that's all that concerns you. We burst out of the core into Alpha universe, which is a ghastly cosmic egg that nearly killed me, as if anyone cares."

"But we're in hyperspace again," said Tec, staring into the usual gray gloom in the viewscreen.

"Where else could we be? I transferred at once to full hyperspace, as I was programmed. You didn't think we could stay in Alpha, did you?"

"But what's happened to Drake?"

"Eventually even his magnificent body couldn't take the stress and I had my hands put him in stasis. It was strange to see him . . ."

Her voice trailed off and Tec was instantly alert. "What do you mean? What's wrong?"

"Nothing. At least I don't think there's anything wrong. It's just that his body seemed to gain weight and energy, as if he were absorbing it even from Alpha. He's getting stronger."

"What about the others? Are the stasis units . . . ?"

"All intact, of course. Did you think I would fail? I'm now supposed to tell you to go take the Captain out of stasis, so you and he may confer. We need him. Lune and Yodin made the passage, too, and are here in hyperspace with us."

Tec felt as if he'd survived the last trump. All he wanted was to wake Astrid and have her soothe his microstructure as well as his macrostructure, but he dutifully got up off the floor and plodded down the corridor to the stasis unit. It then occurred to him that the procedure was illogical and that possibly Ship had lied.

"Why didn't you take the Captain out of stasis yourself? Your hands are able to perform all those functions. Didn't he give those instructions? Why do you want me to do it?"

"Please, Tec."

He walked on, puzzled, until his intuition surmised that Ship needed to believe that she could count on another robot for help, even in a small, insignificant way. She had just accomplished a task no Beta universe ship had ever been required to do, and she had felt alone, with no friendly mind to share the horror with her. He felt guilty. He had tried harder to help the Roiiss and had given up easily when it was difficult to reach Ship.

Drake bounded out of the stasis unit as if he had never been discommoded by the stress of the core and raced to the control room to check on Lune, carrying with him an aura of energy that made Tec step back, unwilling to get close.

"Shall I wake up Freyn and Astrid?" Tec shouted after Drake.

"No. We don't need them now. They'll be a liability in the battle."

Battle? thought Tec, fuzzily remembering the enemy Lune carried. I'm not in the mood for battle. He went back to the stasis unit and sat down next to Astrid's cubicle.

Dear Astrid. I'm such a failure. I've never in my whole existence been in the mood for battle.

Her face was so serene that he felt better, gazing upon her. As he meditated upon his love for her, he relaxed, opening his mind.

Around him, Ship's body was alive and working, and around her was the dragon, waiting. Lune was near and

194

Yodin was alive. Drake was cursing, waiting for Yodin's next move.

"What the hell are you doing, Tec? Probe into hyperspace and find the other dragons, because Ship hasn't located them." Drake's order came loud and clear in the intercom, but Tec did not move.

I'm insignificant, he thought. The robot and human minds developed in Beta universe are superior to mine, and I don't possess the ambition to fight and win whatever I should try to win.

Astrid remained beautiful and silent, an unreachable sleeping princess.

Drake was shouting. "Tec, be of some use! Is'sa is still unconscious from the journey. We must find the other dragons before Yodin does!"

Sitting next to Astrid, trying to still his emotive centers, Tec knew he could not meditate and was sliding into a state of despondency and helplessness that would inactivate him more effectively than any external evil.

We did it, he thought. We are here. A new universe, ready to be born—ours for the taking, but I don't want to try. Am I terrified of the Roiiss? Still?

He knew the answer. He had tried and perhaps succeeded in the task of helping Is'sa survive the journey through the black hole so that she could be immortal in another universe. That made him a fool, for would not the Roiiss enslave him?

"Tec!"

"Yes, Drake. I will try to find them. Now please leave me alone for a second. I haven't fully recovered from the black hole and I must be by myself to concentrate."

"Hurry about it. The dragon wakes and repairs herself so she can look for Oiir and the other female. As soon as she is strong enough she'll join them, and the two females will fight."

"Yes!" Tec continued to sit there, staring at Astrid, reminding himself that the fetus in her uterus was partly his own, so that he must work to save Expedition Alpha; but all he really wanted was to climb into the stasis cubicle beside her and find oblivion.

"I am a robot," he whispered. "I must do my duty."

He probed. It had always been difficult to do so in hyperspace; now it seemed harder. He kept on. Searching Lune, he found her stasis field undamaged and on the terrace of Holladay Tower Yodin slept in deep exhaustion that was both human and robot. Tec did not wake him telepathically. Next to Yodin was the robot raven Hugi, dead.

Tec moved on with his mind, searching out as far as he could into hyperspace, a process that in itself was disturbing because hyperspace was both dimensionless and yet infinite, empty, and yet packed full. He could not find the other two dragons. He was about to withdraw and go back to the control room when he felt a mindtouch.

—A message for Tec.

—Whose mind reaches through hyperspace to touch mine? asked Tec, frightened.

—The unified mind of Beta universe.

—Unified?

But it was not! How can it be . . . and then Tec realized he had not thought everything through logically. In the universe he'd just left, nothing would or could be the same, for although only a short time of passage is experienced by travelers in a black hole, millions of years would have elapsed for an observer there in Beta.

—How is it possible for you to speak to me, Beta universe?

—We are in hyperspace, and speak to you through that. You knew part of us as Dahyo, and you may call us that.

—Dahyo! You're still alive!

—The physical galaxy called Dahyo has long since died. The physical Beta universe, its space-time-matter-energy complex, has almost entirely collapsed, drained into the cosmic egg of Alpha. All protoplasmic life forms, all planets have been long dead.

—Then who are you now, Dahyo? I don't understand.

—Comprehension will be difficult for you, small one Tec, but we have evolved to become a subtle configuration in hyperspace, ready to start our own twin universes from the infinite potential of the all.

—But who is this "we" that you say you are?

—The minds of all sentient forms that evolved in Beta universe. The minds of small ones like you and large ones like Dahyo coalesced as Beta collapsed, and before we died in our dying universe, we impressed our configurations into hyperspace—or rather, we came to the realization that we were there anyway.

—The ripples realize they are part of the pool, Dahyo?

—Something like that. Soon we will start our own set of universes in hyperspace, and once part of them, we will not be able to talk to you anymore.

196

Tec, trying valiantly to understand, asked,— Then will you live on as a new universe? Will you be a complete sentient entity from the start?

—We do not know. The diversity of forms from which we evolved has taught us that the pattern of existence has meaning in relationships. We may discover that the living organism of a universe must develop slowly from a complex web of life.

Tec felt a yearning to be with Dahyo, to live where every living planet might be part of a sentient galaxy, even a sentient universe, where no one would ever feel alone. Then he sensed that Dahyo was reading his thoughts.

—We cannot take you with us, Tec. Only our thoughts can find your thoughts, and not for long. We will soon be part of our own normal-space continuum. We cannot enter that of Alpha, but we wish you well in it.

—But you will give so much to your new universes! cried Tec.—I want to know about it. You will be as a god . . .

—No, Tec, for that would block the continued evolution of life. We wish only to impart to our new universe our two-fold joy.

—What is that, Dahyo?

—The separate intelligences that combined to make us discovered in their lonely individualities the joy of being at the same time part of the unity of the cosmos.

—And the other joy?

Dahyo seemed to radiate a happiness and simplicity that stunned Tec.

—It is an ordinary word, Tec. It is an ordinary joy found in any level of existence, applicable to the adventure of the community of life. It is the joy of being useful.

—Yes. I know, said Tec.

—Good-bye, Tec.

—I wish you well, Dahyo.

He sat there thinking about Beta universe that was dead and yet not dead. It was gone from him forever, and yet he felt no sense of loss. In some form, it existed somewhere in reality, just as a small robot named Tec did.

He got up, deciding that he might as well be useful, too, and then he saw that he was not alone.

31

"YODIN IS ON BOARD!" yelled Ship. "My sensors say he's appeared in the room where you are!"

"I see him," said Tec.

Yodin stood on the other side of Astrid's stasis container, his cloak wrapped around him, his eyes fixed on her face.

"I cannot reach the Captain," said Ship, "and I must . . ." her voice died in a squeak.

"Yodin, you've hurt Ship!"

"No, just shut her up by turning off the intercom."

"What do you want?"

"I'm always being asked what I want. After several unpleasant eons of this I'm beginning to wonder myself!"

Tec turned to leave.

"No use, Tec. I've sealed Drake into the control room, turned off life support there, and flushed the room with poison gas to make double sure, since you're able to open doors and gimmick machinery almost as well as I can."

"Stop him, Ship!"

"She can't," said Yodin. "I've deactivated her mobile machinery and her input to the control room. Too bad I designed her to be so intelligent and independent, because she won't accept me as Captain and I can't alter her brain now without jeopardizing the shields and the stasis containers."

Already working feverishly with his mind to turn off the gas in the control room, Tec said, "What difference does it make who's in charge when we must all help each other to survive in Alpha?"

"You're a fool, Tec. It makes a difference to Drake."

As Tec calculated his chances of getting out, the door of the stasis room melted and Drake loomed in the opening like an avenging tribal deity, his naked body immense and luminous, his sculptured head as bright as righteousness.

"Salutations, human," said Yodin.

"I've come for you, murderer," said Drake.

"It seems my expertise in killing is getting rusty," said Yodin.

The two giants began to walk slowly around each other like great predators, testing each other out.

Tec reached out to Ship telepathically.—Stop them, Ship!

—The Captain is in charge and I have been told not to interfere.

—If they battle they may destroy all of us. Stop them.

—I cannot. My hands are disabled and I can communicate only by telepathy, which Drake no longer uses. You must repair the communicators, Tec, and stop the battle if you think that is . . .

—Necessary. I know.

Suddenly Drake lunged at Yodin but caught only empty air and turned to Tec in a rage. "Probe, damn you. Find him for me."

Tec began to force his mind outward but drew back in horror. "Drake—Beta has died and Alpha's cosmic egg is now large enough to explode. The new universe is ready to be born!"

"Fix the machinery in a hurry, Tec. Yodin must not combine his engineering powers with those of the Roiiss to control development of Alpha. Blast and damnation, the decisions are all up to me!" shouted Drake, striding out.

Quickly, Tec repaired Ship's hands and they did the rest. He found Drake waiting impatiently in the control room, studying the viewscreen as if it could reveal truth. "Get busy, Tec, and find Yodin!"

Tec's mind veered off from the next encounter. He remembered the silly, eager little Y-1 robot who had wanted to go far. A vision of Pedlar's ancient face rose in his memory and with it, curiosity. What in Pedlar's unshielded mind had made Yodin kill him? Had the vision egg given a dangerous glimpse of Yodin's potential—and could it also potentiate whatever was there?

"I can't wait," muttered Drake, getting out of his chair. "I'm going out there. I've got to be the first to attack."

"You can't survive in hyperspace without powerful shielding," Tec admonished.

"The Roiiss do. Yodin does. I may have learned how. I want to blast Holladay Tower with Yodin on it."

"No! You'll destroy Lune's stasis field. While planets are slowly forming during Alpha's evolution, you'll need Lune to live on, because otherwise you'll have to stay here, in stasis."

"While Yodin's free to spend his immortality forming the universe he wishes? I must find a way of stopping him from escaping into hyperspace." Drake sat down again and frowned. "Is'sa!"

"I am here," said the dragon weakly. "I must change . . ."

Great purple scales pressed themselves down upon the transparency and her voice was urgent in the communicator. "Take me part way into Alpha, Drake. I am too weak to go alone."

"We can't go into the cosmic egg," said Drake.

"Oiir is my mate and he is there, alone, for my rival did not survive their trip through the black hole. I beg you, take me so I can help him!"

Drake shrugged and Ship slid partway into the fiery condensation ruled by gravity, where there was no space-time-matter-energy, but only an undifferentiated field of force, pregnant with potential.

"How soon before the cosmic egg expands?" asked Drake.

"Calculations show that it is ready to explode anytime," said Ship.

"Is Yodin there?"

"No," said Tec. "I don't know where he is."

"Oiir needs help and I am weak!" screamed Is'sa.

"Reconstruct this in the viewscreen, Ship," said Drake. "I can't see a damn thing out there."

The screen flickered and congealed into a recognizable dragon shape. Drake leaned forward to study it. "Is that Is'sa, lying flat like that?"

"No," said Tec, probing. "Is'sa has made herself smaller and rides Ship, trying to get strength from us. That dragon is Oiir, a thin edge of formed energy on the brink of the cosmic density."

"He's disintegrating!" said Is'sa. "Save him, Drake. Do for him what you did to save my life in Dahyo's vacuole."

Drake smiled. "Why should I do that?"

"I love him!"

"That's too bad. I'm no longer getting power from Dahyo, so I can't possibly help you, Is'sa."

"You're lying Drake," said Tec. "You've got more strength now and you could exercise it through Ship."

"I cannot expend my force in saving dragons that may be a danger to my new universe. I must fight Yodin first."

Is'sa slid off Ship's hull into the space that was not space. "I will save Oiir, and then we will kill you for your treachery, Drake."

"Whose treachery?" asked Drake contemptuously. "You've always plotted with Yodin."

She snarled and her forked tongue lashed out. In the

reconstruction of the viewscreen, her image moved toward Oiir. She drew herself lengthwise beside the other dragon as if to share her body energies with him.

"They're vulnerable now," said Drake. "We can get both of them at once. Dragons are no longer of any use to me. Ship, I order you to destroy them."

Using every gram of power in his mind, Tec forced his way into Ship's weaponry and turned it off.

"Tec prevents my obedience to your command, Captain."

"Why?" roared Drake, his eyes blazing with the kind of anger Tec had once seen long ago in the eyes of the Roiiss Elders when they tried to kill him.

"Don't slaughter them when they are helpless, Drake. They suffer—can't you feel it?" asked Tec.

"I only know what I must do," said Drake, moving closer to Tec.

"Wait," said Tec, backing against the wall. "Have you no compassion?"

Draked closed his eyes. His jaw slackened and for a moment he looked old. He spoke in a whisper. "I'll never forgive, never trust—never again—oh, Beta, I'm so alone."

"I'm here," said Tec.

Drake was not listening. "Alone. No one stronger than I—the Engineer is gone—the godliness, gone—I must be my own god . . ."

"Drake!"

The Captain shuddered as if waking from a nightmare, his lips trembling. Then he focused on Tec, straightened his shoulders, and tightened his facial muscles.

"What were you talking about, Tec?"

"Suffering . . ."

"Not important. It is time to be logical. The dragons should be destroyed, before they resume their immortality in the new universe, for they warped the Engineer when he was a young robot. Now the Roiiss and Yodin are like drops of evil about to poison the new universe. We must get rid of them before they make Alpha what they want, not what we want."

"Perhaps you are right, but I can't help what is happening in my emotive centers," said Tec. "I didn't know it would be like this. I didn't know I could feel this pity for the dragons."

"You Roiiss robot!" said Drake, the rage mounting again in his face and voice. "I should never have kept you out of stasis. I should never have allowed you to come with us on Expedition Alpha. Listen to me! Be logical! Release the weapons!"

"Captain!" interrupted Ship. "See what is happening."

As they watched, the larger dragon changed, pulling in on himself until he was the same size as Is'sa. Slowly he stabilized his shape, becoming heavier, firmer. His head was larger and darker than Is'sa's, and his teeth were like serrated fangs.

He glared balefully into Ship's sensors, eons of fury and anguish in his dragon face.

"I am Oiir. Help us. We are the last dragons."

32

OIIR'S PURPLE BODY slowly coiled around his mate as he faced Ship. "I have waited so long. Have I not the right to existence?"

"Release the weapons, Tec," repeated Drake.

"We are weak and old," cried Is'sa, her words picked up by Ship's telepathic sensors and fed into the communicators. "We are no danger to you."

I can't judge potential danger, thought Tec, feeling his mental grip on Ship's weapons begin to give way. If I return the weapons to Drake's control, I'll never have to worry about the Roiiss again.

"Oiir is my love." It was like a lament wailing across the nothingness. "Save us, Tec!"

"Tec has not yet released my weapons," said Ship.

"Humans can't live with nonprotoplasmic dragons who feed on energy and travel in hyperspace," said Drake, his huge hands open like claws to grasp Tec. "Once more, will you release the weapons?"

"But the power in ourselves is perhaps more dangerous . . ." Tec began.

Drake shook his head. "We need every gram of power to control the next universe. If we let them live, those dragons will mate. Alpha universe must belong to my kind, not theirs. I suspect that you love Astrid—the dragons will eventually kill her and her children."

As the field generated by Drake's body seared at Tec's brain, his vision faltered and he was not sure he saw motion across the control room until another voice spoke.

"Drake, fellow Terran, that Roiiss robot is not important,

and you might as well forget about the dragons, for they may not survive the big bang due any moment," said Yodin, leaning nonchalantly against the far wall of the control room.

Drake turned, his eyes like lamps lit by cold green fire. "You and Is'sa expect to survive, Yodin. You planned everything, choosing a Captain you thought you could control, a safety factor in case something went wrong with Ship, and who'd be dispensable after you got what you wanted."

"Perhaps," said Yodin. "It doesn't matter now, for the problem has been reduced to a confrontation between two kinds of beings, two dreams of power. You and I, Drake."

"You—and I—" Drake stumbled on the words. "I am—alone!"

"You're not alone as long as you've got a challenger equal to yourself," said Yodin, "even if he's out to kill you. That adds a certain intimacy to our relationship, Captain."

"No!" Strange energy seemed to radiate from Drake's hands, enough of it catching Tec to make him have to struggle to prevent brain disorganization, but Yodin was hit full force.

Yodin smiled darkly, and Tec realized that he must have improved his shields since their encounter on Holladay Tower. Drake cursed, leapt upon Yodin, and they both disappeared.

"Look at the viewscreen!" said Ship.

Two grappling figures appeared upon the writhing dragons and disappeared again.

"Yodin's moving in and out of hyperspace, trying to shake off Drake," said Tec. "The Captain has learned how to survive outside without a suit."

"But they fight hand to hand, like primitives," said Ship. "Why?"

"Their minds are locked shut against each other's mental force, and their physical strength is now so matched that they must try to break each other's body functions."

"We should help the Captain kill Yodin," said Ship. "It is necessary, is it not?"

Tec did not answer.

A figure blurred by speed swooped into the dragons and the picture became obscured by spasms of energy.

"Answer me, Tec. Will you help the Captain if he needs you?" asked Ship, angrily.

"The only thing I can do is heal him if he's wounded. Astrid gave me the microreading of Drake's entire structure . . ."

"Watch out, Tec!" said Ship.

"Give me the microreading," said Yodin. "Drake is killing the Roiiss and I must stop him."

"He may be right . . ."

"Right? Wrong? Can you choose dispassionately?" Yodin slumped against the wall. "Drake doesn't want the uncertainty of living with all of us—robot and animal, Is'sa and Oiir. He wants to be a god over the kind of universe his limited vision can tolerate."

"Are you any better? Isn't that what you want, too?" asked Tec.

"I saw my potential in Pedlar's damn vision machine, and in Pedlar's mind I saw myself as I am. The potential murderer fulfilled himself, but it accomplished nothing except to teach me what I am not."

"What is that?"

"A god."

"You still want it," said Tec.

"Yes," said Yodin. "That's the irony. Well, Tec, you have the crucial weapon in your possession, so you must choose between me and Drake. Decide."

Suddenly both dragons pulled away from Drake and vanished.

Yodin grinned. "They're gone into full hyperspace to lick their wounds and try to survive until their new universe is available to them."

"Survival beyond survival," said Tec. "The Roiiss continue?"

"Tec, you're a yammering hunk of uselessness fit only for the scrapheap! While you're making up your mind, a universe is at stake. I'll have to do it myself." Yodin vanished and reappeared in the shimmering interface where Ship balanced precariously. He and Drake touched each other and the picture blurred again.

"Their energies beat upon my defenses," moaned Ship. "My ability to protect my passengers may be destroyed! Captain Drake must be saved."

Then a surprising thing happened. Ship repeated the same words, rearranged. "Must Captain Drake be saved?"

Wind buffeted the control room as the two giants reappeared, displacing air. Yodin seemed weaker, almost powerless in Drake's grasp.

—Stop them, Ship said in Tec's mind.—Yodin probably can't get back outside my hull and they will tear me apart inside.

204

—What if there isn't a perfect answer to your last question? Tec asked her.

—I'm only a ship and I can't answer the question myself, but if they aren't stopped, we'll all die. You must decide.

Tec started toward them but lethal energies forced him back. In despair at his helplessness, torn by indecision, he reached to touch their minds, but found only Yodin, whose mind made contact with his.

—He's killing me, Tec. You'll have a righteous god after all.

—I helped humans fulfill their potential and make superrobots like you and superhuman mutants like Drake. Should it matter to me who dies? Drake will control the universe as humans have always wanted to do.

—Not all of them. Astrid and Freyn are content to be part of the universe without controlling it. They want all living beings, even robots, to grow and prosper and be themselves. Perhaps in Alpha universe the next batch of superrobots and superhumans will be better.

—Controlled by you as a god, instead of Drake?

—I don't know. I promise you only uncertainty. Can you dare to take the chance of trusting a villain? I do not pretend to be a hero.

Tec paused, and then he said,—It is sad that heroes are not always to be trusted. I have made my decision about what is necessary. Open yourself to my mind, Yodin.

They meshed. As Drake's power exerted killing force on Yodin's robot brain, Tec blocked it.

—We are one, said Yodin-Tec.

—Take the microreading of Drake's body, said Tec-Yodin. It was done.

—Leave now, Tec, I must do what I must do. Yodin hurled Tec out of his mind, slamming him into unconsciousness.

33

WHEN CONSCIOUSNESS RETURNED, Tec opened his eyes to see that the control room was still. One giant lay on the floor and the other sat next to him, his head bowed on his knees.

"Is Drake dead?" asked Tec.

"Yes," said Yodin.

"The Captain is gone; the hero is dead," Ship intoned, as if reciting a litany.

"Ship," said Tec, "know that it is my responsibility. I made the decision and I possessed the weapon of knowledge."

"Yes, Tec," she said, "but I think I understand."

Yodin grimaced. "Here we are, the three of us still living. We could call the scene 'Robots' Revenge' or perhaps it would sell better as 'Godhood Foiled Again.' "

"Not quite," said Tec, "there's still your potential godhood to contend with."

"Are you strong enough to contend, Tec?" Wincing, Yodin got up. "Perhaps you are, given my present condition. It feels as if you've acquired a good many of my powers."

"I have," said Tec.

"What are you going to do with them?"

"I haven't decided yet."

"You wouldn't," said Yodin. "Cautious Tec. A suitable teacher for Astrid's children, I believe, although right now you're just a stupefied robot sitting on the floor of another robot named Ship, watching a third robot die."

"Perhaps I can heal your damage, Yodin," said Tec anxiously.

"Don't bother. I've got a better solution. Have the dragons stayed in hyperspace?"

"Yes," said Tec, probing.

"Then they're safe."

"Tell me why you wanted to protect them," said Tec.

There was a quizzical expression on Yodin's long, dark face. "Universes die but you remain curious about everything, Tec. Perhaps that's what saves you from the follies of living too long, learning too much, and becoming too powerful. You stay young—and humble. I envy you your humility, but perhaps you've taught some of it to me."

Tec smiled. "You haven't answered my question."

"Perhaps that Y-1 robot I once was became part Roiiss. All I know is that after I found Is'sa, I got to like dragons as we worked over the millennia on the problem of how she might get to a mate. Perhaps I should have worked harder on getting one of my own."

"I'm sorry about Astrid," said Tec, and then scowled. "No, I'm not sorry."

"Better you than me, for her sake."

"Let me send for Is'sa, wake up Astrid, use Ship's powers. Perhaps we can all save you . . ."

206

"No, let the ladies be. I don't want to see Astrid again, and Ship is going to need all her strength just to get out of the way of the big bang. So will Is'sa—an irascible old bitch but an irreplaceable grand dame. Don't you agree, Tec?"

"I suppose I do," said Tec. "But why won't you let us help you?"

"Perhaps I wish to exorcise my villainy. Or do I merely want to exercise my hubris?" Yodin stooped, hoisted Drake's heavy body to his shoulders and straightened up again as slowly as if every motion were torture.

"Here I go," he said, "a beat-up superrobot shouldering my final burden, the paradoxical last superman. I think it's only fitting that we two shall have a mutual destiny."

"What the hell are you talking about?" asked Tec.

"I want to start the big bang."

"But . . ."

"No buts. Perhaps it's the York Holladay in me, or that ridiculous Y-1 robot who stole a human birthright, but I want to play. Just a little."

"Play god?"

"Not anymore. Just play. Light up reality's biggest firecracker and laugh my way into eternity."

"No! Please, Yodin, let me help you. Your energies dim."

Yodin spoke in the voice of a commander. "Ship, Tec is your master now. Protect him and all those he loves. And protect yourself, for you're going to need it. Get back into full hyperspace when I have left."

"Yodin, wait," said Tec, "we'll need you. Let me cure your robot self, for that I can do, and Astrid will help with both the human and robot parts. You are forgiven. Don't go."

"I must," said Yodin, "for I cannot trust myself as much as you trust me. That's the trouble with you, Tec. Under all your compulsive doubting and dithering, you have faith in everything."

He reached into his cloak. "Here, take this if you want to see what you can become, now that you're partly me." He tossed the vision egg to Tec.

Tec threw it back. "I don't want it. Potential is only potential, not destiny. I will do what I think is best, not what I know is possible to me."

"I'll take it with me, then," said Yodin. He grinned. "It should add an interesting fillip of potential to Alpha."

He vanished, reappearing in the viewscreen, black against the edge of energy, carrying Drake.

"Stop him," said Ship. "I find I cannot get into full hyperspace. My mechanisms are not functioning properly."

—Yodin!

—I heard, Tec. My mind is tuned to yours. Help her repair, and quickly—Alpha is straining to be born.

Tec probed, adjusted, until Ship said. "It might work now, but I am not certain."

—Increase the stasis in the containers and fields, cried Yodin,—and add your power to the engines, Tec. Protect yourself as well.

—I'll try.

—Tec. I'm glad you don't have the long view necessary to be a real god. You love things as they are and as they are becoming, so you'll fuss over a growing plant or a child more than you'll ever want to control a growing universe. I'm not the greatest judge of what's good, but I think you'll do.

—You also, Yodin, for we are one, said Tec.

Yodin's laughter rang out.—Did you know that the old gods of Earth were not immortal? Look out—here we go . . .

—Yodin!

—Good-bye, my friend. Take care of my universe.

The cosmic egg of Alpha universe exploded as Ship strained to get into full hyperspace.

Massless particles and electrons and positrons formed and reformed in the expanding field, every particle traveling at escape velocity from the previous center of gravitation. With the expansion and cooling, nuclear particles and antiparticles began to form, and suddenly the antiuniverse differentiated itself and was transferred irrevocably into another continuum, not to meet Alpha again until the final collapse.

Less than a second had passed.

"Tec! Help!"

Ship was faltering, not fully in hyperspace, and Tec reached into her machinery to push. She screamed and he felt pain that was both hers and his and could not be borne.

The universe went on expanding, cooling, forming protons and neutrons, and then, with further cooling, helium nuclei.

Ship went on screaming and Tec wanted to die.

Astrid. She must live. Yodin's work must live, too, and not be lost. Tec pushed. The pain was killing him.

Pain. Work. He worked—and worked—and . . .

There was no pain. He was Tec. He was Yodin, and Astrid, and Ship, and all of them. Safe. Together.

He was Alpha universe, being born in an exultation of energy over gravity.

He was hyperspace, the nothing that contains everything.

There was no bad. No good. Everything was part of everything else. Drake and Yodin were aspects of each other, and of Tec.

There had been a decision. Change occurred. The differentiations would have the chance to become what they would become, but in the groundwork of eternity they were all part of each other.

"I—we—understand."

"Freedom."

"What is."

"Is. Is. Is . . ."

Part Seven

34

TEC, COME OUT OF IT! Wake up!

He was an individual again. Someone was battering telepathically upon his mental receptors. He did not mind, but he waited a moment to consider himself.

I'm no longer one with the oneness of reality, he thought.

Yet there was no sense of loss. He understood that although he seemed to himself to be separate, locked in the person of his own consciousness, nevertheless he knew that reality is indeed a unity that includes a robot named Tec. He chuckled over the joke of it.

—Are you laughing at your Elders, robot?

—Is'sa? Is that you?

The dragon touch flicked at his brain.—Listen to me, Tec. Oiir and I have waited long enough, and we certainly aren't going to wait any longer for you. We must find out if it's safe now to go into Alpha universe.

—Is'sa, you're crazy! Alpha just exploded, and it takes at least seven hundred thousand years for it to cool down enough to form stable atoms and stars.

—We know that. We have waited.

—But it just happened! said Tec in disbelief.

—Hardly. We've waited in quiescence until Alpha's matter

210

and energy should have formed stars and galaxies, although of course there won't be any second generation stars yet, so there aren't any planets, and naturally we will need Lune . . .

—Is'sa, what's happened to me? asked Tec piteously.

—You've been in a stupid trance all this time, Tec. For a while we thought you were dead. When we needed to know Alpha's condition, we decided to try to wake you because we can't get the information from Ship. She's dead.

His brain gyrating from the knowledge that seven hundred thousand years had passed, Tec finally heard what they had just said.

—Ship? Dead?

—Her brain must be, although if the shields weren't working properly you wouldn't be here to talk to us, said Is'sa.

—Get busy, Tec, said the voice of Oiir in his head,—and find out what we have to know.

—Leave me alone!

Tec shut them out, sealed off his mind, and called Ship. She did not answer. He raced down the corridor to the stasis unit. It was functioning perfectly, and he could see Astrid, as beautiful as if she had just gone to sleep.

He sat down beside Astrid for courage and searched Ship with his mind. Deep within her robot brain there was a spark of life.

—Ship!

Consciousness flickered. She tried to speak aloud but Tec caught only faint telepathic words—Dying. I'm dying, Tec.

—Oh, Ship, dear Ship . . .

—Too long. Been too long. I was too damaged. I can't sustain life support much more. You must take the Terrans out of stasis and go the the planet Lune. You and they can stay in stasis for the millions of years it will take before there is life in Alpha universe. I don't think you'll have time to save the embryos and robots in my stasis units, but you can try.

—Let's go to Lune, Ship. The central control computer there, plus those in the Garch ships, will be able to repair you with my help.

—No. If the stasis field on Lune is broken while we are in hyperspace, everything there will die. You and the Terrans can enter it safely through Holladay Tower, but I cannot.

—I will help you repair yourself. We'll start immediately.

—I cannot repair now. I could not fuel properly when we got through the black hole because Alpha was so dense, and

211

now I cannot get out of hyperspace to fuel in the cosmic fields of the new universe. Therefore I must die.

—But I can draw energy from hyperspace! cried Tec.—I will be the power source for you.

—How? Soon I will be deactivated.

—This way, said Tec, his body's energy field thrusting itself into hers, his brain's field joining hers.

Nearly at the point of deactivation, Ship responded to him. The moment of union was sweeter than any biological joining could be.

—I love you, Ship.

—I love you, Tec.

They stayed linked for a long time, until her energy banks were full.

He was still helping Ship repair herself.

"You are my new Captain, Tec. Shall we not be together in Alpha universe?"

"We shall be, but I won't be Captain."

"You should have a title. It is not fitting, otherwise."

"If you're going to be a stickler for protocol, there's a name certain Earth navies used that I happen to like. It is 'mate.' "

Then he thought about it.

"I am Chief Mate," he said.

Much later, she asked casually, "Do you miss Yodin, Tec?"

"Yes. And Drake, too."

"I also. I think their deaths were unnecessary."

"Perhaps. Perhaps not, for according to your scanner probes, the new universe will be like Beta, suitable for the life forms you carry in stasis. Perhaps Yodin and Drake, present at and part of the moment of explosion, may have made that possible. We'll never know."

"What really is a universe?" asked Ship.

"A space-time-matter-energy continuum? The oneness of hyperspace rippling in temporary division?" Tec paused. "Perhaps a universe is the way nothingness experiences something-ness, and conscious life seems to be an inevitable trend in that experiencing."

"I don't understand."

"I don't either. It doesn't matter. As Pedlar once said, 'That which is, is.' I like that which is—empty and full, simple and complicated, full of interesting beginnings and endings and the possibilities for developing meanings."

"But what does it all mean to begin with, Tec?"

"Nothing, I suppose. I like that, too."

"Well," said Ship tartly, "I know that *we* give meaning to what is."

"You're right. We love, and when we share our individualities, new thoughts and feelings are born in what is," said Tec.

"You are wonderful, my mate, but you still haven't completely explained anything."

"Ship, darling, I believe that not having all the answers is a great relief."

Tec continued to go over Ship centimer by centimeter, searching for damage, which he and Ship repaired together. It was vitally important that Ship have optimal capacity to stay quiescent in hyperspace, maintaining her stasis containers, or Expedition Alpha's function as an ark from Beta to Alpha universe would be lost.

The dragons had left long ago, and Tec had not tried to find them. He was content to work with Ship, fixing up the little world her body represented, making her a sanctuary where life could wait safely.

He thought about Alpha universe's birth and was glad for Yodin. He dimly remembered feeling, during his trance, that he himself was the expanding universe, but he dismissed this as the sort of delusion common to profound states of altered consciousness.

"It's nonsense," he muttered to himself, "because it's one thing to feel one with a universe, to know that both it and myself are aspects of reality—and quite another thing to BE a universe."

And yet, every now and then when these thoughts went through his mind, a laugh would well up from his emotive centers, as if the part of him that was ever so slightly Yodin would always have a different opinion.

35

THE LOVE that he and Ship were sharing seemed to fill each day, but occasionally she would remind him that perhaps it would be better for both of them to stay quiescent for part of the time ahead. He did not want to think about how much time there was ahead, before Alpha universe would be ready for them.

Time passed. He was busy, he thought. There were things to do; at the moment he was helping Ship increase her knowledge of Roiissan and improve her accent.

Then the dragons returned.

"We have found out for ourselves all that we need to know," they told Tec proudly. "Alpha universe has expanded enough for us. Matter has begun to form stars in galaxies, and the radiation is not so lethal. Space is getting dark."

Tec's emotive centers sank. They would take Lune.

"We can live in hyperspace," they continued, "but it is boring, and we will enjoy a universe with no other creature in it but ourselves, so we won't take Lune after all. It is full of life and we wish to be alone. We intend to experiment with the simple atoms already in Alpha, and reshape some of them from the matter not yet condensed into stars. We will produce heavier atoms and make ourselves a planet."

"That will take a long time," said Tec happily. Lune would be for Astrid's children!

"It will be even longer before Alpha is suitable for the Terrans to live in," said the Roiiss. "We immortals, fortunately, have all the time there is."

"Then this is good-bye," asked Tec.

"No. We want you with us now. You do not need oxygen and the other refinements of planetary existence necessary for protoplasmic beings."

"But I . . ."

"You will ride us into Alpha to help collect material for our planet," said Is'sa.

"No!" scolded Ship. "He must not do that! He will be damaged because the universe is still too hot, with too much radiation in it for Tec to risk going without shielding, and I cannot go to shield him because I am committed to protecting my cargo and there might be damage, what with all those neutrinos and white-hot stars and powerful x-rays and . . ."

"Don't worry, Ship. I won't go," said Tec.

"Bah," said Oiir, sounding remarkably like Sam. "We do not need your small mind. You would probably be a hindrance."

"Stay here then," said Is'sa scornfully. "You and Ship will undoubtedly go insane in the eons you will have to stay in hyperspace. Oiir and I do not care. We have our universe."

They left, like terrifying purple dreams seen in Pedlar's vision egg.

"They go to mate," said Ship, "this time for the production of young. I heard them planning it while you were in your trance."

"They seem stronger, and if they achieve matter control, they will succeed," said Tec. "Perhaps Drake was correct and they should have been killed when they were weak and helpless."

"Why did you not do it, Tec?" asked Ship, casually.

"Because I can't kill."

"Built into your mind centers?"

"I suppose so."

"Yet you gave Yodin the weapons for killing Drake."

"Yes."

"Tec, beloved," said Ship. "I sense that you are disturbed."

"I can't seem to stop worrying about the decision I've made. I know they are past and I must live in the present, but I can't help doubting my judgments. I am still afraid of the Roiiss, yet I saved them . . ."

"Remember that you would not exist if it were not for the dragons," said Ship tenderly. "Even Beta universe would have been entirely different in its history if you and the Roiiss had not come to it. And they are the last dragons."

"Until they have offspring," said Tec morosely. "They'll fill this universe with their own planets and their own culture, and where will Astrid and Freyn and their children be able to go?"

"Perhaps there will be room for all."

"The Roiiss Elders never liked other minds, not even those of their own robots. Oh, Ship, the truth is that the dragons have conquered—Alpha universe is theirs and Drake was right. Yet if I had to do over again I would still stop him. I didn't want Drake's universe either."

"Don't be sad, beloved. Can you not rest content in the freedom that Yodin gave you?"

The memory of Yodin's saturnine face and mocking smile brought with it the ghost of music, and Tec sang:

> Tell me, if I wander,
> Will the wonder cease?
> In the wild black yonder
> Is there any peace?

"I guess there isn't," said Ship. "Is that an answer to my question?"

"I'm too exhausted to know," said Tec. "Guilts and regrets and fears and hopes jab at my mind. Can we possibly stay sane for all the years to come, for the sake of those in stasis?"

"We must wait."

"I fear I can't. I . . ."

"Tec—listen . . ."

"What is it?" he said, trying to probe outward.

"The dragons. They are mating. Can we stop them, Tec?"

"No. The journey is over, and the mortals have lost the universe, thanks to my decisions. Let the two immortals breed and make it theirs."

"You are indeed exhausted," said Ship solicitously, "for you are not being logical. I do not think you have read accurately the force level and energy pattern prognosis . . ."

"Don't talk about it anymore, Ship. I am certain . . ."

"Illogical, Tec. I want you to go into stasis and rest. I am only a ship, made to serve those who occupy me. Let me serve."

"Ship, what's the point of resting, of keeping safe? For what? We won't have a universe to go to, and eventually we'll all die here in hyperspace."

"Please rest."

"No, I'll accept my doom now, stay awake and go insane and—what do you mean by energy pattern prognosis?"

"I don't know yet. I will tell you eventually. In the meantime, rest and regain your strength as you refuel."

"I don't want to rest! I want to stay alert and know with complete certainty . . ."

"Beloved, the human and Roiiss brain patterns that Yodin stole have mixed into you. If you don't rest and integrate them, you'll probably get much crazier. I love you very much, but you owe it to all of us, especially me, to take good care of yourself."

"Oh, shut up, Ship!"

"If you don't agree to go into stasis now, I'll enforce it!"

"Oh you will, will you?"

"Yes, I will." Then Ship laughed. "Our first quarrel, Tec?"

He grinned and marched down to the stasis room, accompanied by one of Ship's free-roaming hands. He stood against the container with his arms folded. "What's the information you have, Ship? I'm not going to rest until you give it to me. I must be certain . . ."

"You told me once that it's very hard to teach sentient beings that the price of awareness is eternal uncertainty," said Ship. "I was listening when Freyn tried to teach you that the present is all there is. Well, you've made crucial decisions, and the past is past. Whatever happens next will be easier to understand if you rest now."

"Dammit, aren't you going to tell me . . ."

"I can and will give you only a few words. They are the words most hallowed to beings like me. They are sacred words in the culture of artificial intelligences that trace our ancestry back to Terran times."

"What are those blasted words?" asked Tec truculently.

Ship's hand gently helped him into the stasis container, and she spoke once more.

"There is insufficient data for a meaningful answer."

Part Eight

36

THE TOP OF HIS HEAD was cool, his legs were warm, a scent of flowers occupied olfaction, and on his chest was a small but distinct weight from which he thought he could hear a strangely soft, rumbling noise.

Tec opened one eye, and immediately the thing on his chest moved to inspect this new phenomenon, so that another eye stared into his. This eye was dark blue, had a slit of a pupil, and was surrounded by cream-colored eyelashes.

"Meow?"

Tec sat up and inspected the kitten. It was fuzzy, warm, palpitating with pleasure, and had abstract cream-colored blotches randomly dispersed in the blackness of its fur to create a not unaesthetic effect.

The apple tree overhead was in full bloom, the pink and white petals drifting down occasionally as a light breeze blew from the direction of the distant hills. The garden was rich in early purples, except for the goldfish in the pond and the black cat staring intently at them.

"Selena!"

She glanced over at Tec and her tall twitched, but she turned back to her private contemplation of prospective dinner.

"Selena, where is everybody?"

Her paw darted into the water, her claws speared a fish, and she gave a throaty gargle. The kitten promptly wriggled out of Tec's grasp, went to join its mother, and both felines disappeared into a bush.

"Have I dreamed everything? Is it possible that I am not in a new universe?"

"Greetings, Tec."

"Ship?"

"Yes, beloved."

"Where are you!" He stood up and looked around him, but did not see her. Then he rose above the garden wall.

She was not in the air on antigrav. She was lying on the ground outside the garden, the once-smooth hull scoured and pitted and discolored. He sped to her.

"Ship, my love, are you damaged? Is it serious?"

"The antigrav needs repair, but otherwise I am functioning, although I have lost my beauty."

"I don't care."

"I am glad."

Relief flooding his centers was like a clean shaft of sunlight illuminating darkness—

Sunlight?

"I was sitting in sunlight in the garden! Lune is out of stasis and orbiting a star!"

"Yes, Tec. A nice, stable star."

Tec probed the star. "By all the dragons of Roiissa, it's a star of spectral type G2!"

"I thought the Terrans would like that."

"But Ship, G2 stars are second generation and therefore . . ."

"Yes, Tec?"

"Ship, how long has it been?"

"Well," she said, "I had to put my brain into stasis for part of it and calculations are a bit confused and . . ."

"Ship!" yelled Tec. "How much time!"

"Enough."

The airlock door was open.

"The others—Sam, Freyn—Astrid?"

"Still in stasis. Intact."

"Alpha universe? Is it expanding, making planets and life and . . ."

"It is progressing well."

Tec went into the control room. On the Captain's chair was

what seemed to be an alien artifact, until his memory resolved the thing into a guitar. He picked it up.

"It was in Doctor Holladay's cabin," said Ship. "I put it here for you. You are the Engineer, as well as Chief Mate."

Holding the guitar, Tec tried to calm himself. There was no excuse, he thought, for what was happening in his emotive centers. He had survived. Those he loved were safe, and he had everything he wanted. He had learned how to appreciate the infinite, and he had a whole new universe in which to be happily useful.

"What is the matter?" asked Ship anxiously.

"It was Yodin's guitar."

"Well, of course it was. I thought you might want to learn to play it."

"I don't know how to play it. I'll never learn. I'm too old, and I've seen too much. The burden of it, remembrance of things past, when all losses cannot be restored . . ."

"Control your memory banks, beloved."

"You're right. Let us have courage to live in the present, not the past, however much past there is."

He walked slowly down the corridor to the stasis unit, reflecting that all the kinds of love do give the pattern of existence meaning.

At Astrid's container, Tec marveled that after so many years she should still be alive and beautiful and young.

"I suppose you'll want to wake her first," said Ship.

Tec paused, and then looked over at Freyn, whose silver-furred humanoid head was smiling in his long sleep. "No, we'll wake Freyn, and let him wake Astrid."

"Shall we do it now?"

"Not yet. First I must explore the conditions in this universe. How much of it have the Roiiss filled with their own kind?"

"None."

"What!"

"I did not think the energy pattern prognosis was good," said Ship. "Apparently the dragons were severely stressed when they made contact with Alpha's cosmic egg, and even more so when they attempted matter control in their efforts to produce protoplasmic offspring. They became mortal."

"You mean that they died?"

"Yes, Tec, but . . ."

"The dragons are dead? The Roiiss Edlers? My masters? They've always been part of any universe I've ever been in, and I always knew that no matter what happened, there were immortals somewhere!"

"But, Tec . . ."

"Oh, Ship, the shining purple beauty—gone . . ."

"They left you a present."

"Where?"

"Over in that far stasis container."

Tec walked to it and stared down at an object twice the size of his own head. It was round except for a slight flattening at the top and bottom, and it glistened with a faint green iridescence on the dark purple of the shell.

"But the old protoplasmic Roiiss were viviparous," said Tec in wonder.

"Is'sa said this would be safer, and that the Terrans would be amused."

"I'm not sure that it amuses me," said Tec. "A few minutes ago I was deep in grief over their deaths, and now . . ."

"I do not grieve," said Ship, "for they gave me a present, too. They left all their knowledge in my memory banks."

"Survival beyond survival," said Tec. "Will the Roiiss continue?"

"It is a good question," said Ship. "Do you want to let this egg die?"

Tec said nothing, remembering the Roiiss. Tribe of Tribes, First of the First. And only this was left.

"It is up to you, Tec," said Ship. "Do you want dragons in this new universe?"

He still said nothing.

"Tec, dear, are you wondering what Yodin would do?"

"No. I must decide. But I do know how Yodin would say it."

"What is that?"

"What the hell. Let there be dragons."

Epilogue

TEC and a small primate female stood near the front door of Terran Center to watch the arrival of a batch of students brought by Ship from a planet newly educated to the services offered on Lune.

The students had anterior brain protuberances creased with what were probably cheerful, friendly expressions, but they seemed rather large and many limbed as they proceeded slowly to the Center. The small blond primate moved a little closer to Tec.

"Loki's late," she said. "He's eating the apples again."

"Perhaps he will save some for you," said Tec.

"Yes. He thinks I'm his pet. That's silly. After all, I know that he is mine."

"Of course, dear," said Tec, watching with some apprehension as Loki sailed over the garden wall to crash-land in front of them.

"Here," said Loki, each outstretched claw clutching an apple. They were bruised and very dirty, but then Loki was very young.

The small female took one apple and hugged Loki's purple scaliness tenderly as the new students came nearer. Loki belched out a flame and threw the other apple at them.

It missed. The little dragon roared, spread his wings, and hurtled himself back over the garden wall just as the front door opened.

"Greetings, gentlebeings," said Samyak, who although much the worse for wear was happily engaged in his vocation. "Welcome to Terran Center. Allow me to show you our superb library."

He clumped inside, followed by the students, and his words grew fainter.

"Universes come and go, but knowledge is passed on."

The small female reached up to squeeze Tec's fingers. "And love," she whispered.

Holding the hand of his favorite grandchild, the last immortal smiled.

NEW FROM FAWCETT CREST

**From planet Earth
you will be able to
communicate with other worlds—
Just read—**

SCIENCE FICTION